MEG EASTON

ALSO BY MEG EASTON

Romancing the Spy romantic comedies

Spies Don't Fall for Their Asset

Spies Don't Fall for Their Rival

Spies Don't Fall for Their Neighbor

Spiced Chais and Secret Spies

Holiday Lights & Cocoa Cookie Nights

How to Not Fall romantic comedies

How to Not Fall for the Guy Next Door

How to Not Fall for the Wrong Guy

How to Not Fall for Your Best Friend

How to Not Fall for Your Ex

A Mountain Springs Christmas

The Christmas Pact

The Christmas Bet

The Christmas Clause

———

Nestled Hollow Romance

Coming Home to the Top of Main Street

Second Chance on the Corner of Main Street

Christmas at the End of Main Street

More than Friends in the Middle of Main Street

Love Again at the Heart of Main Street

More than Enemies on the Bridge of Main Street

———

Love Started romances

It Started with a Sunset

It Started with a Note

It Started with a Glance

———

Silver Leaf Falls romance

Coming Home to Silver Leaf Falls

Spies Don't Fall For Their Neighbor

Spies Don't Fall for Their Neighbor

USA TODAY BESTSELLING AUTHOR

MEG EASTON

For anyone who knows that sometimes the real mission isn't classified—it's next door and wearing a tool belt.

CONTENTS

1. Fire and Flood   1
Charlie

2. Dust in My Hair, Water at My Feet   13
Owen

3. Security Breach   22
Charlie

4. Historic Charm, Modern Denial   40
Owen

5. Caution: Slippery When Seen   48
Charlie

6. Not Flirting, Just Neighbor-ing   63
Owen

7. Let the Record Show: I Am Not Flirting   75
Charlie

8. Race You to Clarity   86
Owen

9. This is Not a Drill   100
Charlie

10. Center Stage Meets Center Crush   111
Owen

11. Spy-dey Senses Tingling   122
Charlie

12. Will Confess for Cookies   129
Owen

13. Packing and Pep Talks   144
Charlie

14. Practice, Pain, and Perspective   155
Owen

15. Believe but Verify   164
Charlie

16. The To-Do List Heard 'Round the Kitchens   172
Owen

17. A Fondue Farewell to the Fake Wall   177
Charlie

18. Aisle Be There   189
Charlie

19. Trial by Lancaster   200
Owen

20. Smoke Signals   214
Charlie

21. Never Mine to Carry   218
Charlie

22. Nothing Says Romance Like a Fast
Escape   233
Owen

23. Candlelight and Shadows   244
Charlie

24. I'm Just Visiting   258
Owen

25. Quiet Yards, Loud Thoughts   271
Charlie

26. Smile and Secure the Exit   285
Owen

27. Procrastination: It's Not Just for Fridge
Leftovers   290
Charlie

28. Spy Mom, Faux Dad, Real Crisis   296
Charlie

29. Halfway Built, Halfway Broken   308
Owen

30. All Systems Overloaded   318
Owen

31. Operation: Find My Favorite Human   323
Charlie

32. Well, That Escalated Quietly   333
Owen

33. Not My First Kidnapping   339
Charlie

34. The Secret Life of Charlie Lancaster   349
Charlie

35. Escape Plan: Trust the Girl   355
Owen

36. Distract and Conquer   367
Charlie

Epilogue One   375
Epilogue Two   389
Read the Romancing the Spy series   393
About Meg Easton   394

CHAPTER 1
FIRE AND FLOOD
CHARLIE

am on fire!

Not literally, of course. But right now, my brother, Jace, is on a critical mission, and it's the final task in what has been a very long operation to take down an evil mastermind, Callid Aragundi, along with his entire network. So many of us here at the Clandestine Services Agency have been working for months to get to this point, so everyone in this room is holding their breath and watching the big screens as I support Jace in the field.

Or, in this case, a super yacht docked in Monaco.

"You've got about ten seconds before that camera resets," I say through my headset to Jace. "So unless you want the ship's security to catch you in that two-sizes-too-small uniform, you might want to—"

"Got it," Jace says as he gets the door open and slips inside.

The urgency in this room is thick as everyone's eyes flick between the big screens at the front and analysts and operatives murmur updates.

So, I'm on fire, and all eyes are *not* on me. Which is exactly how I like it.

But, I guess that means I'm not figuratively on fire, either, or all eyes would definitely be on me. It's more that I'm in my element. Maybe my element is fire.

This is the final phase of the operation, and somehow, I'm the calmest person in the room. I don't look around because I've got everything I need on the three screens at my workstation and in the data coming from the comms. One shows Jace's glasses cam, one has both the yacht's heat signature map and a live feed of every hallway camera I've overridden in the last six minutes, and the third has my screen where I make all the magic happen.

"Take your next left," I tell Jace. "The guard on your right just broke pattern. You've got maybe fifteen seconds before he comes back around."

He moves silently through corridors as I scan my screen for potential problems while getting everything we need for the break-in. I glance at the screen that shows Jace's glasses cam and the heat map.

"You're two doors away from the brain of

Aragundi's criminal empire. Maybe even the key to unlocking who's behind the smuggled artifacts."

"Glove on," Jace says as he finishes tugging it into place.

Seven weeks ago, when we first found this super yacht but Aragundi wasn't on it, my brother, Miles, snuck in and placed a relay node into the ship's network junction at a maintenance panel, cleverly disguising it. A little ghostie in the wires. It's been quietly collecting biometric traffic and system behavior information ever since.

Now it's going to do exactly what we created it to do—make Jace look like a trusted associate of Aragundi's, so we can get past security. I scan the heat map once more as Jace flips open the cover for the fingerprint scanner. I've already loaded Aragundi's print to the reader using the spoof relay, and my finger hovers over the enter key as Jace's gloved hand nears the fingerprint scanner.

The moment Jace touches his finger to it, I press Enter to accept the fingerprint as valid. I think everyone in the room is holding their breath just like Jace and I are. The moment the fingerprint scanner lights up green, we let out a collective breath.

"Okay," I say through my comms, bringing up the retina spoof, "time to dazzle the scanner with your windows to the soul." Timing on these is everything. If I'm off by even a half-second, the system will flag it as a breach. I watch Jace's glasses cam as the scanner does its thing, and I press Enter the same moment it finishes.

A second green light appears, and I can feel the adrenaline coursing through me, clarifying my focus as Jace brushes the ring that's been spoofed to mimic Aragundi's against the proximity sensor on the side of the door frame. The door unlocks with a hiss.

"Boom!" I say as Jace walks in, closing the door behind him. We made it in, but there is no time to celebrate. We've got work to do. "Head to the center rack—row three, second bay. That's the control core. No sudden movements or the temperature sensors might flag you as a 'non-whitelisted presence.'"

Aragundi is an important take-down because he's got his fingers in so many pies. And one of them deals with the fencing of priceless artifacts and aiding in antiquities trafficking. Ancient objects have been getting stolen in large numbers while being transported, usually from archaeological sites to museums or from one museum to another. We've found a few buyers of individual pieces and a few of the couriers, but we haven't been able to find the person behind it all. We haven't even figured out who it is.

But we think that among the information about Aragundi's criminal empire, we'll find more information about the thefts and smuggling. Possibly even the identity of the person orchestrating it all.

When Jace gets to the core, I say, "Okay, insert the jammer first. Move to the left a bit…" I'm squinting to find what I'm looking for. "There! That green port on the far left."

Jace inserts the signal jammer, and I say, "That buys us twelve minutes of blackout." Now, if anyone off-site tries to ping the system, they'll think the yacht hit a dead zone. Which is super important when you know the bad guys will just shut down the system remotely if they catch wind of you tampering with it.

And that would be bad. First, because Interpol is moments away from a raid to capture Aragundi, and we don't want him getting any advance warning. And second, because before he's captured, we want to get that information about the antiquities smuggling, the buyers, and the guy at the top, and we want to take down Aragundi's entire network so it won't live on even without him. And taking it down will surely alert his off-site computer geeks, so we have to get this timing perfect.

Things are getting intense. I feel it. Everyone in this room feels it. Based on Jace's heart rate, he's feeling it, too.

"Okay, the jammer is live. Drop the download drive in that port to the right." This sucker's pulling everything—contacts, transfers, asset routing, call logs, shipment manifests, museum transport schedules, even grocery lists if they're in their system.

A progress bar lights up. *12%, 29%, 41%…*

Jace's heart rate is still a little high, so I start talking to help ease the tension. "If you were wondering, this part of the plan is officially called *Operation: Don't Let Aragundi's Evil Influence Carry On Even After He's Gone.*"

"If this doesn't work—" Jace says.

The bar ticks past 70%.

"It's going to work. Remember when we were kids and I rigged the backyard with trip wires, and you still made it to the tree fort with the intel? It's going to work just like that did."

"Even the bee sting extraction part?"

I laugh. "Even the bee sting extraction." The progress bar reaches 95%, but as it is counting up, our twelve-minute window is counting down. "Get the virus drive ready. When I say go, pull out the download drive and put the virus drive in the back slot. *Not* the blue one. Stick it in there, and the whole bay shuts down before the virus releases." I keep my eyes on the download timer until it gets to 100%. "And… go!"

Everyone in the room watches as the progress bar on the virus ticks up, so I narrate. "Erasing mirrors, corrupting backups, frying the OS… It's basically lighting this place on fire with code." Oh! Because I'm on fire. See? "He's going to feel this."

"It's nice to know that when Interpol drags

Aragundi off this yacht," Jace says, "his empire goes with him."

"Interpol is on their way," my mom, the CSA director, says.

Aragundi's computer geeks are going to discover there's nothing left and know what we did any minute now, which means they'll notify their boss moments after. We don't want them to get that chance.

"And, it's done! Now, unless you want a front-row seat to your own arrest or capture, you need to get out of there *now*."

I watch Jace's glasses cam and the heat map as I direct him through the maze of corridors and up out of the belly of the ship, trying to keep him away from obstacles as Kella remotely guides the eVTOL to the yacht's helipad. It's what will ferry Jace away to safety.

As Jace ascends the stairs to the main deck, I frantically scan the dozens of people I see on the heat map. "Oh, monkey bolts! A hornet's nest has been overturned." I am checking ship schematics against heat maps, looking for any way to get him to the extraction point, but all paths up are blocked. There isn't one. I can't even get him to the upper deck, let alone the top deck.

"Jace, there isn't a way to get you to either of the other two decks. You're going to have to leave from the deck you're on."

Jace is looking casual as he strolls through the crowds of people, heading in the general direction of the stairs leading up, when he sees an officer blocking them and takes a quick left. "You're just going to send a passenger drone right here, to where all the people are?"

I look over at Kella. She nods. "Have him jump. I'll catch him."

I relay the message to Jace.

"She'll…*catch* me?"

"Tell him not to worry," Kella says. "I'm the reigning Microsoft Flight Simulator champion."

I mute my comms and ask, "Like, worldwide?"

Kella shakes her head. "Against my brother."

I unmute and say to Jace, "She seems confident."

I glance at the director, and she nods.

"Okay, then," Jace says, "let's do this."

I guide both Jace and Kella to the side of the ship furthest from where Interpol is pouring aboard. When Jace looks over the edge of the ship toward the water, everyone in this room can see the drone soaring toward him. He climbs up onto the bulwark, waits a beat as the drone nears, and then he jumps overboard.

All of us, me included, hold our breath as he falls. My eyes keep flicking between Kella, whose sole focus is on manning the drone, and the video I'm getting from Jace's glasses. Kella does, indeed, manage to catch Jace on top of the cabin and swoops him away.

A few quick minutes later, seconds after we get word that Interpol successfully captured Callid Aragundi, Jace and the drone land at Héliport de Monaco, where he's going to get into a CSA helicopter and start heading toward home. The operations room here at the CSA erupts in applause. And, honestly, relief. Aragundi has been on *Most Wanted* lists worldwide for ages. After so much tireless work, we just took him down.

I am so relieved that it's Jace they're cheering for, and that they're all looking at the big screens as they're cheering. He's the one who will get credit for the mission, which is just how I like it. With me, not in the spotlight, just executing everything in the background like a boss. I take a moment to revel in the win.

And, since Monaco is six hours ahead of us, we'll all be home in time for dinner. Well, except for Jace.

I meticulously plan for every possibility in every mission. But not all of them go this smoothly. Sometimes one doesn't, and I have to mask a helicopter extraction with a symphony flash mob or remotely reprogram a smart refrigerator to send out a false distress signal to distract some guards. But when it does go this smoothly?

I definitely feel like I am on fire.

———

I step into my apartment after work, and the first thing I notice is water. "No, no, no!" I say as I drop my bag and keys by the door and race over to the big puddle on the floor of my kitchen, right in front of my sink. I fling open the cabinet doors but can't immediately find the source of the water. I race up the stairs to the bathroom and grab all the bath towels, then run back downstairs and start laying them on the puddle.

At work, I may feel like I'm on fire, but at home, I usually feel like I'm drowning. Real life and I don't get along so well. Somehow, a water leak right now feels appropriate. So maybe my elements are fire *and* water. Fire by day, flood by night.

I pull out my phone, my finger hovering over my family group chat. No, I decided I was going to stop running to my mom or my brothers whenever I need help. I am going to get better at figuring things out on my own.

That had been my plan. Right now, my plan doesn't feel like the best idea ever. But still, I manage to not text my family and instead tap on my browser and type in *What do I do if my kitchen is leaking?*

Maybe it's because I'm so flustered right now, but nothing I'm seeing feels like it makes sense. But I do get the gist that I need to turn off the water to my place, find the source of the leak, and clean up the mess.

Not only can I not find the shutoff valve (I have a

great need to always be prepared in case of emergency, so I have no idea how I overlooked learning this detail when I moved in), but I also can't find the source of the leak.

I'm in the middle of pulling out everything from the cabinet under my sink when my roommate, Reese, comes home. She's hanging her keys and her Cipher Springs Middle School lanyard on the hook when she says, "Got a sudden urge to clean enthusiastically?"

Then, she must notice that I'm still in work clothes, the bottom half of my slacks are soaked from kneeling in the water, my sleeves are pushed up to my elbows, and I probably look as rattled as I feel. She rushes over. "It's leaking?"

"Yes. I just can't figure out from where." I've got the cabinet emptied, but none of the pipes I can see are the culprit. Reese sticks her head in, too, but can't find anything.

Then both of our heads turn in the direction of the front of our house as we hear the now familiar sound of our new neighbor's truck pulling in.

Reese grabs my shoulder. "You should go ask Owen to come and look at it! He's in construction. He probably knows just what to do."

I shake my head as I stand, hands on my hips, as I look down at the water mess that is continuing to grow. "We'll figure something else out."

Reese is silent for a beat, so I look over at her. She

gives me a sly smile. "You know, they have therapists you can talk to about your fear of people."

"I don't have a fear of people! I just don't like all their attention on me."

"So it's a vulnerability thing."

"Which makes it just your run-of-the-mill human nature issue. No big deal."

Reese must not like my plan of figuring something else out because she walks straight to our front door. I follow because I'm curious about what she's going to do. She opens the front door, waves, and calls out, "Hi, Owen! Perfect timing."

And then she gives me a push out the door.

CHAPTER 2
DUST IN MY HAIR, WATER AT MY FEET
OWEN

I pull off one of my work gloves and wipe my forehead with the back of my hand before I move to the next seat in the historical theater we're restoring. My guys and I have a good assembly line going. They unbolt the chair, remove the armrests, and pull off the seat and back cushions before it comes to me. Then I inspect it for wood rot, broken springs, rusted fasteners, and the status of the upholstery before bagging and tagging, and another of my guys hauls it off to the appropriate storage container for restoration.

We do it all to some of my favorite sounds—the whine of a power saw, the screech of a nail being removed, the groan of a bolt being turned for the first time in over a century, the whir of a power drill. They're the sounds of exciting things happening.

I flinch when I hear a clatter and a muffled curse before twisting to see a strip of molding fall to the ground and break into pieces. "Oops," Luis says as he climbs down his ladder.

"Careful," I say, "this molding is older than your great-grandma."

"She was one tough lady," Luis says. "She probably would've told it not to be so brittle."

I shake my head, chuckling. I found a manufacturer who can match the design of the molding exactly, and their work is beautiful. So we'll get this place looking like its old, glorious self, only without all the wood rot.

A bit of movement draws my eyes up to one of the ornate balcony boxes, and I squint. It was probably a mouse. Again. Luckily, we've finished all of the foundation stabilizing, roof repairs, window replacing, and fixing most of the masonry work on the outside of the building. Except for days like today when we've got doors open to the outside to haul out the seats, we've got this building all closed up, so we shouldn't have a problem for too much longer.

"We should name them," I say. "The mice. Like tiny theater goers."

"That one in box two is definitely a Harold," Grady says as he removes an armrest.

As I finish up with a seat, I stand to give my back a stretch and give my old knee injury a break. I look at this theater that's been around for more than 112 years, at the high, arched ceiling with its medallions, the hand-carved posts piled against the wall, waiting to be stripped and refinished. The ghosts of chandeliers long gone. The way the afternoon light hits the curved back wall, the delicate relief work just waiting to be uncovered after a century of aging.

It all makes me feel the familiar flicker that I love. This place is going to be beautiful again—I can see it already. Even if no one else can.

I don't notice Luis coming up behind me until he says, "It's starting to come alive again."

I nod. "She's waking up."

"You really do love this part, don't you?"

There's so much potential in broken things. It's hard not to love it. I shrug and say, "Everyone deserves a comeback. Even buildings."

From where he's working to free a bolt connecting one of the seats to the floor, Trent says, "Does your opinion on putting down roots deserve a comeback, too? Because I think Cipher Springs would grow on you if you gave it a chance."

I chuckle and give him a practiced smile. Then I reach out and run my hand gently along the edge of a plaster medallion on the front of the stage, feeling the bumps of its ornate design beneath my fingertips.

Don't get too comfortable.

That's my rule. My very firm rule. I'll be here,

restoring The Shadowridge for maybe eight months. Then it's packing tape, a new zip code, and a new project for me. That's what the job is. That's what my agreement with myself is. Well, with myself and with the contract I signed to restore a historic train station in Philadelphia as soon as I'm done here.

I look up again at the faded velvet of the balcony boxes and the light filtering through the upper windows. I might not stick around to enjoy it, but this place is going to be beautiful again.

———

I pull into my driveway, and the moment I get out of my car, I look at the townhome connected to mine on the left, just as one of my neighbors, Reese, waves, says hi, and pushes her roommate, Charlie, out the front door. They're both looking at me, Reese with a pleased expression and Charlie with a shocked one.

"Hi," I say as I start walking up our common sidewalk before it splits off to our separate stairs. "I'm not used to having a welcoming committee."

Charlie laughs nervously, and I smile. I like Charlie. Ever since the first time I met her, I've found myself smiling whenever she's around.

"We, uh, have a water leak," she says. "I know you're just getting home from spending all day doing things like this,"—she shoots Reese a look—"but do you mind checking it out?"

Do I mind assisting someone who needs my help? Especially if that help is something I'm skilled at and gives me a chance to be impressive in front of a woman I'm attracted to? No, no, I do not mind. "Lead the way. I've been battling legions of dust all day, so a water mystery will be a nice change."

We walk into their townhome, and I can immediately see that the layout is an exact mirror image of mine. I've only been living in mine for a little over six weeks, and I don't plan to stay long-term, so the walls are as plain as the day I moved in. This place, though, is instantly warm and welcoming. Plus, it smells good. And here I am, bringing the scent of old wood, a whole lot of dust, a hundred years of stories, and my best attempt to do them justice with me. But it's not like I can say, "Hang on. Let me go shower and get smelling nice first."

We head past what I know are the laundry room and a bathroom on the right and the backside of a flight of stairs on the left on our way to the kitchen. I'm guessing Charlie and Reese came home and discovered the leak not long before I pulled up, because it looks like they are in the middle of cleaning up the water. A few soaking wet bath towels are spread on the floor, and a couple of smaller towels are draped over the divider between both sinks. The doors to the cabinet beneath the sink are open, and it looks like everything normally stored there has been moved to the countertop.

"Sorry about the mess," Charlie says as she moves the towels to the sink and grabs an unused one from the counter to dry the floor in front of the cabinet.

"It's okay," I say as I kneel down in front of the sink. "This is what a water leak looks like." There isn't an obvious leak from the water lines or the drainage pipe, so I grab another towel from the stack and dry the water lines leading from the hot and cold shut-off valves to the faucet. I give it a moment, and then I test the lines—they're completely dry. I check, and they hadn't already turned off the valves here, so if it was from these lines, they'd still be leaking.

I pull my head out from under the sink to see that water is slowly seeping from under the cabinet onto the floor where Charlie had just dried. I look up at the two women. "Do you want the good news or the bad news first?"

"Bad," Charlie says, biting her lip. "No, good."

I stand. "Well, those flexible, braided stainless steel supply lines are in good shape. So are your drain pipes. The shut-off valves look good, too."

Both Charlie and Reese nod warily, just waiting for the "but." And it's a big one that's hitting me at least as hard as it's going to be hitting them in about two seconds.

"But that means that the leak is either in the wall or coming from my side." My kitchen sink and theirs are back-to-back, connected to the same wall that separates our townhomes.

Reese's eyes go wide, and Charlie gasps, a hand flying to her mouth. As they both stand there, stunned, I ask, "Can I go into your laundry room to shut off the water to the house?"

"Yes, of course," Charlie says as she hurries back toward the front door, I'm assuming to open the door to their washroom. Instead, she races inside first. I come in just as I see she's flinging a few items of clothing into a laundry basket that's sitting on top of her washer.

I smile, just thinking of the first time we met. Her washer had been broken, so she'd gone to the Laundromat and washed her laundry there, then brought the wet clothes back home in a couple of garbage bags to dry them in her dryer. One of the bags caught on a rose bush by our sidewalk, and as I pulled into the driveway, she was leaving a trail of clothes, all Hansel-and-Gretel-breadcrumb-like behind her, including a few unmentionables.

I can tell by the blush on Charlie's cheeks that she's thinking of the same thing. If nothing else, the incident had given me a chance to introduce myself to my ridiculously cute neighbor.

I open the panel in the wall, shut off the valve, and

then the three of us head out of their townhome, down their steps, and up the steps to mine. And as we do, I start wishing I'd washed that pan I'd cooked eggs in this morning, along with the plate and fork I used. Maybe wiped down the counter and scrubbed my sink. Is it weird that I'm hoping for water on my floor to distract them from things I haven't cleaned?

The second we get to my kitchen, which is an exact mirror image of Charlie's and Reese's, we spot water. This time, both Charlie and Reese gasp. The puddle is a good five feet wide.

I run my hands over my face. I take my desire for a distraction back—I'm no longer hoping for water. I open the doors to my under-the-sink cabinet. It's clear it's not coming from my hot and cold water supply lines, which means it is coming from the wall.

I step up to the puddle, stopping right before my boot touches the puddle so I have a marker to make it easier to tell if the size of the puddle is increasing, and I make myself stay still for a good thirty seconds as I watch. Slowly but surely, it gets bigger.

I hurry to my washroom, grateful that Charlie and Reese didn't follow, because with the load of laundry I've got waiting to go in, the room also smells like hard work and buildings that refuse to quit, and I turn off the water to my townhome.

When I go back out to the kitchen, Reese is on the phone with our landlord, explaining the problem. I paste on a smile and say to Charlie, "Well, I have more potentially good news for you. It looks like the pipe coming to my side of the wall is leaking, which means that yours likely isn't. So you might be able to turn your water back on tonight without it causing any problems."

Charlie is looking at me with what I can only describe as a relieved grimace. I'm guessing the relieved part is for her situation, and the grimace is for mine. From what I'm hearing on Reese's end of the line, it sounds like the landlord is going to get someone on it quickly.

So I paste on a smile and say, "I'm sure it'll be fixed in no time. And don't worry about me—I can shower off the scent of 'restoration grit with a side of progress' at the gym."

CHAPTER 3
SECURITY BREACH
CHARLIE

Right now, three things are making me sing along at the top of my lungs to the car radio. I'm adding dancing in my seat at every stoplight, too.

One: I've got a box of lemon lavender cookies on the seat next to me from the cutest little bakery.

Two: Right now at work, we're in the calm between storms. Which means storm prep, for sure, as we work through all the data we downloaded from Aragundi's servers. Being a good intelligence operative means being adaptable, and the only way an operative can really shine at being adaptable is if the person behind the scenes running things—me—has over-prepared. But storm prep also means that I get off at a very predictable time.

And three: Workers showed up at my townhome to get the water leak fixed before I even left for work this morning. I'm a little freaked out to have people working in my apartment when no one is there, but at least everything should be ready to go for the get-together with friends that I'm hosting in a few minutes.

When I get home, I have to park out front. The Lord of the Leaks truck, with its cartoon plumber wearing a crown, is gone. But a truck with the name Demo Daydreams is parked in my spot in the drive-way. This cannot be good. Especially since it means I had workers in my home that I hadn't even met (or vetted) before I left for work this morning.

I grab my box of cookies and head up to my front door. As soon as I open it, I know something is off. Not only am I hearing voices I don't recognize, but everything just sounds weird and echoey. I walk past my laundry room and bathroom to where I can see the kitchen fully, and I gasp, one hand flying to my mouth, eyes wide. My kitchen wall is gone!

The cabinet below my sink, as well as the cabinets on either side of it and the two upper cabinets in the same area, are in the space to the side of my living room, stacked by my small table and on my chairs. The countertop has been removed, too, and it's lying face down across my table, both ends going out well beyond my table, the upside-down sink, along with part of its pipe, just sticking up like a periscope on a turtle's back.

And not only is the Sheetrock missing on my side of the wall, but it's missing on Owen's side, too, so I can see right into his townhome. I hadn't seen Reese pull up, but she rushes in only seconds later and joins me in gasping and staring in horror.

Two workers—one in his mid-thirties and one who looks twenty—are busy taking down the last of the wall on Owen's side, and as soon as the older one sees me, he steps between the upright wood pieces of the wall's frame to come to my side. "Things look a little different than when you last saw it, huh?"

"What happened?" I ask.

"Your plumbers had to cut into the wall to get to the broken pipe, and when they did, they found water damage. That's when they called us."

"And so you decided to take out the whole wall?" Reese asks.

"Not the *whole* wall," the man says. "We're leaving the frame. And it's better this way, trust me. You'll want this fully fixed, not just covered with a bandage that'll cause problems later."

"I have people coming over any minute," I say, my voice coming out more like a squeak.

As if being summoned by the words "people coming," Owen walks warily into his townhome, taking in the destruction with a shocked look on his face that mirrors my own.

"Oh, and there's our other occupant! I was just explaining to your neighbor that we had to take out the wall because of water damage."

When Owen's eyes cut to the side, I notice for the first time that he's got a pile of cabinets and a stretch of countertop on his table, just like I do.

The man turns back to me. "I'm Leandro, by the way. This is Josh. And having guests over is no problem. You won't even know we're here. And look— your landlord left jugs of water for you. We're close to finishing up for the day, but we'll get some plastic sheeting up before we go."

"Plastic sheeting?" I say, not believing I'm actually hearing any of this.

"Yep! It'll basically be a wall. It'll be fine."

Owen and I are staring at each other. I'm feeling a mix of commiseration that we're both in this scenario that I never could've guessed we'd be in just twenty-four hours ago, and feeling incredibly exposed. When surrounded by your home's walls, having your next-door neighbor (who is also surrounded by his home's walls), being able to see you, is just wrong.

I don't get much more than about two seconds to take it in, though, before a knock sounds at my door. Reese takes the box of cookies from me, and I walk in a daze to open the door for my sister-in-law-to-be,

Mackenzie, her best friend, Livi, and who I'm convinced will eventually be another sister-in-law, Zoe. They are each holding a big box containing everything we need to put together the wedding favors for Mackenzie's and my brother Jace's wedding. I just say, "Come in." No need to explain—they're about to experience it.

The moment they reach the kitchen, they all freeze, mid-step.

"Charlie!" Livi says. "Why does your kitchen look like it lost a fight with a wrecking ball?" Then she turns to me. "Was it the Kool-Aid Man?"

The guy in charge waves. "It's a fun and unexpected twist, isn't it? You ladies just go about whatever you have planned. Pretend we're invisible."

As I'm directing my friends around the construction mess to put their boxes on my coffee table, Owen starts talking with the construction worker. I keep sneaking peeks at him. He's dressed in a T-shirt and well-worn work jeans, and has a carpenter's pencil tucked behind one ear and a tool belt slung low on his hips. His boots are dusty, and there's a smudge of drywall powder on one forearm and a streak of something—possibly caulk?—on his bicep. Based on the faint white flecks in his hair and the thin layer of sawdust clinging to his shirt, I'm guessing he was cutting or sanding something at work today. He just looks… I don't know. Manly and adorable at the same time.

He must feel me looking because his eyes shift to me, and it feels like he's seeing right into me. I duck down behind the cabinets that are piled up beside my kitchen table. Do you know what? A bandage over the problem sounds way better than "fully fixed." Let's just go ahead and put my wall back up. What's a little water leak? That's what buckets are for, right?

I have got to somehow overcome my instinct to duck. It's not as if Owen—and everyone else in the room— didn't see me do it. So while I'm down here, I pick up a little chunk of Sheetrock that they missed when hauling out our old wall and stand, pretending that was all I was crouched down on the floor for. Then I go to toss it into the garbage and join the others around the coffee table.

Mackenzie is taking things out of boxes, explaining how we're putting together seed packets. She's got craft envelopes, seeds to scoop into them, a hole punch, ribbon, a stamp for one side that has their names and wedding date, and a stamp for the other side that reads, *The beginning of something beautiful.*

The whole time we work, I keep sneaking peeks at Owen through our suddenly open-concept neighbor situation as he goes in and out of the kitchen area. Whenever he's not visible, I feel both immense relief at having eyes off me and a little touch of letdown that I can't just, you know, see him while I'm in the middle of doing something that has nothing at all to do with him. Which is weird, but I have to admit that I do like seeing his face.

I look again, right when he's looking at me. And I don't duck! I do look away quickly, as one does, but I still think I just scored one for me.

We are all chatting, stamping, and filling seed packets when Leandro and Josh get to the point of putting up the sheeting. I was wondering if the sheeting Leandro said they'd install might be hard plastic sheeting. Like Plexiglas, except solid instead of see-through.

But nope. He was talking about the kind that's as bendy as fabric and comes on a big roll. They roll out a section long enough to cover the open area left to right, then unfold the sheeting and staple it to the wood frame at the top, adding a few staples to the side, too. I'm getting pretty nervous because although the sheeting isn't transparent, it *is* translucent—barely—and I can see body shapes on Owen's side. Which means he can see them on my side, too.

This feels like such a security breach. And not just that, but a security breach designed to poke at my specific insecurities. I take a deep breath. I can handle this. I can.

They add the sheeting to Owen's side of the wall, too, and I pretend that I can't see exactly where everything is on his side of the wall. The two men clean up, and then the one in charge comes over to tell us that they're finished and leaving for the night. Then, just before he turns to leave, he says, "We'll see you again bright and early on Monday morning. Have a great weekend!"

Reese and I turn to each other. "Monday?" she says.

"We have to go *all weekend* with a fake wall?" I'm trying not to panic.

"It probably won't be too bad," Zoe says. "It almost feels like an actual wall. I had blankets hung instead of walls in one place I lived as a kid."

I can handle this.

"I still can't believe they took out the whole wall," Livi says.

Reese nods. "Well, their name does suggest they dream about doing demo. Otherwise, their company name would be *Restoration* Daydreams."

"Maybe they should rename it Open Concept Daydreams." Mackenzie spreads her hands like she's picturing it on their van.

Zoe says, "I think they should've named it Collateral Damage Daydreams."

"Or Oops-All-Demo," Livi says.

The hostess in me hates that the disaster surrounding us happened on the same day as this get-together, but I'm glad everyone is here, talking and laughing about it. I might be freaking out right now if they weren't. Or, I might be freaking out more. I still am a bit.

Can Owen hear us talk? He might be able to, which would be more than I can handle. Although the double layer of the plastic is probably enough to muffle sounds. Plus, I can see shadows on Owen's side enough to tell when he's in the room, and he's currently not.

Livi is Mackenzie's best friend, and I'm Mackenzie's best (and only) sister-in-law. She asked both of us to be co-maids-of-honor, which is great because Livi is fun and doesn't mind being in the spotlight. Plus, the girl has an almost magical ability to never let a bad boyfriend experience dampen her enthusiasm for hunting down her Mr. Right. And oh, boy, has she had some doozies when it comes to bizarre boyfriend experiences.

Eventually, the conversation turns to guys, and I peek over at the plastic wall. I don't see any Owen-shaped blobs, so I think we're good. Livi tells us about how she and a guy she's been dating had plans to go walk around a park where a bunch of artists were painting. Before they got there, though, he asked if they could go to the hardware store instead. "And he pulled out his growly voice to ask, so of course, my resolve turned to jelly and we went to the hardware store."

"Ah, yes, the growly voice," Reese says. "Gets me every time."

Zoe shakes her head. "Not me. I'm immune."

"I've met Ledger," Livi says, "and he seems like the kind of guy who'd have a great growly voice, so I don't buy that for one second."

"What's the growly voice?" I ask. Surely I can't be the only one who doesn't know what they're talking about.

"It's when they use that deep, kind of gravelly voice that's also kind of sultry." Livi clears her throat, then says, "Like this," which is kind of deep and gravelly but not at all sultry, especially when you factor in the waggling of the eyebrows that she's doing.

"No," Reese says, and then changes her voice, "it's more like this."

We're each trying to pull off the growly voice and all failing, but we're all laughing so much that it makes me forget about how exposed I'm feeling when it comes to my neighbor.

"Does Jace ever use the growly voice?" Zoe asks Mackenzie.

I'm not at all sure I want to know this information about my brother.

Mackenzie gives a sly smile and says, "Why do you think I said yes to marrying him?"

Maybe it's from doing the same task over and over as we make these, but we've all apparently reached the stage where everything is funny, and I find myself laughing just picturing it. And, of course, talking about Jace and Mackenzie brings up the subject of the wedding that's happening in just two weeks.

"Who are you taking to the wedding?" Zoe asks Reese.

"Miles and I are playing the best friend card and taking each other. I'm not dating anyone right now, and he doesn't want to bring a woman he's only going to take on one date to a big family event, so it works out perfectly for both of us.

"Oh, but it was so funny. We had gone out to lunch, and just as he was taking a drink of his soda, I asked, 'Hey, do you want to be my date for the wedding,' and he nearly choked on his soda! I was like 'Relax, big guy. No one is trying to endanger your prized bachelor status.' It was the greatest. I think I really had him going for a second."

Then, of course, Mackenzie asks me, "Do you know who your plus-one is, yet?"

No. No, I do not. "I haven't figured out if I want to bring someone. I'm not sure I even want to date at all right now." I say it casually, like it's not stressing me out in the least, even though it totally is. I'm thinking of just telling her to seat me at the single table.

"You should ask Owen!" Reese says.

I motion for her to keep her voice down while we're without a wall.

"You should," Mackenzie adds in a (thankfully) quieter voice. "I've seen that look on your face every time your eyes land on him."

"And make all of this…" I motion at our lack of a wall, "even more awkward?" Being seen—either through a wall or because someone like Owen has X-ray eyes that feel like they can see into a soul—feels unsafe. "'Hey, Neighbor,'" I say in some voice that just comes out weird. "'Since we can see what's going on in each other's place, what do you say to dating, too?' Yeah, that's not going to happen."

Reese shakes her head slowly. "I just don't understand you."

Without even taking her eyes off the ribbon she's trying to tie, Zoe says, as if it's nothing, "It's because she was kidnapped as a preschooler. That kind of thing has long-term effects." Then Zoe looks up, notices everyone's reactions, and says, "Oh, do we not talk about that?"

"No, it's okay," I say. I wouldn't have brought it up, but it's not that big of a deal. "But that's not what's going on here—I mean, the kidnapping happened over two decades ago!"

Zoe raises an eyebrow and goes back to tying the bow.

"You were kidnapped?" both Reese and Livi say nearly in unison. Yeah, I guess I really don't bring it up.

"Why?" Reese asks. "For money?"

I shake my head. "They wanted information from my dad."

"Information?" Livi asks. "From someone with a business solutions company? What information did they need? Steps on creating a spreadsheet?"

I laugh just picturing things through Livi's eyes. Her best friend, Mackenzie, knows all about the Clandestine Services Agency and our cover as Lancaster Business Solutions because my brother told her. I mean, I guess it's important information to know before you marry a guy. Mackenzie swore she'll never tell the secret to another living person, and based on Livi's reaction, it's clear she's kept her word. Of course, being obsessed with spy movies has probably made it easier for Mackenzie to cover for any minor slip-ups.

Reese doesn't know about the agency or that our "family business" and my job as an IT systems coordinator are covers, either. Zoe does, of course, since she works for the CIA and has had a lot of mission crossovers with my brother, Ledger. That was how they met. But she can keep a secret with the best of them.

I don't talk about my kidnapping often. I have before, though, so I know the cover story to use well. "No, not spreadsheets. Our company has secure servers that house sensitive data from our clients' companies. The kidnappers wanted him to turn over information belonging to our clients that they didn't want shared." It's not exactly the truth, but it's close enough.

"Okay," Reese says, looking like she's still working through details, "I guess I kind of see how that relates to feeling exposed when you're in the spotlight."

I really don't want to get into this in more detail with Reese right now, in front of everyone. So, instead of letting her continue to think about it and come to conclusions that don't have anything to do with anything, I redirect. "I'm fine having eyes on me—it's not that." Okay, it's definitely part that. It just isn't related to the kidnapping. "And I have nothing against dating. I date for fun all the time. But I don't feel like I'm old enough for a serious relationship. I'm only twenty-four."

"Almost twenty-five," Reese cuts in.

"Plus," I say in a voice I'm sure is low enough that it won't carry, "I'm the youngest of six, and Jace is my first brother to get married. So I've got four brothers older than me who aren't getting married yet. It's not my time."

"Whoa, girl," Livi says. "Who's saying anything about getting married? We're just talking about going out with the guy."

"Oh, I know. It's just that we've established that it's not going to end in marriage, which means, eventually, there'll be a breakup and much awkwardness. You know how things are with an ex! Now, imagine if he lived next door." I can tell by everyone's flinch that they get it.

"But for the record," Mackenzie says, "I think you're plenty old enough for a serious relationship."

"Thanks. I think I don't feel like I am because everybody else seems to have everything figured out, and I just… don't. I mean, you've seen my life." I gesture at our kitchen. "It's kind of got the flooding theme going on. I'm not good at any part of it, including relationships—they all kind of crash and burn." I pause. "Wait. That doesn't really go with the flooding theme… They all *capsize*. Like Ty! And I don't want to date our neighbor, deep six our relationship, then have to see him daily."

Reese shakes her head. "Ty can't be used as evidence because you didn't deep-six your relationship with him. That relationship flopped like a dead fish all on its own. It was obvious from the start it was going to happen because he wasn't a good fit."

Livi tilts her head. "Is he the guy who thought your nickname for Charlotte should be Chuck instead of Charlie?"

"That's the one."

"Owen, though?" Reese says. "He seems like a good fit. Plus, he's super cute."

"He is. And maybe someday, when I get life things

figured out more, he might be a good fit. He isn't right now."

———

Saturday morning, I stumble my way down the stairs from my room after staying up way too late laughing and chatting with the girls, and then convincing Reese to inspect our place with me. We had workers in our house all day—two different sets of them. One could've left the doors unlocked when leaving for lunch, and someone snuck in. And yes, after Reese went to bed, I used my equipment to sweep the place for bugs because any of them could've planted one of those, too. It's better to be safe than sorry.

The only reason I'm up already and wearing running shoes is that I'd already promised Reese I'd go jogging with her, and the girl has a magical ability to wake up at the same time, regardless of when she went to bed.

I'm most of the way down the stairs before I remember the state of my kitchen. And more importantly, my kitchen wall. At least our landlord left us water. The cabinet that holds the water glasses is on the floor by my table, so I crouch down to open it and grab a glass.

As I'm pouring water from the jug into my glass, I hear Reese coming down the stairs at the same time that my attention is pulled to the plastic sheeting. I can see the blob that is Owen coming toward his kitchen, *and* I can hear something. After a second or two, I realize he's listening to a podcast on his phone.

Then he gets even closer to where his kitchen cabinets usually are, and I realize I can hear every word of his podcast. Every. Single. Word.

I turn with wide eyes to Reese just as she gets to the bottom of the stairs and point frantically toward our plastic sheeting wall. I mouth, *I think he could hear everything we said last night!*

Her eyes go wide, too. Probably thinking about how very much we talked about Owen.

She doesn't say anything—she just follows my lead and gets a glass from the floor cabinet, pours herself some water, and drinks it, looking cute in her navy and honey yellow running outfit and her navy glasses with the little honeycombs on the sides. Then she nods toward the front door. Yes. Let's wait until we're out of this space where Owen can hear everything to talk about it.

Except he has managed to get outside even before us. He's about ten steps ahead of us, heading toward his truck, when we step out onto our porch. He hears me pull our door shut and turns as we're walking down our steps.

He gives us a nod and then says in *a growly voice,*

"Good morning," before he gets into his truck and pulls out of the driveway.

Reese nods as she watches him back up. Then she turns to me. "Yep. He definitely heard us."

My face is flaming hot.

But I've got to admit, my friends were right—that growly voice is definitely irresistible.

CHAPTER 4
HISTORIC CHARM, MODERN DENIAL
OWEN

I may not have a wall anymore, but I do have running water again. Not in my kitchen sink, of course, but I was able to shower this morning after my run. Showering at my place has never been more refreshing.

Scratch that. One time, I misjudged a broken pipe angle and ended up wearing two gallons of standing water that had been collecting since Nixon was president. That shower still holds the title of *Most Refreshing*.

I drive straight to the job site for what I like to call Dreaming Day. It's what I do on Saturdays, making it my favorite day of the week. I do it alone so I can really focus and plan. Whatever site I'm at, I set up an office somewhere. For this site, once we got everything structurally sound, I set up a folding table to serve as my desk in one of the balcony boxes. I like having it there because I can look out at the theater while I work.

I start with reviewing my scheduling and budget, which usually means figuring in the hidden costs we've come across over the past week that we didn't know about until we pulled things apart. I have a general schedule, and on Saturdays, I make a very specific schedule for the coming week and a bit more vague one for the week after.

I managed to secure funding for the entire restoration from a single source—an Italian billionaire. That's so rare. It gives me fewer people I have to keep updated, which is nice. But the budget still has to be managed. As much as my crew would love the overtime, I can't afford to pay it often. And there are definitely parts along the way that have to be accomplished more quickly, so I need to save it up for then.

I go over paperwork, make sure that invoices are paid, building materials for the coming weeks are ordered, deliveries are scheduled, and take care of all the other project management details I can. That way, during the week, I can spend the bulk of my time working with my crew.

Then comes my favorite part: dreaming. I walk the space slowly, letting the past rise up around me. I imagine the velvet curtains drawn back, the seats full, the lights warm and golden across the stage. I picture gleaming chandeliers, crown molding that's crisp and whole again, and the wood under my feet polished to a mirror shine. I think through every step it'll take to get there—the materials, the order, the hidden work behind the visible beauty.

I realized early on that I can see what things are trying to be. Not just buildings, but the stories they used to hold. Most people see what's crumbling and broken. I see what's waiting. And when I can describe it well enough for other people to glimpse it too, that's when magic starts to happen. It's how I got funding for this place. And every time I finish one of these restorations, I take it as proof that something broken has the potential to become something breathtaking.

And usually, I can do all of it without constantly thinking about a spunky brunette living next door. Not today.

I didn't mean to eavesdrop on Charlie and her friends last night, but with the missing wall, it was hard not to. Plus, they weren't exactly being quiet, and after a physically taxing day at work, I was starving. Because of the state of my kitchen, I couldn't cook a meal, but I could make a hearty sandwich. My kitchen was about the only place I could make it, and it was so close to Charlie's living room, where they were all hanging out.

It wasn't like I hung around all night, listening. It

was just during the times when I had to be in my kitchen. I purposely tried to stay away the rest of the time. Even still, sometimes they were loud enough that I heard them no matter where I was.

But, on the plus side, I unintentionally learned a lot. The effects of "growly voice" on a woman, for one. A lot about Charlie, for two. And copious amounts about wedding seating politics, who fell for a guy just because of his voice, and what bakeries make the best éclairs. I also learned the tone and volume of laughter that only happens when people feel safe and comfortable together.

And I learned that I really love the sound of Charlie's laugh.

———

Some of the guys from my crew—Grady, Luis, and Trent—invited me to play disc golf with them, so when I finish my admin and planning work for the day, I head toward the park.

I like that they asked me. I've only played disc golf a few times, and I'm bad at it, but when you move into a place where you know no one, it's good to make friends. I don't mind leaving friends behind when I move on to a new place, because then, if I'm ever traveling in an area where I've lived for a job, I have friends there. I have friends sprinkled all over the Mid-Atlantic.

Relationships are a different story, though. Those you don't just sprinkle around and come back to if you're ever in the area. I try to never forget that I'm only here for the short term, nothing permanent.

Not like Charlie. She obviously has roots. I don't. No matter how attractive she is and how pulled I am toward her, I'm not going to be in Cipher Springs long enough to make deeper connections.

When I meet up with the guys at the disc golf course just past the edge of town, the four of us step onto the first tee. It's still warm and bright, and the breeze is just enough to make us second-guess every throw, which makes it even more fun, because then chaos can win over skill. We each pull a driver disc from our bags.

"Let's make this interesting," Trent says, stretching his arms behind his head. "Loser buys chicken wings. Winner gets to gloat with zero consequences."

"You say that like you're not the reigning king of double bogeys," Grady says, already digging into his backpack for a disc that looks suspiciously too light-weight to go far.

"All part of my strategy," Trent says. "I lure you in with mediocrity, then unleash the perfect flick on hole six."

Luis takes the first throw. He winds up with an

exaggerated hop-step like he's about to launch a javelin. The disc hooks left immediately and clatters into a cluster of saplings. "That was just a warm-up. And a warning to the trees."

Grady's up next. He does a slow, theatrical wind-up with a pirouette flourish at the end, releasing the disc with the elegance of a man who thinks he's starring in a deodorant commercial. His disc sails a solid distance and lands with a satisfying skip just a few feet short of the basket. He smirks and bows like he's been waiting all week for this one moment.

I step up to the tee, eye the slight right curve of the fairway, and let my disc fly. It glides with a surprising precision that makes it look like I might actually know what I'm doing before it catches a breeze and veers off course, landing behind a boulder.

Trent's throw goes high and wide, his whole body spinning dramatically with the force of the toss. He stumbles on the follow-through, windmilling his arms before catching himself. The disc lands somewhere between a patch of tall grass and what might be a shallow drainage ditch.

"That's a bold strategy," Luis says as they start walking down the fairway. "Going for aquatic terrain so early in the game."

As we walk toward my disc, since it's the furthest from the basket, Luis asks what my hobbies are. Maybe he's wondering if I'm likely to play as beautifully as the first half of my disc's flight went or the second half.

The truth is, when it comes to hobbies, I'm a history buff. Especially history in relation to architecture. That particular skill comes in handy in exactly three situations: trivia nights, when writing epic poetry, and while shooting the breeze with other historical restoration specialists.

There are zero trivia nights held around here. I checked. Ditto to nearby historical restoration specialists. So, instead, I answer Luis's question by listing things that I enjoy that I think he might enjoy, too. Playing pool, bowling, darts, axe throwing, cornhole, whatever.

"Did you hear that, guys?" Luis says. "It looks like we're going to have to have a cornhole competition at some point!"

I grin. "I don't know. My bean bag game puts my disc golf game to shame." When we reach my disc, I squint at the awkward angle I'll have to take.

"This is what you get for not bribing the wind gods," Trent says.

Grady shrugs. "You could go over the boulder. If you enjoy failure."

I opt for a low, backhand curve. The disc somehow makes it through a tight gap and lands within putting range.

Luis slow claps. "That's the kind of redemption arc we love to see!"

Trent's second throw lands somewhere in the weeds. Again. "I swear this course is tilted," he says. He seems to get over it quickly, though, because he turns to me. "So, did you leave a girlfriend behind at your previous job?"

"Nope. It's been a good long while since anyone was brave enough to date a guy who smells like nineteen-twenties basement insulation half the time."

They laugh, and the moment passes easily. But as we walk to the next disc, my mind drifts. Charlie's the only one who's made me even *consider* wanting a relationship again, and I heard enough of her conversation with friends to know she has her own reasons for steering clear of relationships, especially with me.

And I've had too many failed relationships to believe I can make it work. I might be able to see the potential in buildings, but when it comes to relationships, it's easy to believe they're meant for everyone but me.

CHAPTER 5
CAUTION: SLIPPERY WHEN SEEN
CHARLIE

Somehow, I made it through the weekend with a translucent wall separating my townhome and my very cute neighbor's. It was tough. After realizing how much Owen could hear, I felt like I had to spend the rest of the weekend whispering whenever I was home.

Within moments of my alarm going off, a knock sounds at our front door, and I know it's Leandro and Josh, here to finish the job. Reese wakes up even earlier than I do, so she went down to answer the door while I got into the shower. Since I'm not downstairs, where there is no real wall, I've got music playing, and I'm singing along. There's nothing like rocking out in the shower to start your day off energetically.

When I start washing my hair, the song *Unwritten* by Natasha Bedingfield comes on, and I am lathering up the shampoo like it's never been lathered before, all while releasing my vocal inhibitions. Reese and I have our own rooms, but we share this bathroom, and we always joke about how the water from the shower head comes out like gentle rain, so I especially belt it out at the line about feeling the rain on my skin.

And with an impressive but unfortunate feat of timing, the water stops allowing me to feel the rain on my skin at the exact moment I'm singing about it. It just… *stops.* I mess with the faucet, turning it off and back on. Hotter and colder. But nothing comes out of the shower head besides a few straggling drops.

Did the workers seriously just turn off our water without even giving us a warning? I've got a giant beehive-shaped lathering of shampoo on my head right now! And not just on my head—it's running all down my body.

There are very few things that make me really mad. I'm talking like maybe three. I can't think what the other two might be at this exact moment, but I do know that the third is turning off the water while I'm covered in shampoo. I step out of the shower, grab my towel, wrap it around me, and storm down the stairs, ready to give those guys working on our house an earful.

Normally, there's not much anyone could possibly do to get me to appear in only a towel in front of *anyone.* The only way I'm doing it now is because a) I don't know the workers, and they'll go off and forget about me the moment they're done here, and b) because I've got the fuel of anger, frustration, and righteous indignation propelling me down the stairs.

I start saying, "Did you seriously just turn off the water right in the middle…" before I even get far enough down the stairs to see into the kitchen. Once I do get to where I can see, I try to take in everything at once. The plastic that used to be my wall but is currently lying in a heap on the floor. The plastic on Owen's side all folded up. The water that has sprayed everywhere in my kitchen and is still dripping in some places. The workers that are looking up at me sheepishly.

And Owen. Standing like he'd just been talking to the two men, his eyes frozen on me. Me and my piled-high shampoo suds that are probably not quite so high now, based on how much is running down my torso and arms. And me, standing there wearing only a towel, with nothing but the thin railing of the stairs between me and Owen's gaze.

This is a nightmare. It has to be a nightmare.

Leandro scratches the back of his neck. "So, um, funny story. We were taking down the plastic so we could work on your repairs. We got your neighbor's side down just fine. But when we were pulling the staples loose on your side, Josh reached a little too far, fell off his step-stool, and wouldn't you know it? He landed right on your pipe. Not only that, but the hammer in his tool belt hit at just the right angle to puncture the line. That's why there's water everywhere. And because I knew you didn't want to come down to a swimming pool, we, uh, had to shut off the water to your place.

Reese, whom I hadn't noticed had followed me down the stairs, holds a towel out to me and asks, "So, what does this mean for repairs?"

I take the towel from her, and with a hand on each of the top corners, hold the towel in front of me like a screen, blocking the view of my body all the way up to my eyeballs.

Leandro lets out a sigh. "It means we'll need to bring your plumbers back to fix this before we can continue. But don't worry—we're going to get you taken care of. Eventually."

Josh, looking extra sheepish now, wordlessly grabs a gallon of water from the one part of my counters that is still intact, walks over to the stairs, and hands it up to me with a grimace. I have to let go of one of the corners of the towel to take it from him, which makes it less like I'm hiding behind a big shield and more like I'm hiding behind a small tree's trunk. Then I brush some of the shampoo from my eyes and say, "Thank you."

They'll get it taken care of… *Eventually.*

I breathe out a defeated sigh, then take my gallon

of water and head back upstairs to finish off my shower in a less rain, more garden-hose kind of way. While I'm trying to rid my body of this much shampoo using a single gallon of water, I become more and more determined to avoid Owen at all costs, at least while the wall is down. And let's be real, probably for weeks after because that's how long it's going to take for my dignity to recover.

———

Work today was busy. And not the "Oh, wow, it's quitting time already?" kind of busy. More of the "I'm so exhausted, I can barely drive myself home" kind. I do manage to drive myself home, though. And when I get to my front door, there's a sticky note on it from Reese that reads *BRACE YOURSELF.* And then in smaller writing below it, it reads, *Just a reminder that I'm going to a concert with Miles tonight and won't be back until late.*

I take a deep breath and go inside. I don't head to the kitchen first—I stop by the downstairs bathroom and turn on the water, then let out a breath of relief when water actually comes out. I was finding soap suds in random places on me all day.

Then I brace myself and head to the kitchen. There is no new wall up, which I had already guessed, and the thin plastic is back up. The place actually doesn't look too different from how it looked all weekend. I assume they fixed the pipe, since we have water, but not a swimming pool amount of water.

This time, though, there's a door cut into the plastic just to the side of where my sink usually is. It's about as high as a regular door, but only as wide as the space between studs. I'm guessing they did it so they can travel between the two townhomes without having to go outside. The only thing holding the plastic sheeting door closed is four pieces of blue painter's tape.

It's fine. I can handle this. No big deal. I'm too exhausted to *not* handle it, anyway.

I search upstairs in both my room and Reese's for any sneaky people hiding, change into my comfiest clothes and fluffiest socks, order Chinese food, do a quick sweep for bugs, and when my food comes, I sit on the couch to eat it. In fact, sitting on the couch feels so good that when I'm finished, I decide to stay there and just read a cozy mystery. It's not often that I get a quiet night like this, and I'm going to just soak all the relaxation in.

I'm in the middle of chapter four when I hear Owen answer his phone and say, his voice getting more muffled as he walks further from our makeshift wall, "Oh, hi, sis! Do you mind if I put you on speaker? I'm in the middle of doing laundry."

I'm trying very hard to pay attention to my book as the main character is realizing that the victim was someone she knew, but all I can seem to picture is Owen doing laundry. Is he sorting his clothes before putting them in the washer? Folding them? Dang, if the image of him sitting on his couch, folding clothes on his coffee table, isn't getting me right in the feels.

You are avoiding him. Focus!

And I can. Mostly. That is, until he comes back out of his laundry room, and I can hear their conversation better. They're mostly just talking like brother and sister, shooting the breeze. It's obvious that they have a good relationship, and it's cute hearing him in this role.

I'm ignoring. I'm totally ignoring.

Then I hear Owen say, "Oh, Mom is calling."

"Don't answer it!" his sister says in a rush. He asks why, and she says, "Because I want to tell you first." Pause. "But I don't want you to panic."

"You do realize that saying 'don't panic' is the easiest way to get someone to panic, right?"

She lets out a tight chuckle. "Okay, but seriously, don't."

"Where are you?" he asks warily.

"The hospital."

"What? Why?"

I close my book. There's no way I'm going to be able to focus on it now.

"I was hanging out with a bunch of friends just in front of the KOBL building. It's right by the quad, and there's a BBQ and a table, and some good cement. Several of the guys were riding on skateboards, doing tricks, as we were all just talking. There's kind of a half wall going up on one side of the area where we were, because there's a sidewalk up there. So, of course, there was also a railing. But the railing wasn't right at the edge, and the space between it and where the wall dropped off was wide enough for a skateboard."

I can tell that Owen is up and pacing by the way the sound of his sister is changing, like it's getting closer and clearer and then further and more muffled. He hasn't said a word throughout her story, but I can almost feel his nerves.

"Then one of the guys bet another that he couldn't skateboard along it. The guy said, 'You're right.' But they were ribbing each other, and I don't know. I just kind of said that I could do it in my sleep."

"You didn't."

"I can't help it if I get accidentally competitive sometimes."

"You can barely walk in platform shoes! Please tell me you didn't actually try it."

"I would, but I know how much you value honesty."

Owen takes a deep breath. "What happened?"

"Well, I went up to that sidewalk, climbed over the railing, and put one of the guys' skateboards on the ledge. Then I got on it, and… kind of proved that I was wrong."

"You fell?"

"Right onto the cement below."

"Tessa! How badly did you get hurt?"

"Now, see? You're panicking. You're supposed to *not* panic."

"Tessa," Owen says in a tight voice that seems to be taking everything he has to sound less panicked. *"What happened."*

"In a nutshell? My friends got me to the hospital, where they did surgery to put a pin in my broken leg. They say I'll get out of the hospital soon, and I'll get a cool boot to wear around campus for a while. I called Mom first, and then I called you."

I know just from hearing Owen's footfalls that he's hurrying around his townhome. "I'll hop on the first flight they've got to Denver and hopefully be there tonight."

"No."

"No?"

"Owen, I barely finished talking Mom out of 'hopping on the first flight to Denver.' That was exhausting enough. Don't make me do it all over again. I mean, *I just got surgery.* Making me expend that kind of energy wouldn't be a very brotherly thing to do."

"Tessa, you're going to need help. Whatever they gave you during the surgery is going to wear off, and you'll be in a lot of pain. You'll need someone there with you."

"You do remember that I share a dorm with *seven* other girls, right? Trust me, I've got plenty of help. There's always someone around. Plus, the guys with the skateboards feel terrible about what happened and are already smothering me with offers of help. I'll be okay."

There's silence for a moment, and I don't know if it's because Owen's pacing has taken him too far away for me to hear or if he's just busy trying to control his breathing. I realize it must be the latter when I hear his sister say, "I mean, really. If you want to be worried, it might be better to worry about my academic probation."

"What?" Owen says, clearly taking her advice to worry now.

"I mean, at least that's what I'm hearing through the grapevine. It's not official yet. But skateboarding on that ledge is against the rules."

"And *you knew*?"

"I didn't think anyone was watching!"

Their conversation continues for a few more minutes, and I can tell that Owen is trying to be a patient big brother and be there for his sister. But I can also tell that it really stresses him out. Especially because even after their phone call ends, I can still hear him pacing. I can still sense his worry.

I should do something. I am practically being pulled toward him.

No. I'm avoiding him at all costs.

I stand and walk closer to our wall. Maybe I should ask if he's okay. Or maybe I shouldn't. Maybe he would rather pretend I'm not home, or that I wasn't really able to hear any of his private conversation.

I'm debating with myself for a long minute before it hits me that these walls aren't exactly opaque. With his pacing, I'm sure he's turned to see me standing next to the wall, unmoving. Like a giant eavesdropper.

Since it's a good bet that he's been made aware that I've overheard everything, I throw all caution to the wind and knock lightly on the wood stud. Then I say, "I can offer a listening ear if you'd like it."

There's a pause in his pacing, then his blurred silhouette nears. A moment later, I hear the sound of painter's tape being pulled off plastic sheeting, so I pull it off the door cut into the plastic on my side, too, and we each open our floppy doors. He just looks at me for a moment, and then he nods. "Come in."

He holds his piece of plastic open, and I walk through the narrow opening to his place and follow him to his living room. And my mental image was right! There is folded laundry on his coffee table, and a basket half filled with clothes sitting on the couch. I'm still reveling in that swoon just a bit.

That is, until I spot a pair of his underwear peeking

out in the basket, which not only reminds me of my towel incident earlier, but also of the very first time that I met Owen—when a laundry bag mishap made me leave a trail of my underwear on our shared front yard for Owen to discover, and my face heats up.

I force the thought away. I'm not here to be embarrassed. I'm here because Owen is sad.

"So I'm guessing you heard all that?"

"Most of it," I say. "Sorry—I was just sitting on my couch, reading a book, so it was kind of hard not to."

Owen sits on the couch, and I sit in a side chair. With his elbows on his knees, he drops his head into his hands for a few minutes, his fingers in his hair. It hurts to see him like this. I feel such a strong need to do something that I get up and move to sit next to him on the couch. I do manage to keep my hands to myself instead of patting or rubbing his back. It's the closest to 'avoid him at all costs' I can manage.

Eventually, he lifts his head and says, "I just worry about her, you know? She's always been more of a risk-taker and doesn't make the best long-term decisions. And now, she's at a university that's over sixteen hundred miles away, so if anything happens, I can't even be there quickly to help. And I worry about the friends she's made if she feels like she has to break school rules and do dangerous things. I mean, why didn't they stop her?"

"You didn't make any bad choices in college?"

He chuckles and shakes his head, and it releases a bit of the tension in the room. "Okay, you're right. I made my fair share. Several that I wish I could take back."

"Everyone makes bad choices in college. Well, we do every day, too, but college has its own special brand of them. You just have to hope she isn't making catastrophic choices."

He nods.

"I think you should be proud of her."

Owen turns to look at me. "For riding a skateboard along a ledge with a drop-off to cement when she has no skateboarding experience?"

"No," I say, playfully swatting at his upper arm. "For being independent."

He studies me like he can see right into me, trying to figure out just what I'm thinking.

"Listen. I am well-versed in Protective Older Brother. I've got five of them."

Owen's eyebrows rise. "Five?"

"Yep. And all are overachievers who see protectiveness as the most important skill to develop. And let me tell you: having a protective older brother is the greatest thing in the world." I pause a moment. "It also makes it incredibly difficult to be independent, since they're always willing to step in and solve any problem you have."

Owen looks down, thoughtful.

"Yes, she is injured, and she will need help. I think she gets that. But she didn't call you the moment it happened, begging for help. She's working it out on her own. Figuring out how to best deal with the consequences of her actions. Instead of looking at it as her making choices that are going to lead her down a path to… I don't know, living in a ditch or whatever your worst case scenario is, you could always view it as her taking an opportunity to exercise some independence. Be impressed. Cheer her on. Heck, I'm impressed. If I were her, I might've called you from the ground where I landed."

He's just looking at me, and I don't know what to do. It's an uncomfortable feeling, having someone see me so thoroughly.

After a long pause, he says, "Thank you. I hadn't thought of it that way. It feels good."

"Yeah?"

"Yeah."

Now he's giving me a look, and I'm sure I'm giving him a look, and it feels like the very opposite of avoiding him at all costs. Although at this exact moment, I'm not so sure I'm as willing to commit to that plan.

Well, at least until my next embarrassing lack-of-a-wall moment. I work to clear my mind of the haze it's in from being right next to Owen as he's being all protective, brotherly, *and* domestic. Then, I clear my throat and make myself stand. "Okay, well, I'll let you get back to…" I gesture at the basket of clothes on his other side and the folded clothes on his coffee table, "laundry, and pretending not to worry."

"And I'll let you get back to… pretending that I don't exist."

So, he noticed that, huh? I force a grin. "Exactly. Just as soon as I tape back up my side of the door."

CHAPTER 6
NOT FLIRTING, JUST NEIGHBOR-ING
OWEN

We got the remaining theater seats removed last week, which has made The Shadowridge feel pretty cavernous and echoey. Today, we're making enough dust that it's a little less so. But only a little. We're also making plenty of noise. I've got some guys removing some damaged plaster so they can begin the rewiring, and I'm up on some scaffolding, cataloguing and carefully removing the decorative features on the front of the balcony boxes so when we restore them, they'll look exactly as they did originally.

Normally, on a day like today, my thoughts go something like this: thinking deeply about what I'm currently doing and the best way to do it. Thinking about what everyone else is doing. Thinking about what the next steps are and who I'm going to put on what jobs. Shifting my position to help my hurt knee. Thinking further down the schedule, about what building materials I need to order next. Thinking about how to deal with an upcoming area that's going to be tricky. Repeat.

Today, though? My thoughts are more like this: scoring the caulk and paint seal along the edge of some trim. Thinking about Charlie. Inserting the trim removal tool and carefully prying it loose. Thinking about Charlie. Glancing down at my guys removing plaster to see how things are going for them. Thinking about Charlie. Starting to ponder what the next steps are, but getting distracted by thoughts of Charlie.

Why? I don't know. I decided long before I came to Cipher Springs that I wasn't going to get involved with anyone while I was on a job. Not three days ago, I reminded myself that I'm in no shape for a relationship, and that based on what I'd heard from Charlie when she was with her friends, she doesn't want a relationship, either. I'd decided that we could be friendly but not flirty.

"Owen!"

I quickly shift where I'm standing on the scaffolding to glance down at Grady, who's looking up at me like maybe he's been trying to get my attention for a bit. "What?"

"You've been awfully quiet today, boss. Thinking about blueprints or brunettes?"

I chuckle and admit, "A little of both. Whatcha got?"

"We've got wires runnin' right where the old duct was. Want me to reroute, or have you got a plan for that?"

"Reroute," I say, then turn back to the front of the balcony box, the trim I'm removing, and, unsurprisingly, thoughts of Charlie.

Maybe I'm having so many thoughts about her just because of last night. A small, far-away part of me knew that Charlie was home when Tessa called. But I was so concerned about my sister that I didn't have brainpower left for wondering if Charlie could hear. Part of me is embarrassed that she did.

The other part of me, though, is glad she did. I didn't realize how badly I needed someone to literally step in and put things into perspective until Charlie did just that. I didn't ask her to. She just somehow intuitively knew I needed it. And she knew exactly what I needed to hear. I still can't get over it.

When I called Tessa today to check on her, she was clearly in more pain than when she'd called from the hospital. But the pain was manageable, and she was getting tons of help. She even had her friends on a rotating schedule to check in on her and help her with the things she needed.

I told her that I was proud of her, and I was impressed at how well she was taking care of everything. That seemed to be exactly what she needed to hear, too. I swear I could feel her beaming right through the phone. I have Charlie to thank for that.

Or maybe I can't stop thinking about Charlie because of what I have planned to give her after work. When I first chose this theater as a potential project, I checked out the whole town. I remembered going into a little shop near the theater that made custom-painted wooden signs. The kind you hang on a wall in your house.

I stopped by on my way to work this morning and told the shop owner about my current wall situation and what happened last night. I asked her to make a sign for me that reads, *Eavesdropping Level: Expert.* I don't know Charlie as well as I'd like to, but from what I do know, I think she'll get a kick out of it. The shop owner was so excited to get started on it that she said she'll have it ready for me to pick up when I leave work. I can't wait.

As I'm doing a building sweep and locking the place up at the end of the day, I get a call from my landlord. He tells me that it seems some of the electrical wiring was damaged in the leak, especially in the oven area—I'm not sure if he's talking about the initial leak or the one caused by Josh's hammer—and that an electrician will need to come by and fix that first.

"But that's not all," he says, and I get the sense that he really doesn't want to say the rest.

"You can tell me," I say. "I do construction for a living, so I know how many things can delay a job."

"True. Okay, so you might have noticed when they were doing the demolition that the insulation between the walls had some water damage and a bit of mold. Obviously, it had to be discarded. But the insulation needed between units like yours is on backorder for a week or two." I can practically hear the grimace in his voice.

"I talked to the restoration company to see if they would put the Sheetrock back up on one of your walls and just wait to do the other side until the insulation came in. That way, you'd at least have something more closely resembling a wall. But the younger of the two guys got injured on a job, and he'll be out for at least a week."

"From when he fell and broke our pipe?"

"Um, no... it was another job. Apparently, that wasn't his only time being clumsy. Since they're a man down, their schedule is a little too tight, so they aren't willing to come until all the building materials can be there. I tried to line up a different company, but there aren't any that are free. It was hard enough getting Demo Daydream as quickly as we did."

None of the problems happening are within my landlord's control, so I tell him that I understand and thank him for trying to get everything taken care of. "Have you told Charlie and Reese yet?"

"I'm calling them next. Wish me luck!"

When I stop to pick up the wooden plaque, the shop owner sees me walk in and excitedly goes over to a counter and picks up the sign she made, showing it to me with a big grin on her face. I've noticed that Charlie wears a lot of pink, so I had her do the base color in pink and the lettering in white. And she's done a fantastic job. *Eavesdropping Level:* is in blocky hand-lettering, and *Expert* is in a fancy script.

The shop owner even puts it in a fancy box with tissue paper and everything, and she adds a pink bow. I thank her profusely and promise that I'll stop back in and let her know what Charlie thought of it.

When I pull into my driveway and see that both Charlie and Reese are home, I start to second-guess everything. What if Charlie doesn't find it funny? What if getting the call from our landlord saying that it would be longer before we get a new wall has just left her angry or frustrated, and this will only make it worse?

Instead of knocking on Charlie's door and handing the box to her when she answers, like I had planned, I opt for leaving it on her doorstep. I tell myself that it's the kind of gift that's best if it's not opened in the presence of the giver, and not that I'm doing it this way because I'm worried about whether she'll find it funny or not. I knock on her door, then race into my own townhome so I can hear her reaction through the non-wall.

Both women start by wondering what it is, who it's for, and who it's from. Then one of them opens it, and Charlie immediately knows the answers to those questions. Their laughter is loud, long, and joyful, and it has me grinning from ear to ear.

This is good. I gave a very neighborly gift, not a flirty gift. I'm still on track.

———

It's nearing nine p.m., and I'm sitting on my couch, going over the blueprints for the historic train station in Philadelphia that I'm under contract to restore next, and perfecting my final restoration proposal after getting the structural assessments on my laptop, when I hear a small noise come from my kitchen. I glance over to see a blurry silhouette of Charlie, crouched down and pushing a little basket of something through the untaped flap at the bottom corner of my fake door, next to the floor.

A second later, Charlie stands, and I see her hand slowly maneuvering its way between two of the taped sections of the door, right about eye level. She sticks a pink Post-It note to my side of the plastic and then removes her hand. A second later, I hear a small knock before seeing her race away from the door.

I walk over to the note, and I grin as I read it.

Thank you for your very thoughtful gift. I will treasure it always.
P.S. Look down.

I bend down and pick up the wicker basket she left. It's filled with muffins sitting on tissue paper printed with a wood design. Was she just able to guess that wood is my favorite color? There's a little card attached, so I open it to read, *From your nosy but adorable neighbor.*

I shake my head. It's been a long time since I've had a neighbor I've had this much fun with. I take a bite of one of the muffins and nearly moan. I'm aware of the state of her kitchen, so I know she didn't bake these. But I had no idea that there were places that sold muffins that taste this good!

I find the cabinet that houses my office supplies over by my table and shift everything a bit so I can open the drawer and pull out a pad of sticky notes and a pen. I go to the one cabinet and countertop that wasn't removed—the one that used to be the bottom of the L in my L-shaped kitchen but is now more like a small island—and I think about what I want my note to say. I'm left-handed, and when I'm not paying enough attention to my handwriting, it slants a lot. I make sure to slow down and make all my letters upright.

And thank you for your very delicious gift.
My taste buds will fondly remember it forevermore.
From your neighbor who talks on the phone too loudly.

I reach through a space between the tape on my side, snake my hand through the space between the studs, in through a space between the tape on Charlie's side, and I stick the note to her plastic.

Then, I head back to my couch to work on my proposal, smiling.

———

The next morning, as I keep pulling things out of my closet, I realize I should have spent a bit less time perfecting my proposal last night and a bit more time deciding what to wear during my presentation. I've got it down to two very different choices, and I can't decide which one.

Charlie is insightful. I bet she'd know. I look down at my watch. It's seven-forty. One thing that no sound deadening between you and your neighbor does is let you easily learn each other's daily routines. So, I know Charlie is currently standing at the one part of her cabinets that's still in place, eating breakfast. From a part of a conversation I overheard, I'm guessing yogurt with granola and maybe blueberries.

So I put on my first option, which is a navy suit that's well fitted with a white shirt and a light blue tie that has a subtle design of architectural blueprints. Then I go downstairs to my kitchen and knock on one of the studs. "Charlie, are you nearby?"

"Yeah," she says, sounding a bit surprised to hear my voice.

"Can you help me figure out what to wear?" I already hate that I said that out loud.

"What to wear? Um, sure."

As we are both pulling the tape away from the plastic so we can open the door, I start talking. "I am presenting at a historical preservation society about my plans for my next project. What?" I stop explaining when we each open our side's door and I see the expression on her face.

"Nothing. I just, wow. You, uh, look mighty spiffy

in a suit." She clears her throat. "Seriously, good job on that."

I look down for a minute, smiling. And then I have to remind myself that my goal is to act neighborly, so I should stop thinking of the flirting responses I really want to reply with. I meet her eyes again. "Thank you. So, I want them to say yes to my proposal, and I know that what I wear can make a difference. Do you mind if I come back in a few minutes wearing my other option?" And here I am, feeling all stupid again for asking.

She says she doesn't mind, and in my head, I keep replaying her reaction to my first option as I'm changing into the second. It wasn't flirting—it was an honest reaction, which makes it so much better. Maybe the navy suit is the right choice. It's professional-looking. Especially when I take Charlie's reaction to seeing me in it into consideration. I mean, that has to be good, right?

This time, I put on a vintage-inspired crisp white shirt and camel-colored trousers that are slightly tapered and cuffed just enough to show off my brown leather brogues. My tie is a dark gray, leaning slightly toward brick red. Then I put on a charcoal tweed vest with a faint herringbone texture, and add a deep forest green sport coat with leather elbow patches and brass buttons, and look in my mirror. It's a well put-together outfit that feels slightly… academic. It makes me think of cedar and old books.

I go back downstairs, knock on the stud again, and Charlie and I both open our bendy little doors.

This time, Charlie doesn't say a word—her eyes just widen. Then she swallows, nods, and says, "This one." Except the words come out sounding a little choked.

"Yeah?"

"Definitely. The first one looked like you were going on a fancy date or to a benefit or something. This one says, 'You can trust me with your beloved building.'"

I smile. "That's exactly what I was hoping it would say."

"Now if you'll excuse me," Charlie says, "I need to go remember how to… not…" She says as she's closing and re-taping her door. Then she turns around to rest her back against a stud, and I swear, her mumbled sentence finishes with, "…spend all day drooling over those two mental snapshots you just gave me."

CHAPTER 7
LET THE RECORD SHOW: I AM NOT FLIRTING
CHARLIE

had a crazy dream about needing to hack into the International Space Station's climate control system because someone smuggled a vintage violin aboard, and the wrong humidity would ruin its tone. Which isn't even remotely plausible. I mean, they run proprietary encryption that auto-bricks your system if you even sneeze near the login screen. But it has made ideas of ways to code a program to cloak agent heat signatures from motion sensors run through my head all morning.

I'm almost ready for work and am just coming down the stairs to get breakfast when there's a knock at my front door. The electrician is here already? I answer the door to see a man in his fifties who's wearing a tool belt and holding a clipboard in one hand and a toolbox in the other. There's a truck parked out front. It's not one of the box trucks, like the plumber and the restoration guys have—it's a white work truck with a tool chest in the bed and a *Bolt & Beacon Electric* logo on the door.

"Hi. I'm here to fix some electrical issues in your kitchen caused by a leaky pipe."

I still can't believe that I'm letting a worker in here again when I'm not going to be home. I may have freaked out that the plan had changed from plumbers at Lord of the Leaks to Demo Daydreams while I wasn't even home and without getting a chance to vet them first. At least I got a chance to thoroughly vet this one. Both the man and the company he works for. He's clean. I guess going without a wall is enough to help me let down my defenses a bit.

And I am pretty proud of myself for making all the progress I have on being okay with workers being here. Jace wouldn't have let them in at all.

Of course, if it were happening to my mom, the CSA would've lined up their own people from the start. They can't have their director being targeted by anyone with a fake company truck and a convincing uniform.

"Come in," I say. It'll be fine. I'll get Reese to do a thorough check with me when we get home, and then I'll sweep for bugs when she's gone.

I lead the electrician into the kitchen, and he sets down his toolbox without taking his eyes off the plastic draped and stapled to my wall frame. "They took down all the Sheetrock, huh?"

"Yep," I say as Reese comes down the stairs, looking adorable in red tights and a bright yellow cardigan over a navy blue dress with a pattern of illustrated books. And, of course, she's wearing matching bright red glasses, too.

"This sheeting is all that separates you and your neighbor?" He looks at me. "And you're okay with that?"

No. No, I am not. Instead of voicing that, though, I say with a shrug. "I wasn't at first, but…It's not so bad."

"Only because our neighbor is cute and Charlie is crushing on him," Reese says.

I turn to her and hiss, "Shh! Owen can hear!"

Okay, I *might* be crushing on Owen. But only because he's adorable in every way, and it'd be hard not to. And it's true about the wall not being so bad. I've learned way more about Owen than I ever could have by going through his garbage, like Zoe once suggested. You can hear a lot through this wall, and with the fuzzy shape of him that I can see as he moves around—at least when he's within about ten feet of the fake wall—I've got a pretty clear picture of how his day goes.

I know what time he wakes up and goes to bed, how many times he reheats his dinner in the microwave because he forgot about it, that he mutters when he is puzzling through work plans, and that he always stops at 9 p.m. to make a cup of hot cocoa.

I also know that every morning, he sings his to-do list. And he doesn't simply read his list in a sing-song voice. He picks a random tune but makes up his own words. Like yesterday, he sang about removing plaster and decorative features on balcony boxes to the tune of Queen's *We Will Rock You*. And this morning, he was singing about checking on some insulation to the tune of *Hey Jude* by the Beatles. A few days ago, he was a little further away and harder to hear, but I'm pretty sure I heard him singing about double-checking that a ceiling fan wasn't haunted to the tune of *Uptown Funk*.

But last night, after realizing how much I know about Owen, a stab of panic hit me. Because if I know way more than I should know about Owen, then he knows way more about me than what I'm willing to share.

And the truth I try to hide from everyone but am not always successful in doing is that I'm a big, fat, scaredy-cat, and I just want to go hide under the couch and pretend I don't exist until someone brings snacks. I don't want to be seen deeply. I want to be seen surface-ly. I want to choose what is seen. Being seen deeply feels vulnerable. And vulnerability feels dangerous.

So I'm trying hard to keep things on the surface. Just fun, neighborly flirting. Nothing more. Like leaving notes for each other, ever since I left that sticky note on his side of the plastic two nights ago.

Our notes have mostly said things like *I hope your day's more functional than our kitchen wall,* or *Thanks for not judging my cleaning playlist last night,* or *Today's forecast: 20% chance of rain. Indoors.* I've kind of been living for it. Just harmless surface banter. Nothing deep.

My reward for keeping things light and neighborly was coming downstairs this morning to find a little gift bag waiting for me at the foot of our makeshift door. The tag said, *Because I interrupted your reading with my phone call.*

Inside the bag, I found a candle with a label that said, *Smells like shared wall.* Then, in smaller print below, *(Just kidding. Smells like brown sugar and vanilla.)* There was a colorful bookmark with the words *Good fences make good neighbors. Shared walls make romantic comedies.* I think I might've laughed even harder than I did when he gave me the wooden plaque.

And there is nothing like starting the day with a good laugh. Soon after, I put a sticky note on his side of the plastic that said, *If your goal was to make me belly laugh before breakfast, mission accomplished. (And thank you.)*

I keep telling myself that I am thrilled to live next to a fun and neighborly neighbor. But boy, does my stomach flutter every single time I see a note or a package from him, or hear his voice, or see his fuzzy silhouette, and I'm having a hard time just keeping things neighborly here. Reese is right. I'm full-on living in Crushville. Even though I said I wouldn't. And even though it freaks me out that he can see so much into our lives.

I'm trying to hold back. To put the brakes on things. But also, I got an idea for a little something to leave Owen tonight, and it's really exciting me. I just need to pick up a few more items on my lunch break.

Okay, maybe my resolve to hold back is weakening. I need to work on that.

I say goodbye to the electrician, ask him to lock up when he leaves, and tell him that if he needs to leave for lunch, to make sure he locks up then, too. Reese seems to have no problem leaving while someone is in our townhome. Is she the normal one? Or am I? I grew up in a family of spies. What do I know?

Reese and I leave for work at the same time, each of us pulling out of our driveway and heading in different directions.

All morning, we've been going through the info that we downloaded from Aragundi's servers that relates to the stolen artifacts we've been tracing, trying to figure out how to track down who is behind it. I've been working with my brother, Emerson, since he's the lead analyst, and my brothers Jace and Ledger, since they—along with Miles when he returns from Marseille—will be the ones to run the missions.

Emerson swipes to a heat map on his tablet that shows thefts across Europe and North America. Red and orange markers blink like angry pinpricks. "There's been a rise in high-value thefts from museums, private collections, and archaeological transports. Mostly small, portable items: coins, scrolls, religious relics. Entry methods are inconsistent, security footage is conveniently fuzzy, and—fun twist—none of the items have shown up on the black market."

Ledger leans back in his chair. "Let me guess. Ghosts? That would explain the fuzzy security footage and the fact that no alarms go off."

"Nah," Jace says. "I think it's more along the lines of time travelers with really niche hobbies."

"I don't know," I say as I scroll through my tablet. "I've been running the timestamps against local calendars. Weirdly, a lot of these thefts go down during festivals, street fairs, or major city-wide events. So my guess is a history-major-turned-criminal who only feels truly alive around fireworks and funnel cake."

"Not to dismiss any of your theories," Emerson says, "because those are all...creative, but on a slightly more serious note, one of my analysts flagged a private sale of three fifth-century coins. They were never reported stolen and never listed for auction. Yet somehow, a buyer in Monaco knew to inquire."

"No, wait—I found a listing I think is related to that sale." I start searching for the info on my tablet, and my brothers each do the same.

"This?" Emerson asks, tipping his tablet to show me.

"That's it!"

"There were three listings, and they each used euphemisms like 'legacy medallions' and 'heirloom coins of European persuasion.'" Emerson side-eyes me. "Which I flagged for suspicious language, and you flagged…with fourteen exclamation marks."

"That's how I process concern. With punctuation."

Jace rubs his jaw. "So we've got stealth thefts, mystery purchases, and a buyer list we can't trace."

"Correct," Emerson says. "So I've been tracing shell companies that have moved jurisdictions recently on the off chance one might be connected."

I bring up my list. "Three companies pinged this week alone. All recently changed locations. One moved from Florence, Italy, to Alexandria, Virginia. I'm keeping an eye on it."

Emerson smiles. "Which is code for: she's already started three background checks and created a shared folder titled 'sketchy and suspicious.'"

"Technically, it's called 'Sketch-a-saurus.'"

"Oh hey," Ledger says, "speaking of suspicious activity. Anything happening between you and your neighbor yet?"

"Okay, that has nothing to do with high-value targets." Unless we're talking personal high-value targets that I am finding myself setting my sights on.

Emerson raises an eyebrow. "Yet you've still managed to casually bring up Owen four times in this meeting, even when we're talking about the theft of relics."

I have? And here I thought I was doing really well. I swear I've gone at least five minutes since relating something to him. "Alright, then. Has anything been happening between us? Just coexisting in a drywall-free zone and swapping notes through a plastic flap. You know, neighborly stuff." I'm not lying. I'm just leaving out the part about what it's doing to the butterflies flapping around in me.

Jace leans back in his chair, folding his arms. "From what I saw when we did that very professional, not-at-all intrusive stakeout of him at his job site right after he moved in, it seems like things could turn from 'neighborly' to 'unintentionally married' real fast."

I laugh. "Okay, I will keep an eye out for accidental vows."

Our meeting takes hours. But by the time we're done, we've divvied up the biggest red flags: Ledger will pose as event security for a museum gala in Paris that's a perfect fit for the recent theft pattern. Miles will head to an archaeological dig site where equipment has been tampered with. And Jace is heading to Prague to meet a whistleblower who claims someone's paying off customs agents. I've got a dozen surveillance feeds to set up, some backgrounds to falsify, and some creative firewall cracking in my future.

I do still manage to take off during lunch and pick up the items I need for Owen's little gift and to print out the tags. But the day is long. I end up having to eat dinner at work, and it's nearly bedtime when I finally pull back into my driveway.

When I get inside, I empty onto my coffee table the bag of everything I got to make a "Flood Survival Kit" for Owen, including a plastic container with a latching lid to put it all in. Reese helps me attach the tags to each of the items. I got him an ultra-collapsible umbrella, "For unexpected indoor precipitation," a pack of waterproof bandages, "For emotional wounds caused by sudden plumbing betrayal," a rubber duck, "For morale," a toy boat, "In case evacuation is needed," comfy socks, "To keep your toes dry," and a badge-type pin that I got at one of those make-your-own places that says, "Official member of the *No Wall, No Problem Club*."

We have a hard time not giggling loudly enough

that Owen might hear us the whole time we're tagging them and placing them into the kit.

As I'm taking it over to our little flimsy door, Reese whispers, "Do you think he'll see it tonight?"

I shake my head. "I'm sure he went to bed an hour ago."

I pull a little flap of the plastic aside and slide the container onto his floor, and then I head upstairs to bed and set my alarm for a bit earlier than normal, just to make sure I'm awake when he finds it.

CHAPTER 8
RACE YOU TO CLARITY
OWEN

drop my keys on the side table by my door and run my hands over my face as I head to my room to change into pajama pants and a t-shirt after an extremely long day. Once my crew left for the day, I stayed to try to fix a big mistake. When I order building materials, I try to keep the delicate balance between having everything when we'll need it with not having more than what our limited storage space can hold. Today, I discovered that I messed up, and no matter how many ways I tried to rearrange things, it just wouldn't work.

I head into my living room/kitchen area and look toward the plastic sheeting separating my townhome from Charlie's. She must've worked late yesterday or gone somewhere right after work, because I didn't see her fuzzy silhouette over there all day. It surprised me how much I missed seeing her.

As frustrated and as bummed as I am right now, I still smile, though, just thinking about the package I found by my plastic door this morning. Every item in it made me laugh. I can't think of anyone I'd rather share a makeshift wall with.

Everything is dark on Charlie's side of the wall, so I must've missed her today, too. I go over to where the *Flood Survival Kit* is sitting on my one section of counter, pull out the pair of socks, and put them on. I like that they make me feel like I got a little of her tonight.

Why do I like it? I have to admit that it's because I like her. *You have to move once you finish The Shadowridge*, I remind myself. *You signed a contract. So, stop liking her as more than a neighbor.*

I should go to bed, but my newly discovered problem at work is still running through my brain, and I don't really want to try to sleep while so focused on that. Instead, I slide open my patio door and step into the cool night air, breathing in deeply, hoping it and the sound of crickets chirping will help to clear my head. The night is only slightly cool. It's a good temperature, actually. The patio isn't big—it could probably fit a couple of chairs, or maybe a grill or a meat smoker. My patio is empty, though.

I walk forward and spread my hands wide on the

railing. There are townhomes that are very similar in a row on my side, along with three other sides that form a square with a big grassy area in the middle, along with a small playground at the opposite end from me. I just look out at it, trying to regulate my breathing and think peaceful thoughts.

"Are you okay?"

I simultaneously yelp and jump at the sound, turning to see Charlie sitting on a chair on her patio, her feet up on a second chair. There's only about a five-foot gap between the railings of our patios. "Sorry —I didn't realize I wasn't alone out here."

"Did you want to be alone out here?"

"Please, no. Stay."

The neighbor on my other side has their patio light on, and between the light of that and the light of the moon, I can see Charlie pretty well. She's also wearing pajamas, and she's got her hair pulled up, but there are many strands still hanging down, which I love. And she's wearing glasses. I didn't know until this moment that she normally wears contact lenses.

I walk over to the railing at the side, facing her patio. "Rough day?" she asks.

I nod. "Yep. You?"

"Very much so. What are you in for?"

"I made a bad call. A shipment of building supplies I ordered was unexpectedly delayed, and they won't be here when we need them. Not only does it mess up our schedule, but it means I have to tell my crew that they're going to have their hours cut for this next week. I know that's a really big deal to some of them. What are you in for?"

"I also made a bad call at work. I like to be overly prepared because I think that things go the smoothest when I am. Then, when things don't go according to plan, which they often don't, I'm already prepared for the backup plan. And plans C, D, and usually E.

"I made the call that we weren't ready yet and that we should wait another day to meet with someone who had information on a high-value… client, and because we waited, the guy got cold feet and bailed completely." She shakes her head. "And we really wanted that client. We'd already put so much work into getting them."

"That's rough. I'm sorry. What is it that you do?" It's weird—in some ways, I feel like I know Charlie well. I know what time she wakes up because I can hear her alarm from my bedroom, and I can hear how long it takes her to shower because our upstairs bathrooms share a wall just like our kitchens do. I know how long it takes her to get ready in the morning, whether she brushes her teeth first or blow-dries her hair, and when she eats breakfast. I can't believe that I don't already know what she does for a living.

"My job title is IT Systems Coordinator, and I work for my family's business solutions company. I set up, troubleshoot, and monitor integrated systems for secure communication and data handling."

"That sounds… complicated."

"Only when I have to do something like remotely override building security at a top-secret facility."

There's a playfulness in her voice that tells me she's joking around, and it makes me smile.

"I can't even get my laptop to stop auto-connecting to someone's Wi-Fi nearby that's named *FBI_Van_42*, and you're hacking firewalls for breakfast."

"If your laptop suddenly starts blinking Morse code at you, just blame the socks. They might be bugged."

I look down at my socks. "Thanks again for these. My toes are definitely warm and dry. They apparently also have a magical ability to chase away some of the day's frustration."

"I'm glad they helped. I figured anyone who's battling rogue Wi-Fi and wall-less living could use some backup. Oh, and I've been meaning to ask you— how did your proposal go? And also, *what* was it for? I was so distracted by how you looked in a suit that I forgot to ask."

I chuckle. I think the expressions on her face when she saw me in both suits are burned into my memory, and it makes me smile every time I think about it.

"I was presenting the proposal to a historical

preservation society in Philadelphia about my plan for restoring their beloved train station."

Charlie sits up a little straighter, looking alarmed. "Already? Will you be leaving Cipher Springs to start on that one soon?"

"First, no, I'm not moving on so soon. It could take another eight months to finish the theater. But the process of going from finding an old building I'd love to restore to getting approvals and funding to actually starting to restore it is an extremely long process with many steps along the way."

"And second, I am kind of digging that you got so alarmed at the thought of me leaving soon."

She smiles and looks down for a moment before meeting my eyes again. "In case of any future aquatic misadventures, it's nice to have a neighbor who is already experienced in flood management."

I chuckle. When Charlie smiles, it isn't reaching her eyes, so I figure her mistake at work is still weighing her down. I know that morning can bring great clarity and perspective. I also know that it can be hard to get to that morning clarity when beating yourself up about it keeps you from getting the sleep you need.

She's dressed like me—in pajamas and socks. I say, "Go grab your shoes."

"My shoes? Why?"

"Because there's nothing like increasing your heart rate for a bit to pull you out of any doldrums. You'll need that if you want to sleep tonight, so we're going to race around the grass."

She raises an eyebrow. "We are?"

"Yep. You've got thirty seconds to meet me back out here."

She gives me an amused look for a couple of beats, and then she hops up and hurries inside. So I do the same. I race to my bedroom, slip on my shoes, then grab a folded blanket from my closet and race back out to my patio. I find Charlie sitting there with both shoes on, tying one of them. When she finishes, she nods at my blanket as she stands. "Do you plan to use that as a cape?"

"Only if it looks like I need to tap into some superpowers to help me win the race." We each head down our own stairs, and I drop the folded blanket onto the grass. "Okay, we go to that corner, along that side, turn left just before the playground, down the far side, and the first person to get back to the blanket wins."

Charlie nods. "Ready? Go!"

We start running, and Charlie is playfully acting like she's trying to push me out of bounds or something, and I'm playing right back. By the time we reach the halfway point at the back left corner, though, Charlie starts full-on sprinting. She pulls away quickly, and I start sprinting, too, in order to keep pace. We reach the blanket at nearly the same time.

We're both panting, and Charlie is laughing, so I start laughing, too.

"Wow, that really does work!" she says, grinning and panting and laughing practically simultaneously.

I spread the blanket on the grass, and we both flop onto it as we catch our breath. Before long, we're both staring up at the clear night sky, and I wish I could reach out and turn off every townhome's back light so we can see the stars better.

As much as I keep telling myself that I only like Charlie as a neighbor, I know I'm lying to myself. I like her as much more than that, and I don't want to lie here, looking at the sky with my neighbor. I want to lie here next to the woman I am hopelessly falling for.

We are looking up at the stars when Charlie asks, "So, what made you choose to be an architectural restoration specialist?"

Well, I can't say it was because I wanted to start falling for someone, but I know I can't because I'm already under contract to move to another state before long. I don't tell her that, though.

I'm lying on my back, elbows out, fingers linked behind my neck. There's a rock under the blanket that's digging into my back, but I don't want to move because our legs are touching, and Charlie hasn't pulled away. "My dad is a carpenter. He's really good. His workshop is in the backyard, and I spent a lot of time in there with him, learning everything I could.

"That might have led me slightly toward my career, but what really did was a building in my town that's kind of a gathering hall and reception center. It's been around since the early nineteen hundreds and used to be a courthouse. When I was ten, a historical restoration specialist and his team came in. He needed a skilled carpenter, and he asked my dad.

"I spent every day there after school and every second I could during the summers, watching it happen. I was mesmerized. The restoration specialist's name was Hudson, and he never seemed to be bothered by a little kid shadowing him everywhere he went. I think he saw that I was interested in a lot more than the regular construction stuff that most boys are interested in—power tools, tractors, stuff like that.

"So he told me what he was doing, why he was doing it a specific way, what his thought process was, everything. He also talked a lot about how important it was to care about the past, to honor history because it was what helped us understand the present, and about how we were all standing on the shoulders of the people who came before us.

"Seeing that building restored, and learning everything I did along the way from both Hudson and my dad, was transformative to me. I loved everything about seeing it go from old and damaged to restored and beautiful. It was proof that broken things could be made whole again.

"But it was my grandpa who sealed the deal for me. When he saw how interested I was in restoration, he brought me here."

"To Cipher Springs?"

I nod. "To The Shadowridge, specifically. My grandpa had grown up in Cloakwood, but he came here to watch a musical at The Shadowridge—*My Fair Lady*—and that's when he met my grandma. She played the lead, and my grandpa said that when she sang 'I Could Have Danced All Night,' he was entranced. He stayed after so he could meet her, and the rest is history."

"That is so sweet!"

I nod. "While we were looking at The Shadowridge, my grandpa said, 'She's run-down now, but I'd love to see her shine again.' I was only ten at the time, but I told him that I was going to be a restoration specialist when I grew up, just like Hudson was, and that I was going to restore The Shadowridge for him. I've never stopped wanting that ever since, so choosing my college major was a no-brainer.

"I worked in construction part-time through college. In college, I got an internship with a historical restoration specialist. A lot of what he was doing at the time of my internship was securing funding, which is arguably the hardest part. I learned so much from him. Right after college, I started working full-time for a restoration company, and did for a couple of years until I was ready to go out on my own."

The whole time I'm telling the story, Charlie has her head turned to me, looking like she's soaking every bit of my story in. I've probably been talking way too much. It's just not often that I find someone who is as interested as she seems to be.

"Those two parts of your job sound like they require very different skill sets," Charlie says, the breeze catching her hair and blowing a few strands away from her face. "Well, it sounds like there are a lot more than two parts of it, but I mean everything related to working on the building versus everything that happens outside of the building, like getting permissions and funding."

I chuckle. They definitely require different skill sets. And there are parts that I like more than others. "Yeah, there are a lot of meetings with planning commissions, historical preservation societies, and code enforcement. Plus, grant applications. Sometimes presentations or speeches made to city councils, a development board, sometimes the public, at galas for private donors, things like that."

"Wow. I would totally fail at that part."

"What are you talking about? You would charm everyone! They'd be eating out of your hand."

She shakes her head. "No, I wouldn't, because I'd be freaking out about being in the spotlight. I'd never actually make it to the point of talking to them because I'd be in the bathroom either throwing up or passing out from hyperventilating."

I look at her curiously, wondering why she might worry about being in the spotlight. Everything about Charlie is delightful, and I imagine that whatever she did, she'd be well received. "What about you?" I ask. "What drew you to your job?"

"I can't really pinpoint an exact source of my desire to work with computers like you can. It was just something I took to easily. And because the family business is business solutions, I naturally took my love of computers in that direction.

"Plus, I just like to help people. I enjoy being in the background, quietly supporting the people in the spotlight, helping them to have everything they need to really shine.

"I did an internship with a cybersecurity consulting firm during college. They worked with hospitals, financial companies, and government agencies to stress-test their internal systems and set up backup protocols. I was the one sitting in the corner with too much caffeine, flagging anomalies before the pros did."

As she's explaining, she hesitates a few times, probably trying to decide how to put into layman's terms things that are way too technical. I'm glad, because what she does say is still above my level of computer knowledge. My computer knowledge is all related to architectural software, project management software, and researching on the internet. If anything goes wrong beyond that, I'm at a loss.

"And then Lancaster Business Solutions recruited me right out of college. Which, okay, I know it sounds like I'm just saying, 'And then my parents hired me.' But they didn't hire me—hiring is done by the board with no input from the directors, so they couldn't even suggest that they consider me. They found and recruited me all on their own."

"Oof. Your parents own and run the business, and that doesn't even get you an in? No automatic hire because you're the boss's kid? Not even consideration? That's rough."

She chuckles. "I get how ridiculous it sounds. It's just that..." she pauses. "My job requires some very specialized skills, and if the person in my position doesn't have them..." She pauses again. "Just trust me when I say that bad things would happen. So they couldn't just hire me because I am a Lancaster—I had to have those skills.

"Anyway, with the exception of today, I love it, and I'm really good at it." She looks at me from the corner of her eye, like she's trying to hold back a smile. "Probably because no one sees the person behind the computer."

I chuckle.

"You know, you were right."

"I love being right," I say. "What was I right about?"

"About needing to get out of my own head if I ever wanted to sleep tonight, *and* about this being an excellent way to do it."

The night air was a good temperature right after we'd run around the grass, but now it's getting chilly. Charlie looks at her watch, which prompts me to look at mine. Oof. It's way later than I thought.

"Morning is still going to come just as early," Charlie says, "so maybe we'd better head in."

We both get up, and I grab the blanket. As we are almost separating to go to our own stairs leading up to our patios, I blurt out, "Come and see my job site. I mean, I know you did once before, but a lot has changed since then." Including how well I know Charlie. I'm not even sure I knew anything about her at all when she appeared at the theater my first week there.

She smiles a wide, genuine smile. "I'd like that."

I don't know about Charlie, but I'm going to be heading to bed feeling much more blissful than I would have if I had never come out to my patio tonight. Especially because the image of Charlie, running around the grass in her pajamas, will also be forever burned into my mind.

CHAPTER 9
THIS IS NOT A DRILL
CHARLIE

I am wearing a fun pink top and my one pair of jeans that are both super cute and super comfortable, my belly is pleasantly full of street tacos, and I just got to relax at the movies with Reese and my brother, Miles. I lean back in my seat in Miles's car. "Thanks for tonight. After this week, I really needed it."

Miles glances over at me. "Are you referring to work or your water woes?"

"Work. Other than the fact that our kitchen is completely unusable, the water woes have been manageable."

Reese laughs. "She's only saying that because it has provided her with ample flirting opportunities with our neighbor, Owen."

"Oh, yeah?" Miles says.

At one point, I might have hated that Reese brought the subject up with a protective brother present because then I'd have to answer too many questions. But lately, I've loved every chance I get to gush about Owen.

"He's just so cute! And sweet and funny and thoughtful."

"You should hear her when he's not around," Reese says. "She's basically one heart-eye emoji away from knitting his name into a throw pillow."

I laugh. "He's worth the embroidery."

Miles chuckles. "Okay, but let's talk about that flimsy wall of yours for a moment. I've trusted Owen ever since we fully vetted him after spying on him at his work when he first became your neighbor."

"You guys spied on him?" Reese asks.

Miles seemed to have forgotten that we have someone *not* in the family business in the car. "We just did a little recon at the theater. A little hiding behind bricks just to see what he was like. You know, to try to tell if he was good enough for Charlie before she really started falling for him."

They did a bit more than that. I found out later that my brothers had *fully* looked into Owen. He came back clean enough that they gave him their stamp of approval, as long as he's treating me right. And predicated on whether my little crush grew into something big enough to need their approval, which it hasn't yet.

"Anyway, Owen being a good guy doesn't negate the fact that the plastic wall you share doubles your chance of a break-in. Because if someone breaks into his side, they would see that plastic wall, and who wouldn't also break into yours? And if they wanted to break into your place specifically, that'd be the easier way to do it. Or if Owen just plain forgets to lock his door sometime, it'll put your place at risk, too."

Tonight was such a relaxing night! What is he thinking, going and getting me all scared about danger possibilities like this? It took me so long to get unfreaked out about it when the wall first came down.

"I don't think you need to worry about that," Reese says. "Our neighbor has quite the crush on Charlie, so if someone broke into his side, he'd stop them from coming to ours."

"But would he be able to?" Miles asks. "The guy hasn't been in a fight in his life."

I don't want Reese to question how Miles could possibly know that. So I ask about the other part that caught my attention. "You think he has quite the crush on me?" It feels stupid to say out loud, like we're pre-teens or something, but hearing her say it still gives me happy flutters.

"No," Reese says, deadpan. "Guys always leave fun and thoughtful gifts for a woman they don't have a crush on." Then she turns to Miles. "You know,

Cipher Springs isn't exactly known for its high number of break-ins."

"There are always exceptions to the rules." Then, to me, Miles adds, "Plus, your chances are higher, considering your job."

Reese gives him a look like he's being ridiculous.

"What?" Miles says. "Sometimes clients can get disgruntled."

"Because her clients might go, 'My computer crashed and I hadn't saved my work, so I'm going to break into the IT person's house.'"

Miles is hiding a smile, knowing that Reese has no idea what kinds of "clients" he's actually referring to. But to keep the focus off that, he says to her, "You never know. It could be someone from *your* work."

Reese gives him an amused smile. "A disgruntled middle-school-aged bookworm? Or are you talking about my side hustle and are referring to someone I sold delicious, healthy, taste-bud-pleasing honey to?"

"I just want to make sure that nothing bad happens to my best friend and my sister. What do you say we run a drill?"

Reese and I look at each other, and Reese shrugs. "We'd love to," I say. I know Reese will be on board because Miles is her best friend, and it's clear this is important to him. I'm actually grateful for it. Worrying about safety is the kind of thing that keeps me up at night.

And not just worries about someone breaking in, but about other dangers, too. Fire. Earthquakes. Floods. (The big kind, not the kitchen floor kind.) Things that require evacuation from your home quickly. Things that impact an entire area and can make you get separated from your family.

I wish Reese was willing to do roommate drills with me. Like what to do in a fire. But if my brother and her best friend, a guy who can charm the socks off anyone, can barely talk her into doing some kind of drill, it's not likely that I ever can.

Owen's truck is in the driveway, and I look at my watch as Miles pulls up in front of our townhome. "Oh, but it's late. Owen likely went to bed an hour ago."

"You know what time he goes to bed?"

"We know everything," Reese says. "What time he wakes up, how long he takes in the shower, that he paces and sighs about every 7.8 seconds when he's thinking through a problem, all of it. We know way more than we should know. That wall is *thin*."

I try to quell the panic that the reminder gives me about how much Owen has inadvertently learned about me. I have bigger things to panic about right now, like someone breaking in. Or earthquakes, fires, or floods.

"Just humor me, okay? I can be quiet." I nod, so Miles adds, "You two just go in. Do whatever you'd normally do. Leave the door unlocked or don't—I can always pick the lock. I'll wait an undetermined amount of time before sneaking in. I'll be so quiet you won't hear me coming. I want to see how long it takes you to notice me and how you fend me off. Give me your best."

I take off my seatbelt. "We can do that."

I grew up learning self-defense moves, but Reese didn't. Miles has spent enough time teaching her, though, that she can get herself out of a pickle. He turns to look at her. "Remember—palm strikes to the nose or chin with the heel of your hand are very effective. I can counter it well enough that you don't have to worry about hurting me. Since I'm not wearing any protective gear, I'd appreciate it if you stay away from defending with a knee to the groin, though. Elbow strike to the jaw or ribs, or a foot stomp or shin scrape with your heel are good options."

Reese turns to me. "Your brother loves us so much that he's willing to sacrifice that pretty face for us."

"Now that's some confidence thinking that you might be able to actually hurt this pretty face."

We both laugh and tell him goodbye—for now— and head into our house. There haven't been any workers inside today, so I don't feel compelled to go check for intruders. Although now that Miles has gotten me thinking about intruders coming through our plastic wall, I still check under my bed when we both go upstairs to change into pajamas.

When Reese comes out of her room, she says, "So, he's going to expect palm strikes, elbow strikes, and foot stomps. I say we give him something he isn't expecting. Something no one trained would actually do."

"Ooh. I like the way you're thinking," I say. "What about if we hide somewhere close to the front door, like maybe in the laundry room. He won't be expecting us there. Then, when he passes by, we jump onto him like spider monkeys and just hang on tight."

"Oh, fun!" Reese says. "I'm digging this plan."

I am, too. It's less stressful. As grateful as I am for the drill, just knowing that Miles is going to be coming to fake break in spikes my adrenaline.

My brother, Ledger, is an adrenaline junkie. If you put him on one end of the spectrum, I'm on the complete opposite end. *All* my brothers are on Ledger's side of that spectrum, just not quite as extreme. If Ledger is 100 and I'm 1, Jace and Miles are probably 95.

When I'm leading Jace through a mission that is adrenaline-filled, and I'm guiding him from a safe room behind my computer, everything is fine. But if someone actually broke into my townhome (which, honestly, isn't going to happen in Cipher Springs), I'd be very afraid. And I don't like feeling afraid.

I don't like watching scary movies. I don't like walking down dark alleys. I don't like vacuuming out my car (because when I'm holding something so noisy, my head deep in my car, unable to see anyone coming up behind me, I'm always convinced I'm seconds away from being ax-murdered). I don't like roller coasters. I don't like haunted houses.

Staying away from manufactured horror is what makes me able to be in the dark, because then I don't have to worry about all the fears they brought up. I only have to worry about the fears coming from my own head. And I've got enough of those on my own! I'm not looking to overpopulate the place.

When we get downstairs, I glance at the plastic sheeting. Yeah, Owen's side is very dark. He has definitely gone to bed. I dim our lights so Miles won't be able to see us as well when he breaks in. Then Reese slips into the laundry room, and I go just inside the bathroom door, hiding in the shadows, and we wait.

It's a full fifteen minutes before we hear the faint sound of Miles picking the lock on our front door. He wanted to make sure we had plenty of time to get distracted and let our guard down. I am holding my breath as he opens the door and then silently sneaks down our hallway toward our kitchen.

We wait for him to pass by us, then Reese races out and leaps onto Miles's right side. He spins, and the second his left side is aimed in my direction, I also leap onto him. We both have our arms locked around his neck to hold on, our legs pinning his arms to his side.

Miles grunts as he moves down the hall, trying to brush us off against the wall as he goes. But he's not trying as hard as he would if we were actual attackers, so we hold on just fine. "This is *not* a palm strike to the nose," he murmurs.

"Exactly," Reese says.

I am grinning as our weight throws him a bit off balance, and he bumps into our only remaining counter. This isn't the easiest position to remain in, though, especially with mine and Reese's legs trying to occupy some of the same space. But my focus is 100% on keeping his arms pinned down. If he can get them loose, he'll easily pull us off.

The sound of a guttural and very loud roar makes us all freeze and turn in the direction of the sound. Owen has come through the floppy doors that separate our townhomes, a cordless drill in his hands, raised high and threateningly as he races toward us, shouting, "Get away from them!"

"Wait! Stop!" I yell as I release my grip on Miles and drop to the floor, my hands outstretched. Reese drops also, and I can see that she and Miles have their hands out as stop signs, too, as Owen comes to a stop just three feet in front of us. The cordless drill in his hand is still raised in the air. "This is just my brother,

Miles. I'm sorry—I thought we were being quiet. This is just a drill."

"A drill?" Owen says, as he looks up at the drill in his hand, sleep obviously making him not think clearly.

"He was just testing us to see what we'd do if anyone ever broke in. You know, for safety," I finish, faltering at how it sounds.

Owen lowers the drill and runs a hand through his hair. "No one is in danger?"

I shake my head. "We're all fine. But oh my gosh, you waking up and barging in here to save us is so sweet!" And endearing. And disarming. And a little too intimate. And I love everything about it.

"How did you even manage to wake up?" Reese asks. "I swear we didn't make enough sound."

Owen shrugs. "I don't know. I think my body just knew something was off."

My brother reaches out and claps Owen on the shoulder. "You're made of good stuff, Owen. Untrained, your body couldn't have woken you up like that if you weren't."

"Thanks," Owen mumbles.

"I can't say your weapon of choice was the most effective," Miles says with a friendly grin, nodding at the drill. "But, in the heat of the moment, you grabbed something and came running. That counts for a lot. If you want, I could give you a few tips sometime. Like making sure the battery pack is in it so it has a little heft to it."

Owen is still looking like he's in a daze, and he just nods.

I guide Owen close to our wall and away from Miles and Reese. "Sorry about waking you up in a panic. If we do a drill in the future, I'll make sure it's during waking hours."

Owen nods. "I'd appreciate that. I, uh, think I'll go back to bed now." He turns to leave.

"Wait. Owen?" When he looks back at me, I say, "It was really amazing of you to run in here to save us. Thank you." Because it really is the sweetest thing ever. My brothers will come running to save anyone, but they've been trained for it. Owen knows nothing, not even what random objects can be used as a weapon, apparently. Yet he still came running. "You didn't wait to be ready. You just acted. That's courage."

I see a hint of a smile before Owen goes back to his side of the wall, taping the door closed behind him. Me? My smile is wide as I sigh against one of the wall studs.

CHAPTER 10
CENTER STAGE MEETS CENTER CRUSH
OWEN

am rarely at the job site on a Sunday afternoon, but when the investor who is paying for the entirety of renovation expenses says he is in town and would love to see the site, you do whatever you can to get there. So I'm at The Shadowridge, walking through the mezzanine and the balcony boxes with Giovanni Vitale.

Usually, visits like these are stressful. I always want to show my investors, donors, and owners that their money is being well spent and that I'm being a great steward over what's been entrusted to me. I understand what it takes to trust someone with a project that you care about.

I'm glad I was able to arrive before Giovanni so I could review all of my schedules and have them fresh in my mind, because he asks so many in-depth questions about materials, timelines, and restoration techniques. He seems to really care about the bones of this place.

Some investors only want to see the flashy parts. Some panic when they see things in the demolition stage, all torn apart, looking its worst. Some just want to be reassured with schedules and cost allocations. Sometimes, all they really want is to see that you have lots of data and seem confident in it.

But everything with Giovanni has been amazing. I've taken him on an extensive tour of the entire place, even showing him little nooks and storage areas, and he's been interested in all of it. The entire time as we've been walking through The Shadowridge, I've been feeling energized and proud. Not nervous or stressed. I can't believe someone from across an ocean is willing to fund my vision for this restoration. I'm lucky to have him as an investor.

We're back in the main part of the theater, where the seats will go again once we get them restored, chatting, when Charlie walks in. My smile spreads wide at this unexpected surprise. Any clouds must've drifted away just at that moment because I swear the room is brighter.

"I was driving by, saw your truck out front, and since I told you I'd come and check out the place…Oh, but I see you're busy."

"No, please, stay," I say as I beckon her the rest of

the way to us. "Charlie, I'd like to introduce you to the man financing The Shadowridge's restoration, Giovanni Vitale. Giovanni, this is Charlie Lancaster. She lives in the townhome next to me—we, uh, share a wall." And I can't help but share a smile with Charlie.

"I am charmed to meet you," Giovanni says. "Owen has been showing me all the ways in which he's going to bring this place back to life."

"And I'm happy to meet the man who is making it possible. I love your accent. Did you grow up in Italy?"

"I did. I still live there, in fact."

"And this project drew you all the way here?" Charlie asks. "You must have incredible historic theaters back home."

"We do. But my wife grew up in D.C. She loves the stage, loves historic buildings, and loves a good surprise."

"What does she think of the restoration?"

"She hasn't seen it yet. I want to unveil it when it's complete."

"Oh, that's so sweet. Do you have a picture of her? It must be so hard to keep a secret so exciting from her!"

I love that Charlie and Giovanni are chatting so much. He gets to see how great Charlie is, and she gets to see how excited he is about this place. I'm not sure I've ever had someone I've dated come to a site

I'm working at before. At least not to come check out what I do. And they definitely haven't ever made such an effort to make a client or investor feel welcome.

As they talk, I look at Charlie. The light coming in from the high windows shines down on her, making coppery strands in her brown hair and her cheeks glow with her smile.

Giovanni pulls up a picture on his phone and turns it to show us both. "This is Margot. The love of my life." The picture of Margot is of her on stage, performing in what looks like a play. She's got long brown hair and a face that's somehow both sweet and mischievous.

"Oh," I say, "I can see that she's definitely a huge fan of the theater. You didn't tell me that she's also a stage actor."

"It has always been her passion."

I suddenly want to know more about Charlie's passions. What does she love that I know nothing about? What else don't I know about her yet?

Charlie asks, "What has been her favorite role?"

As the man is slipping the phone back into his pocket, he says, "Oh, I'm sure I couldn't guess."

"She probably has many," Charlie says. "You're here alone? No assistant?"

"I told him to go check out the town so I could pester Owen with questions in peace."

"Did you fly in just for this visit? Or are you traveling in the area?"

"I have other business meetings in the area that I'm seeing to, for which I'm grateful. It gave me a good excuse to come check out my baby and see the progress in person." He gives me a nod. "I'm glad a man who also has a love of restoring old buildings and of the theater sought me out. He's been the perfect fit for this project.

"It really is time for me to go see to other obligations, though. It's been nice meeting the person who lights up Owen even more than this building does, Ms. Lancaster."

As he shakes Charlie's hand, I can't help but wonder what all Giovanni saw in me when Charlie walked in, because I hadn't mentioned her to him at all. I catch her eye for a moment as Giovanni turns from her to me, wondering what she thought of Giovanni's comment. I don't get enough of a glance to tell, though.

"And it's been great seeing your progress, Owen," Giovanni says as he shakes my hand, then gives me a business card that has only his first name and a phone number. "I look forward to your updates. Do let me know if anything changes along the way."

Once he's gone, I turn to Charlie. I'm so energized by Giovanni's visit that I'm practically buzzing. "Isn't Giovanni great?"

"It sounds like he was asking a lot of really specific questions."

I grin. "I know! Isn't it amazing? Most people just say, 'Looks good' and leave. But not Giovanni. It's rare to find someone who just gets a project this much. And he wanted to see everything, even more obscure things, like trapdoors and backstage catwalks, probably because of his wife's acting background. He even looked like he was interested, down to the hidden alcove behind the stage that I found!

"He wanted to know the timeline on each part, too. I love that he's so invested in it. I mean, he's *literally* invested in it." I point up to the cameras in the main area. "And I'm glad we got the cameras installed to ward against vandalism from the start, because he even asked about that. And, I mean, the man is a unicorn. It's so rare to get someone who will bankroll the entire project."

"I bet," Charlie says. "He must be investing a *lot*. What is in it for him? Just the resale value of the building? Or does he think he'll make back his investment through ticket sales?"

I shake my head. "He doesn't own the building. He sees it as more of a donation than an investment, since you bring up an entire community when you build up the arts. And it's so generous of him to do it in a place that's so far from home. I hope that his wife loves it, and that they travel here often to see the fruits of his donation."

Charlie nods. Not like she's so impressed that Giovanni would do that. More like she's just taking in the information, filing it away. I'm not quite sure what the expression is on her face, but then she steps closer, grinning at me, and it's all I can do to not wrap my arms around her waist and pull her in close. "I love that you're this excited about it," she says. "And that you got to share your enthusiasm about this place with someone who seems just as passionate about it."

"Me, too. Okay, enough gushing about my investor. I want to take you on a tour!"

I loved showing Giovanni around, but it is nothing compared to showing the place to Charlie. Giovanni wanted to see everything, to know the timeline, to know my plans.

But Charlie notices all the little details that make this place amazing. She understands the craftsmanship and the care put into every part of its original design. Instead of just taking it in as a whole, she imagines an actual person designing each part and wonders aloud what that person must've been like. She ponders how many people worked on the design. If, when they went to bed at night, they dreamed about the design.

Then she asks me if I dream about it at night. (I do.) When we stop at the railing that curves around the grand staircase leading up to the second-floor balconies that we are in the middle of stripping down to fully restore, she asks how long it takes me to work through what might be the best way to get each part looking like it once was. So I tell her about my process.

I take her through the theater, the stage, backstage, the dressing rooms, the balconies, the ticket counter, the offices, the grand foyer, everything. Basically, all the things that I just showed Giovanni. I tell her about plans I have, what's coming next, and the biggest challenges I have coming up. She seems excited and interested in it all. The whole time we walk around, my bad knee is really aching, but I don't even care. Charlie is here, appreciating all the things I'm passionate about.

"Okay, so now you've seen what I'm interested in. I want to hear what you're interested in, and if I can come see." Her eyes go wide, almost in alarm, like she very much doesn't want me to show me what she loves to do. So I backtrack. "Or not. It's not a big deal."

"No, it's not that. It's that most of my hobbies are related to work, and we deal with a lot of client confidentiality stuff. It isn't exactly something I can show."

I nod. It's okay. Maybe someday I'll get to find out what really makes Charlie who she is.

"Oh," she says, "but I am passionate about safety."

"Safety? Like seat belts and bike helmets?"

"Well, yes, but more like being prepared. Which…

is...also something that's hard to show." She sounds almost apologetic. But being passionate about safety is something. I tuck the info away.

As we've walked through The Shadowridge, we've passed several battery-powered drills. All without battery packs, since they're currently plugged in for when my crew shows up ready to work tomorrow morning. And every time we do, I have flashbacks of my attempt to rescue Charlie and Reese from the intruder.

What had I planned to do? Poke him with the little Phillip's head bit sticking out of the end of the drill? I'd been deeply asleep when I sensed a problem. I like to think that if I'd actually been awake, my weapon of choice would've been a better one. A framing square, perhaps? Nothing says "back off" like right angles and rage.

Charlie has a family thing she needs to head to, but she seems reluctant to leave. I feel the same. Having my favorite person in what is currently my favorite place is pretty sweet. We head back toward the grand lobby and stop near what was originally a coat check but was later turned into a concessions area.

If I'd have noticed that stopping here would've put a drill, sans battery pack, right in plain view of both of us as it sits on the concessions counter, I'd have directed us anywhere else. But now, it's the elephant in the room. So I say, "Sorry about barging into your place in my misguided attempt to save you from a terrifying adversary. It was a total breach of—"

"—a door that was practically unbreachable?"

She smiled through her words, and I chuckle, rubbing the back of my neck. "It was more of the unwritten rule that I won't pass through a piece of plastic as thin as fabric, held together by painter's tape and a wish, without your express permission."

"I still think it was sweet. And brave."

"You know, come to think of it, I *was* brave. I mean, that could've been a diabolical serial killer I was rescuing you from, and I went in with what amounted to an inch-and-a-half-long screwdriver with a big handle."

"You also had the element of surprise and the moral high ground. No villain can withstand that."

I chuckle, and the only thing I can think about is how much I want to kiss her. And how at odds that is with my date-no-one-while-on-a-job plan. Especially since after this job, I'm under contract to leave. I don't get long to think about it, though, because her phone suddenly starts blaring the song *Born to Be Wild*.

Charlie hurries to pull her phone from her back pocket and sends the call to voicemail. "Sorry—that's my brother, probably wondering why I'm not at..." she pauses like she was going to say something else, making me wonder what she was about to say, then finishes with, "my mom's yet."

"Is this the brother who I thought was an intruder?"

"Miles? No. His ringtone is *Sharp Dressed Man*. This is Ledger, and I really need to get going." Before she leaves, though, she says, "Thank you for taking me on the tour. I can see why you're so passionate about this place."

And I'm smiling long after I see her walk out to her car, get in, and drive away.

CHAPTER 11
SPY-DEY SENSES TINGLING
CHARLIE

know exactly how busy work is going to be today, so I left home extra early. When I turn off the tree-lined street to the front gates of the Clandestine Services Agency building—or, as the small metal sign at the gate reads, *Lancaster Business Solutions*—the sun still hasn't poked its head up.

I stop at the gate house, and when the guard comes out, I say, "Good morning, Moss!"

"Good morning, Ms. Lancaster," Moss says in his very deep voice as he holds out the scanner.

I tap my badge to it, and then I put my hand on the fingerprint screen.

"You're getting quite the early start."

I shrug. "There's just too much fun to pack into a normal-length day, and I don't miss out on any of it."

Moss laughs, I'm sure fully knowing that no one

shows up to work before the sun because they're expecting fun at that time of day. "Well, toss some confetti for me, will you?"

As the gates open, I say, "Will do!" before driving through them, then down the cobblestone road to the side of the building, and then down underneath it to the parking garage.

The second I get up to my floor and over to my desk, I schedule a 10:15 meeting with Emerson during the one fifteen-minute window I'm free today.

———

I'm just finishing up with a final security sweep on Jace's cover identity when I see Emerson standing in my peripheral vision, a tablet in hand. I hold up one finger, hurry to close out the secure server connection, then lock my screen and head back to one of the conference rooms with him.

"Yesterday, I stopped by The Shadowridge, and Owen showed me around."

"Nice! I take it things are going well?"

"Please hold all relationship questions until the end. That isn't what this meeting is about. And I've only got twelve minutes, because Jace is on an airplane right now, headed to that high-end antiques fair in Marrakesh to pose as a buyer, so I need to be ready to support him soon."

Emerson holds up a hand in surrender.

"When I walked into the theater, Owen was just finishing up showing around the investor or donor or whatever he wants to be called. He introduced me to the guy, and I'm telling you that something is off about him. With all I've got going on with Jace's mission today, there's no way I can look into him. Do you have time to?"

"Anything for you, sis. What's his name?"

"Giovanni Vitale. He doesn't own the theater—he's just paying for renovations. He lives somewhere in Italy. That's also where he grew up."

"Got it. Okay, tell me what seems off."

"I don't know. Little things. Like the way he stood just a little too straight, his emotions too tempered. The way he glanced at the exits and the security camera. That he was hyper-aware of his surroundings. That he didn't mirror Owen's posture. You know, the things your subconscious picks up on that your conscious mind doesn't always. I'm telling you, my spy-dey senses are tingling."

Emerson is smiling.

"What?"

"I haven't heard you use the phrase 'my spy-dey senses are tingling' for a long time. I'd forgotten about it."

"You know, we should use it more often. Make it part of CSA lingo."

"I don't think you'll get Jace to agree to being called a spy. Probably not Ledger or Miles, either."

"I don't know. Since Mackenzie stepped into Jace's life, I think we have a chance. But if not, maybe it can just be for analysts and officers."

"Agreed. It should be a thing." Emerson looks down at his handwritten notes on his tablet, which don't contain a whole lot. "Anything else you can add?"

"Yes. I got the sense that he was sketchy right away, so I asked lots of questions. Luckily, Owen just interpreted it as me being interested in his investor. I think the investor bought it for friendliness, too.

"Okay, so first off, he didn't come with an entourage or even an assistant. He's got enough money to bankroll an entire restoration project in another country, and he doesn't even travel with anyone? A bodyguard, even. It just seems like he's the kind of person who would."

I don't even wait for Emerson to respond because he wasn't there—he didn't catch the vibes, and I know that part is very thin evidence. "He asked Owen a lot of questions about his timeline for repairing different sections, and he wanted to see every part of the place, even hidey holes. And he never put his hands in his pockets."

"That's not just a spy thing."

"It's not. It's also a bad guy thing as a way to

throw suspicion off them or to show you that they aren't armed.

"Oh, and he showed me a picture of his wife, whom he's restoring the building for, but he hasn't even told her about it. It was one of those professional photos they take of the cast while they're on stage, performing. And, yeah, he could've shown me that one because he'd just said that she loves the theater, and it would back up that story. But he didn't show me one with the two of them together. The woman in that picture could've been anyone. He could've found it online. Maybe it wasn't his wife."

Emerson is writing all this down.

"It was his answers to questions, too. Like when I asked if he flew here just for the tour of the theater, he said he had other business in the area. I'm thinking it's sketchy business. And why did he invest in a building on another continent? Owen thinks it wasn't to earn back his investment—that it was simply a donation to the community. But why would he care about a community that's four thousand five hundred miles from home instead of his own community?"

Emerson is still writing, and I wait quietly as he does. When he finishes, he looks at the notes for a long moment, and then he meets my eyes. "Your job is to find danger lurking in dark corners. Are you sure you're not just seeing danger where there isn't any?"

"As I was lying in bed last night, I asked myself

that same question so many times. I could easily convince myself that I was. And I could just as easily convince myself that I wasn't. But here's the thing. I'm *trained* to sense what things are off. And I've had enough experience watching for danger through video when Jace is on missions to know I can trust my gut. I really, *really* hope that I am seeing danger where there isn't any. I'll gladly accept being wrong! I will cheer. Heck, I will throw a party. Until then, I've got to go with my gut."

Emerson nods. "That's good enough for me. I'll look into it." He pauses a moment, then asks, "How much time do you have until your next meeting?"

I glance at my watch. "Four minutes. And it's in Sub-level One."

"That gives us about two minutes." Emerson leans back in his chair. "So, have you asked Owen to be your date for the wedding yet?"

"No."

"Why not? You clearly really like the guy."

I take a deep breath. "I don't know. Because I'm scared." It isn't the reason I would tell any of my other brothers, but with Emerson, I know I can always get real.

"Of what?"

"Of… starting something, I guess. I don't know if things with him will even work. Or if I can even do a long-term relationship. And if I start something and it's anything other than a long-term thing, I'm afraid of just how awkward things are going to get, since he's my next-door neighbor. He moves for every restoration job, too. And my job isn't the kind where I can just move away.

"Plus, asking someone to a wedding and introducing them to the entire family at once is kind of a big step, you know? And I'm a little step girl. What about you? Have you asked…" I search my brain to think of the woman's name that Emerson mentioned maybe once. "Kara?"

"Kira. And no—it turns out that we weren't a very good match. There's a woman, though, Delaney, whom I'm thinking about asking. I'm just not going to let it be a big step."

I grin. "I can't wait to meet her."

"And I can't wait to meet the guy who was willing to take on Miles with nothing more than a juice-less drill."

I smile. "Isn't he just the sweetest?" I look down at my watch. "Okay, I've really got to go. Thanks for being willing to look into Giovanni, Emerson. If I think of anything that might help, I'll let you know."

When I get to the door, Emerson says, "Charlie? For what it's worth, I've always thought of you as a Big Steps girl."

I smile, then head down to my meeting with Abraham.

CHAPTER 12
WILL CONFESS FOR COOKIES
OWEN

I am working on a grant application when the room goes dark, and all electrical humming, including from my refrigerator, goes silent. Is this related to the flooding issues? Or is this just a cursed townhome? I go over to my patio door and move the curtains aside. Okay, so the lights are out everywhere. That's actually comforting.

I hear a muffled bang from Charlie's place, followed almost immediately by an "Ow." A couple more minor crashes and bangs. I think I can hear her walking, maybe even toward the patio to check to see if the lights are out everywhere, then a louder bang followed by an even louder crashing sound and a grunt.

"Charlie? You okay over there?"

She sighs audibly. "Yes." Then after a short pause,

she says in a more frustrated tone, "No. It's just really dark, and I left my phone on the coffee table when I went to the fridge, so I don't have any light. Which normally would've been fine, but I panicked and really needed to see if the power outage was just me, because that's a whole different issue if it is, and there are cabinets in all the wrong places and, well, now at least one of them is on top of me."

I gasp. "Are you hurt?"

"No. Just trapped."

"I've got a flashlight. Do you want me to come over and help?"

"Yes. I've got one in my safety kit, but it's in a cupboard. I don't even think it's in one of the ones on me. Owen?"

"Yeah?"

"I give you my express permission to come through our door-shaped, fabric-thin plastic that's held together by painter's tape and a wish."

I use my cell phone to find the flashlight in my toolbox. And on the way to our shared wall, I grab the plate of cookies that Luis brought me today before pulling the tape back from the "door" and heading to Charlie's side of the wall. The light from my flashlight finds her next to her table, with a cabinet on top of her and a second one fallen onto it.

I set the cookies and my flashlight on the one cabinet that's still in place so I can see what I'm doing.

I lift each of the cabinets and put them back where they should go, then I give Charlie a hand up and help her to the couch. She's moving like she's a bit achy, but she says, "I'm okay. Really."

"You're sure?"

"I'm sure."

"Is Reese here?"

Charlie shakes her head. "My brother is her best friend, and they're both at a musical in Baltimore. She won't be home until Elphaba defies gravity and Miles defies the traffic back from Baltimore."

I remember that Charlie said she was passionate about safety, and I wonder if the power going out has triggered some safety fears for her. So, I ask, "Do you want me to check your door locks?"

"Yes," comes out in almost a whimper.

I go to her front door, open it to take a look around, then shut and lock it before grabbing the cookies and my flashlight on the way back and checking the lock on her patio door. "Power's out as far as I can see out the front door and the back."

"Thank you," she says very earnestly.

I stand my flashlight upright on her coffee table so it's giving the room a dim glow. "Cookies?" I ask, holding the plate out to her. "One of the guys on my crew made them with his little girl last night. His wife suggested that he bring me some, since I haven't had use of my kitchen and was probably craving something homemade. I can't say I've ever used my kitchen here for baking cookies, but I have definitely been craving something homemade."

"Oh my gosh, me, too." She grabs one and takes a bite. "And these are *so* good."

So we aren't sitting in the dark and the silence, I ask, "What were you doing before the power went out?"

Charlie leans back into the couch. "Work has been exhausting lately, especially with how many extra hours I've been putting in, so I've been coming home and crashing. I decided to read more of that book I had started when I overheard your phone call with your sister." She motions to the book on the coffee table as she talks, and I glance at it and smile to see that she's using the bookmark I gave her. "How is she doing, by the way?"

"Great, actually. She got off with a warning from the school, and the leg is healing nicely."

"Oh, good."

"*And*, I told her I was proud of her for showing so much independence, and that seemed to make her really happy. I don't think I ever did thank you for that."

Charlie holds up her cookie. "This is a great way to do it."

I chuckle, remembering she was on her way to the

fridge when the power went out. "Do you want to play a game or something? I've got a few."

She still has about one-third of her cookie left, but she reaches out with her other hand and grabs a second one while shaking her head. "Can't. My hands are busy with cookies right now. It's vital."

"Okay, then, nothing that will use hands. How about a Q and A?"

"As long as I can keep eating cookies," she says, and takes a bite.

I try to think of a random question that might help me to know Charlie better. "I've got one. What's your earliest memory?"

"Pass."

"Pass?"

"Yep. It's not pleasant."

"Okay, then, how about *any* early memory? Your choice."

"Playing hide and seek with my family. No, correction. Being *the best* at playing hide and seek with my family. One of the perks of being the littlest is that you can fit in so many great places. What's yours?"

"Jingle bells."

"The song, or the sound like when Santa is near?"

"The sound."

Charlie nods. "That's a good one. My turn." She looks up, thinking, biting her lip as she does, and I've lost all ability to think. "Okay, tell me about a proud moment from your childhood."

"That's easy. Football. I started playing when I was little, and by the time I hit my teens, I realized that I was fairly decent at analyzing the strengths of the people on my team and knowing how to use them. I was also good at being able to quickly scan the field and know how to adjust. It made me a good quarterback.

"My family came to every one of my games. I think they were the loudest ones in the stands every time. I loved it. Especially when I got to my senior year of high school, because I was on top of my game. My team did so well. We might not have started off that way, but by senior year, we all understood each other well and fully trusted each other on the field."

Well, that was until Cordell broke that trust. My bum knee starts hurting just thinking about him, and I have to push my negative feelings away. "Okay, let's hear one of your proud memories."

She thinks for a bit. "Mine isn't nearly as flashy, but it was a huge moment for me. When I was a kid, feeling safe was super important to me. I'm the one who always made sure all the doors were locked, that we had a first aid kit in the car whenever we went anywhere, stuff like that.

"I also hated being away from family. I wasn't a fan of anything unknown, really. So anytime I got invited to a sleepover, it was a hard pass for me. But afterward, I would always hear my friends talking about how much fun they had and all the things they did, and I knew I was missing out on so much.

"I got invited to a sleepover when I was twelve, and I knew my friend's family pretty well. So I decided that I was going to do it! I was going to say yes. And I even managed to stay there through the whole night."

"Nice! That must've felt like quite the accomplishment."

"It did. I never told anyone, but I waited until everyone was asleep, and then I got up and checked all the doors to make sure they were locked before I fell asleep."

"You didn't wait to be ready. You just acted. That's courage."

Charlie gives me a playful push for quoting exactly what she said to me when I tried to save her from an intruder.

"Okay, my turn." I think for a moment, and then say, "Hmm, we covered the proudest moment. What was the scariest thing you did as a kid?"

"Attempting to read an essay."

Her answer comes quickly. I raise an eyebrow. "Really? I have to know more of this story."

"Okay, when I was thirteen, for my English class, I had to write an essay about something I learned when

I was younger. So, I wrote it about a time when I was shopping for school clothes with my mom when I was eleven. We'd stopped for lunch in a café, and a man came in, *very* angry about something, and it looked like things might get a little scary. Well, remember how I'm great at hide and seek? I was also great at disappearing and keeping myself from being noticed.

"My mom? She's great at diffusing tense situations. Before she stepped forward to help, though, she put me behind a young couple and said to them, 'Protect her.' So, in the essay, I told about how I'd learned that being able to keep the focus off me wasn't enough— when there was danger, I needed to be protected by someone bigger or stronger than me.

"What exactly the essay said wasn't important. The important thing for you to remember is that the essay was about my fear of being seen."

I nod. She's telling the story with a big smile, so I'm smiling, too, just hearing her tell it.

"Anyway, I turned the essay in. I had really bared my soul in it, but it was just words on paper, you know? I didn't think anyone would read it. I didn't even think the teacher would—I mean, she had a lot of students! Who would want to read all those papers? If I had thought it might get read, I probably wouldn't have turned it in.

"But... I found out that my teacher *did* read it, thought it was great, and entered it in some districtwide writing contest without telling me. I didn't even know that she had until she told me that I had won."

"Oh, sweet! Why wasn't this in your proudest moment story?"

"Because winning meant that other people had read it, too. And that wasn't even the worst part— there was an awards ceremony, and I'd need to be on stage with the other winners. *In the spotlight.* And I'd have to read my essay."

"Okay, okay. I'm seeing now why this is your scariest moment story."

"I still can't believe I ever agreed to do it. What can I say? I was a people pleaser. And everyone at school was just so excited for me. I didn't want to let them down.

"Three other people went before me. The whole time they were at the podium, reading their essays, I was getting more and more nervous. It was like my body got its signals crossed and sent moisture to my hands instead of my mouth, so I was wiping my hands on my dress constantly and licking my dry lips.

"My parents knew I was nervous and had gone over breathing techniques with me before, so I practiced those. Plus, those spotlights were really bright, so I managed to convince myself that no one was in the audience. And it worked for a while.

"But then it was my turn. I walked up to the podium, my legs so shaky that I was surprised they even got me there. I was barely breathing. I squinted at the crowd, which helped me to see that there were actual people out there. I was feeling incredibly exposed and vulnerable, so I looked down instead, at my essay, which was all about a time when I felt exposed and vulnerable.

"I glanced at the crowd again, and everything got blurry. Then I full-on passed out."

"Oh, no."

"Yeah. It was probably because of the extreme stress and, you know, not breathing, so it didn't take long for my body to regulate, and I came to. But I was out long enough that the other winners on the stage with me were already to me. So I woke up, saw I was lying on the ground and surrounded, and I reacted by windmilling like I was being attacked by invisible bees.

"My parents were almost to me, and they got the crowd to give me space. My dad picked me up and carried me off the stage and out of the spotlight. Once we were out in the empty hall, he set me down, but I held onto both parents tightly for a while."

"I can see why 'Attempting to read an essay' came to you so quickly when I asked about scary moments."

"Yep. I got better, though."

"Yeah?"

She nods. "Once in college, I gave an entire presentation on the impact of social media on society, and I didn't even pass out once."

"And no paramedics were involved? See? Now that's what we call growth."

"You know it," Charlie says, grinning. "Okay, now let's hear your scariest moment."

"Pass."

"You can't pass after I told that whole story! Come on. Where's the reciprocal soul-baring through the darkness of a power outage?"

"Still pass."

"Not *the* scariest, then. Maybe the second scariest."

I shake my head. "You had a full stage faint, some surprise ninja moves with that windmilling, plus a dramatic rescue. That's going to be tough to follow."

"You're not going to leave me emotionally vulnerable out here alone, are you? I'll have to file a complaint."

"Okay, in the interest of reciprocal soul-baring through the darkness of a power outage, I'll share the second scariest." I take a deep breath. "My grandpa died."

Charlie sits up straight. "Oh, Owen. I'm so sorry."

"It was fourteen years ago. I'm okay. I was thirteen at the time—apparently, that's the age for scary moments. My grandparents lived next door, and he and I were really close. I hung out with him almost every day, and he used to tell me stories about where everything came from. Like, he'd point to a dent in a banister and say, 'That was your dad, age six, trying to skateboard indoors.' He made every scratch feel like part of a legacy. That's probably why I got into restoration. He helped me to see that life wasn't just about fixing things—it was about holding onto the stories.

"Anyway, one day, I went over to his house after school. He and my grandma sat me down and told me that they had just found out he had stage four cancer and didn't have long to live. He died a week later."

Charlie gasps.

"I hadn't realized how much of a source of stability he'd been in my life until he was gone. But I *had* realized how much I loved and appreciated him. And how much I loved spending time with him. When he was gone, it made me realize that life isn't predictable. That it isn't always stable, even when it seems like it always will be, and that the more you love someone, the more it'll hurt when they go away. And that they will always go away."

I feel the sting of his loss all over again, just telling Charlie about it.

Charlie doesn't say anything right away. She just reaches over and lays a hand gently on my arm. "He sounds like the kind of person anyone would be lucky to grow up with. I'm so sorry you lost him," she says softly. "That kind of loss... it gets in your bones, doesn't it? You can move forward, but it never really stops mattering."

I meet her eyes, which are lit up in the darkness by the soft glow of the flashlight. I can tell that she truly gets it.

Before I get a chance to ask more, though, she says, "Okay, I think maybe it's time to lighten things up. Tell me something you love about work."

I swallow and then clear my throat. "Working with my hands. It reminds me that I have control over my own future."

"Ooh, I like that. Okay, mine is when I'm in the zone. I just feel as if I can do anything. Like I have super powers."

"I have no doubt that you do. Okay, tell me something that makes you smile."

"Live, outdoor music."

"Yeah?"

She nods. "There's the community aspect of it, of course. Everyone coming together to hear the same thing, feeling the beat of the music deep in their chests. But I'm also so impressed that the band is willing to get up on stage and have all eyes on them. It's inspiring. What's something that makes you smile?"

"Getting an opportunity to use my vast knowledge of obscure or random historical facts, whether it is for work, for writing epic poetry, or for winning trivia contests."

"Really? I did not know this about you."

"True story. I even won a trivia night once. It was highly prestigious. I think it took place in a bar called something like Ale's Well That Ends Well, and my trophy was a taxidermied squirrel wearing a crown. I still have it in a box somewhere."

She's laughing, which makes me laugh, and now I think we're both just laughing as a byproduct of the sharing of emotional things we just did. It's been a very long time since I've felt this close to someone outside of my family.

We talk some more, but the more we do, the more Charlie yawns. "I'm sorry," she says. "I'm just so tired from work."

"You should get to bed. It's the one thing that is easy to do during a power outage."

We both stand and make our way toward the kitchen.

"Thank you for coming," Charlie says. "I really don't like being alone in the dark, and you made it so much better."

"I'm happy to be your professional flashlight-holder slash emotional support neighbor anytime." She smiles, and I add, "You made it better for me, too. Power or no power."

We are standing in her kitchen, less than a foot

apart, and for there being no electricity, I can sure feel a buzz between us. My flashlight is aiming downward, so I can't see her face as well, yet I'm still searching it. I think she can feel this thing between us, too.

We both jump when Reese opens the front door and drops her keys on a little table. "Why are you two hanging out in the dark? Oh. Power's out," she says as she tries to flip on a light. There's a small pause as she walks toward us, followed by, "*Oh!* Sorry. You two were, um…I'm just going to head upstairs now." Then she practically races to the stairs and runs up them.

I smile at Charlie and then brush my knuckles along the side of her jaw. "Goodnight, Charlie."

"Goodnight, Owen."

I head to our door cut in the plastic, and just as I reach it, Charlie says, "Wait!"

I turn around.

"Do you want to be my date at my brother's wedding on Saturday?"

I grin. "I would love to."

CHAPTER 13
PACKING AND PEP TALKS
CHARLIE

love Mackenzie's place. It's so cool that she lives in an apartment built inside her sister's garage! But only for a few days longer. Livi, Mackenzie's sister, Maggie, and I are all here with her, in the bedroom part of her apartment, helping her to pack up everything before the wedding.

Well, everything except for the laundry basket, where she's put everything she'll need between now and the wedding, and the suitcase already packed for her honeymoon to the Azores Islands in Portugal. The Azores are remote and peaceful, and they're off the radar in the best way. I'm excited that they're going there.

"Check this out," Mackenzie says as she grabs a big manila envelope from her suitcase that has *Top Secret* stamped across the front. She opens the flap and pulls out a briefing folder. "Knowing how obsessed I am with spy movies, Jace made our honeymoon itinerary into an operation briefing!"

Of course, I already know this—Jace put everything together himself, but he needed a good amount of help getting it all formatted just right and looking official. And since computers are my jam, I got to read it all. It's fun to hear Mackenzie talk about it, since I didn't actually get to see him give it to her. I miss having him on comms when he does cute things.

"It's got 'Important Mission Contacts,'" Mackenzie says and turns the folder to us, showing a photo of Jace with the words *THIS GUY* written under it. "And then each of the next pages lists what we're doing each day of our honeymoon, each as a 'Mission' with its own 'Mission Objectives.' And it has time-stamped ops schedules! We've got things like taking in the volcanic islands and lush greenery, checking out crater lakes, hot springs, black sand beaches, doing some whale watching, hiking through calderas, scuba diving for shipwrecks, and canyoning.

"And there are micro operation objectives, too. Like 'Successfully kiss operative while laughing' and 'Execute three swoony glances.' And it has an Operation Gear Checklist with things like 'Standard Issue Sunglasses (for surveillance and sunset admiration), Evening Attire (in case of emergency tango needs), and Backup Flip-Flops (in case of beach-based ambushes).'

"And look! There's even a map of the area!" Mackenzie says, turning the page and putting the folder on the bed for us all to see. "It has locations marked and labeled—Known Rendezvous Points, Suspected Scenic Overlooks, and Potential Extraction Sites."

Maggie, Livi, and I are all looking at it with wonder. And, okay, longing. This place looks amazing! And I love that Jace had the idea to create this for Mackenzie. It's so sweet.

"This is the greatest thing I've ever seen," Livi says, poring over the briefing.

"Remember back before Jace," Mackenzie says, "I used to ask every guy I dated if he could choose to go on a vacation to the beach or the mountains, which he would choose?"

Maggie nods. "Because you wanted to know if they wanted to relax on vacation or have an adventure. And you always hoped he would choose adventure."

Mackenzie grins. "My biggest dream was to find someone who would hike with me. Or maybe even canoe. Can you believe that I get to go on an adventure honeymoon like this? This is so far beyond my wildest hopes and dreams!"

It's so fun seeing all of Mackenzie's excitement as

she's moving on to the next stage. I can tell that she loves this place, but she loves my brother even more. So, she's leaving a place she loves to move onto something better, doing things she loves even more. It's kind of beautiful.

And it makes me want it, too. It surprises me how much I want it, because I've never really felt its pull before. I don't know if it's because of Owen or not, but it makes me want to be more open to a relationship with him.

Livi finally tears her eyes from the operation briefing to meet Mackenzie's. "Someday, I tell you, I'm going to find a guy who will be just as perfect for me as Jace is for you, and we'll go on a honeymoon this perfect for us."

"Speaking of which," Mackenzie says, "how did your fancy date with your boyfriend go last night?"

"Not awesome," Livi says, flipping through more of the briefing. "We broke up."

"You did?" I asked. "I thought you really liked him."

"Well, I did, but sometimes it just doesn't work out." She hands the folder back to Mackenzie and then goes back to folding the clothes hanging in the closet and putting them in a box, like she didn't say that she just broke up with the guy she's been gushing about for weeks.

"And?" Maggie says.

"Get back to packing, and I'll tell you."

I swear, we all forgot that was what we were doing for a moment. I keep working on boxing up Mackenzie's shoes—the girl has a *lot* of shoes. Super cute ones, too.

"Okay, so Javier planned this fabulous date—a murder mystery on a yacht in the Baltimore Inner Harbor. We got assignments of what character we were supposed to play ahead of time, and I was a nineteen-twenties courtesan. So I was wearing a scandalously short flapper dress, and Javier was dressed as a nineteen-twenties gangster.

"As part of it, during the dinner, they handcuffed me and Javier together. I didn't think it was such a big deal, but apparently it was to Javier. I knew he was claustrophobic, because we played 'Guess my phobia' once." She stops in the middle of folding a blouse to give us a look. "Guess what his clue was? 'I don't like being trapped in small spaces.' I'm like 'Come on! You're not even making this hard!'"

"What was the first clue you gave him about yours?" I ask.

"That I don't like hiking in rainforests."

"Ooh. Good one," Maggie says.

"Right? Because then you're like, what could it be? Giant spiders? Snakes? Heights because there might be cliffs? The fear of forests? Or trees? Of animals? Heck, even what humidity does to hair.

"Anyway, I thought the key phrase in that sentence was 'small spaces.' Nope! The key word was 'trapped.' So, the handcuffs made him feel trapped, and claustrophobia—or, I guess, *cleithrophobia*—was activated and on steroids. I noticed at first that he was really focused on his breathing and nothing else. I asked if he was okay, and he said, 'No.'

"Then he started full-on hyperventilating, stood up, and started pacing away. I followed, of course, since we were handcuffed together. Then he started really freaking out and shouting, 'I need these off! I need these off!' So the woman pretending to be the officer hurried over with the key to free us, and the key *broke off in the lock*."

"Oh, no," Mackenzie says.

"Luckily, a guy from the yacht came over with some big ole bolt cutters. He was in the process of using them—the cutters were open, the chain between our cuffs was in the open part of the cutters... And Javier passed out."

I gasp.

"He fell forward, taking me down with him, which was totally fine. But he landed on the bolt cutters, cracked a rib, and the pain from the cracked rib woke him up, screaming.

"Of course, we didn't know it was a cracked rib yet, so someone called nine-one-one, we docked at about the same time the ambulance arrived, and I took him down to the ambulance."

Livi gets distracted by trying to figure out how to fold a jumpsuit, and it seems like she's done with the story. So I say, "Wait. You said you guys broke up. That doesn't sound like a breakup."

"Oh, that's the best part! So, right as the EMTs were saying that they thought Javier had a cracked rib, *his mom showed up*. I don't know how she even knew to come. Javier never pulled out his phone, so he didn't tell her. She must've been listening to a police scanner for the area where he was.

"And she was glaring at me like the broken rib was my fault. Then her eyes went to the one half of a pair of handcuffs that each of us was wearing like they were bracelets, then to my courtesan outfit and his gangster outfit, hardcore judgment in her eyes.

"She stayed quiet until the EMTs blocked Javier's view of us. Then she came up to me and said in a low voice, 'If you are ever around my son again, I swear I will send self-exploding glitter bombs to your place weekly for the rest of your natural life.'"

"She did not," Mackenzie says.

"So what did you do?" I ask.

"I told him we couldn't see each other anymore. I mean, if there had been a lot of potential in our rela-tionship and I could see marriage and babies in our future, then we could've addressed the threatening mom issue. I didn't, and I decided I didn't need the kind of toxicity she was exuding in my life." She finally figures out the jumpsuit and puts it in the box, then looks at us. "It's okay, though. I'm going to find the right guy, and I won't stop looking until I do."

I grin at her determination. "I hope you find someone who is the best of the best."

"What about you?" Livi asks. "Anything happening with you and your cute neighbor?"

Is it crazy that my heart gets all fluttery just by Livi mentioning Owen? "Yes and no. There have been so many little things happening daily. Like last night, the power went out, and he came over, so I wasn't alone in the dark. He brought cookies with him, and we told some soul-baring stories. We even shared a moment at the end that might have turned into something amazing."

"But you got interrupted?" Maggie asks. I nod, and she fans herself and says, "Oh, I love a great interrupted moment!"

"And we've been leaving sticky notes on each other's side of the plastic wall. When I woke up this morning, there was one waiting for me that said, *In case of another blackout, please consult your emergency neighbor kit: 1. Flashlight, 2. Cookies, 3. Me.* Is it weird that I'm wishing for another blackout?

"And then just before I came over tonight, I needed a new roll of paper towels from on top of my fridge, and I couldn't reach it. We don't have a stool, so normally I would just drag over a chair from my kitchen table and stand on it. But since they're all currently holding or trapped by my cabinets, I couldn't.

"I knew that Owen was home, so I just asked him through the plastic if he could come over and help. And I swear the guy bounded right over in two seconds, happy to do it."

"And?" Livi prompts. "When he reached up high, did his shirt rise a bit and show you a sliver of stomach?"

I look down, blushing but totally smiling. "Yes. Okay, but what if he ends up *not* being the right guy? Because you can't totally figure out if they are the right guy before you start dating them. And then if we broke up, cue a lot of neighbor awkwardness because we'd still see each other every day. I mean, we'd still share a wall. One that will hopefully be a real wall again soon." Plus, there's the part where I am investigating the guy who is paying for the restoration on the building that means so much to him. That makes being interested in Owen at all feel so wrong.

"I dated and then broke up with a guy who was my neighbor once," Maggie says.

"You dated a neighbor?" Mackenzie asks, seeming incredulous that there was information like that about her sister that she didn't know.

"Yeah. It was a secret relationship."

"When?"

"In high school."

"Seriously? *Who*?"

"Brady Rigsby."

Mackenzie gasps. "You dated *Brady Rigsby*? Brady Rigsby, as in the guy who peed in our garden?"

"Okay, that was one time, and he was four."

"I can't believe you didn't tell me!"

"It wouldn't have been a secret if I had. Anyway, since I'd been obsessed with Brady before the breakup, I knew his schedule well. So after we broke up, in order to avoid the awkwardness, I timed my comings and goings so precisely that for six weeks, I didn't so much as catch a glimpse of him. It was like emotional air traffic control. I could land a plane with those avoidance skills.

"And then after that, I just mastered the 'neighborly nod.' Not too friendly, not too cold. Just a perfectly neutral chin lift. It's the international signal for 'I no longer emotionally spiral when I see you.'

"Here's the thing that took me way too long to figure out: awkwardness doesn't last. Regret does. If you're scared it won't work, that's okay. But don't let that stop you from finding out if it could."

"That's a very good point."

"So you're going to go for it?" Mackenzie asks, with way too much hopefulness in her voice.

I nod. "Well, I kind of already committed to that, so yes. That's the other thing I wanted to tell you—I asked him last night if he'll be my plus-one at your wedding."

I'm suddenly surrounded by hugs and very excited women. Mackenzie is grinning at me. "I bet you're really not going to regret it."

I'd like to think that she's right.

CHAPTER 14
PRACTICE, PAIN, AND PERSPECTIVE
OWEN

've only got half of my crew working today because of the hold-up in getting the insulation we need, which has put a stop to so many tasks. My guys don't like to be off when they should be working, and no building supplier is showing any in stock on their websites.

In a last-ditch effort to get my crew back on the job, I started calling suppliers, and I found one that has as much as we need, about a forty-minute drive from here. I paid for it over the phone right then, told the rest of my crew I would be gone for the afternoon, and jumped into my truck to go and pick it up.

I like the feeling of having everything I need lined up. To see all the building supplies we'll need over the next couple of weeks, just waiting for us. But the feeling is even sweeter as we load all the insulation into my truck and trailer and get it tied down, just knowing that it means my guys can be back to work tomorrow.

I'm in a city near Baltimore that I've never been to before. As I'm making my way back through a residential part of town with my window down, the unmistakable sounds of football practice happening nearby carries on the wind. I slow down to figure out where it's coming from.

I turn down a street leading to a high school and pull off to the side in the parking lot right next to the football field. I was just going to watch for a moment from my truck, but I decide to get out and walk around to the bleachers. Since it's just a practice, there are only a handful of people watching, scattered throughout the space. I take a seat near the side.

I have missed this! The sharp blast of the whistle, the thud of cleats pounding against turf, shoulder pads clacking as they hit, the dull impact as the offensive linemen hit into the padded blocking sleds, plays being called out, coaches barking instructions, all of it.

The team is split into groups, and I take them all in. The running backs are doing the gauntlet drill, trying to keep their ball from being knocked away. Quarterbacks are on the far end, dropping back and passing to receivers who are also practicing their routes, defensive backs are running break-and-react drills, and a couple of punters are practicing kicking point after attempts.

It's when a quarterback throws a tight spiral that arcs perfectly through the air, landing in the hands of a wide receiver who lets out a triumphant whoop that the nostalgia really hits deep. Man, I loved being the quarterback. The scent of the grass and sweat, the adrenaline rush as we went out onto the field, the camaraderie. The way Friday night lights used to make everything feel possible.

I find myself mindlessly rubbing my knee. It's funny how just watching football makes it hurt, even when it wasn't a football injury that gave me the lasting pain. But the knee injury was what changed everything with football, so they're still closely tied in my mind. Especially because it was a fellow teammate who caused the accident. The familiar sting of anger toward the guy who did it surfaces, and I work to push it out of my mind.

I keep watching as the coach calls everyone in to run a scrimmage, but watching them has gone from giving me happy nostalgia and a longing for those days to a sharp reminder that everything is fleeting. Those things in life that you love are only there long enough to make you think they could be a part of your life before going away. It doesn't seem to matter how much you wanted it to stay or how tightly you were holding on. In fact, those things just make it hurt worse when it does go away.

I stand, my knee protesting extra for a bit as I walk down the stairs at the side of the bleachers and head back toward my truck.

I can't help but wonder if things might be the same with Charlie. If I'm just going to want her in my life more and more until the day when she's not. And will it hurt as badly as having football taken away did?

I get into my truck and see the sticky note that Charlie left on my side of the wall this morning. *Thanks for rescuing me from the dark last night. 10/10 would let you break through the painter's tape again.* I brought it out to my truck when I left home this morning because it makes me smile, and I wanted the feeling of her being with me today.

Experience has taught me that I shouldn't get more invested in a relationship with Charlie. But I'm just so drawn to her. I really like her—it's hard not to. And I love spending time with her.

I am hopeless.

I just sit in my truck, not ready to turn it on and drive away yet. There's an unseasonably cool breeze coming through my window that feels good. So I just sit while my mind wanders to thoughts of my grandpa, especially after telling the story to Charlie last night. I know my grandpa hadn't chosen to die, yet I still felt betrayed by his passing, and I'm suddenly wondering how my grandma felt about it.

It's been fourteen years, and to my knowledge, she's never even dated anyone else. We are probably pretty similar—we both got burned and learned. But she's managed to keep from putting herself into that position again, and I am failing at doing the same thing. Right now, I need to talk to someone who understands exactly how I feel, and who can tell me how to just step away from Charlie.

So I pull out my phone and call her. When she answers, I say, "Hi, Gram. Are you busy?"

"Well, I was halfway through organizing my spice drawer alphabetically, but for you, kiddo, I can pause the thrilling saga of 'tumeric vs. turmeric.' What's on your mind?"

"I just… want to talk. About life."

I hear a squeak that tells me that she's stopped doing whatever she's doing and is settling into her favorite chair. "I'm ready. Tell me everything."

"There's a woman who lives next to me. We haven't started dating yet, but it's heading that way. Her name is Charlie, and I like her. A lot. And I know I shouldn't, because, well, you know how it is from losing Grandpa. Every time I get close to something I care about, it disappears."

"Ah. The old 'love-is-a-trapdoor' fear. Runs in the

family. Just like our stubborn knees and unreasonably high standards for cinnamon rolls."

"I'm serious, Gram. I just watched a high school football team practice, and it hit me again how fast something can be gone. Football. Grandpa. And so many other things along the way. They all just left. And even though I've had a lot of experience with that, I still haven't figured out how to avoid that kind of loss again."

"Sweetheart, you don't avoid grief by avoiding joy. That's like refusing hot cocoa because it might burn your tongue. Sure, it might. But it's also warm and sweet and might have marshmallows."

"The problem is, Charlie is the hot cocoa, and I'm really pulled to the hot cocoa. She's kind. Funny. Bright. I feel like I come alive when I'm with her. But I've had my tongue burned pretty badly before. I'm not looking to do it again."

"Owen, listen to me. If something lights you up, you don't run from it. You follow it. You chase it down like the ice cream truck on a ninety-degree day."

I exhale a breath through a laugh. "That's the most *you* thing you've ever said."

"I haven't even warmed up yet."

I look out over the field, watching kids running drills like they're indestructible. "But what if I lose her?"

"Oh, honey, you're going to lose a lot of things in

life. Socks. Your favorite pen, over and over. Your ability to eat a plate full of tacos without consequences. People you love, absolutely. But let me tell you something. I spent forty-four years waking up next to the love of my life, and even though he's not here now, he's still in every part of this life I've built. And I'd rather have forty-four years and this heartache than zero years and a nice, quiet, unbroken heart that never really beat."

I'm silent for a long moment, just taking all that in. And Gram doesn't feel the need to break the silence before I'm ready. Eventually, I say in a quiet voice, "I miss him."

"I know, sweetheart. So do I. And he was worth every tear. Still is." She pauses, then adds, "Listen to me, Owen. If love didn't come with risk, it wouldn't be nearly as rare or beautiful. You want a guarantee? Buy a blender. You want a life that matters? Pick the people who make your soul light up and go all in."

"And what if things with Charlie don't work out?"

"Then we throw a 'well-that-was-a-learning-experience' party, serve bad fondue, and move on. But you don't quit before the first dance just because you're scared the music might end." She pauses a moment, then says, "Let me ask you something—if you'd have known when you were a little boy how much it would hurt to lose your grandpa, would you have chosen not to love him and spend time with him?"

"No. Never."

"And that's how you know. If you look at Charlie and think, 'Even if I lose this someday, I'll still be glad I had it,' then don't waste your time trying to walk away. Love her with everything you've got."

I find myself smiling. "You always do this."

"Do what?"

"Say something slightly ridiculous and then hit me with the truth like a freight train."

I can hear the grin in my grandma's voice as she says, "That's because 'ridiculous' is the sugar that makes the truth go down smooth. Now go after that woman, Owen, and do it fully committed. You don't need a guarantee. You just need your heart, your courage, and freshly brushed teeth."

I chuckle. "I love you, Gram."

"I love you more, kiddo. Oh, and Owen? Thank you for understanding how important The Shadowridge was to me and your grandpa. He'd be so proud of you to know what you're doing with the place. I know I am."

I get a little choked up but still manage to say, "Thank you. The Shadowridge is important to me, too."

"And I expect a full report about you and Charlie. Preferably over cocoa."

"With extra marshmallows?"

"Always."

I end the call and look back over the field. That wasn't the advice I was expecting to get from Gram today. But I absolutely should have expected exactly that.

I nod. Almost like an acceptance of her advice. I'm all in when it comes to Charlie. I'm going to pursue her with my heart, my courage, and, of course, freshly brushed teeth.

CHAPTER 15
BELIEVE BUT VERIFY
CHARLIE

'm in a conference room at the back of the CSA bullpen, just finishing up a meeting with Emerson, Kella, and Miles. Kella is going to start running some missions with Miles after two years of being a tech op, like me. Even though I never want to be a field operative, I think Kella will be great at it.

Since Jace is getting married in two days and isn't even coming in tomorrow, I won't be running any more missions with him until after he gets back from his honeymoon in two weeks. Until then, I'm helping out with other field operatives. Hopefully, my next two weeks will be less stressful than the last two weeks have been.

As Miles stands, he says, "If all else fails, I'll just charm the regional security attaché."

Kella starts gathering up her things. "When are

you going to stop being a player and settle down with someone?"

"When the regional security attaché falls hopelessly in love with me and we bond over secure comms and trust issues."

"Ha ha," Kella says.

"Charlie, want to stay after?" Emerson asks. "I've got some information for you."

As soon as Kella and Miles leave, I ask, "About Giovanni Vitale?"

"Yes. It seems that he does, in fact, have a wife." He taps some things on his tablet and then holds it out to me. "Is this her?"

I look closely at the image. "The picture he showed was on his phone, and since it showed her whole body, I didn't get a close look at her face, but I think so. She looks different now. She's got longer hair. And it's lighter."

"Well," Emerson says, "I found her Instagram profile. She does a lot of gushing posts about going to the theater. I looked into her—she was born in New York and moved to a few different homes there in her childhood. She spent four years in Washington, D.C."

I nod. "That's where he said she grew up."

"I guess if it was an important four years of her childhood, you could say that was true. She met Vitale while studying abroad in Florence for her Master's program. They got married a little over two years later. I checked—the FBI doesn't have anything on her. The closest thing was her grandfather for some smuggling nearly fifty years ago."

"Huh," I say, leaning back in my chair.

"I can't answer anything as to why Vitale didn't have security or an assistant with him. I did find that The Shadowridge isn't his first time investing in a restoration project in another country. He has also funded the restoration of a historical market hall in Morocco and an opera house in Romania.

"As far as him mentioning he had business in the area—that one is thin. He does have a luxury import/export business in Alexandria, Virginia, that he could've been checking in on. Or he could've been looking into new business opportunities, or even just meeting with business associates who were also in the area. All we know was that he was in the States for a total of three days before he flew back to Italy. We don't have anything more on him, and I checked—the CIA doesn't, either."

"So, he's clean?" My voice is full of hope. Yes, that would mean I was wrong, which might mean that I can't trust my gut as much as I thought I could, but I really want to be wrong.

"Hard to say."

It feels right. Of course, it's hard to tell if it feels right because I want it to feel right or because it's actually right. I pause, try to clear my mind, and listen to my gut. Not what I *want* my gut to tell me, but what it's legitimately telling me.

And I realize that it's telling me that I was right the first time. Giovanni can't be trusted.

"If I come across anything more, I'll let you know."

"Thank you." As Emerson is gathering up his things, I say, "I asked Owen to be my plus-one at the wedding."

Emerson gives me a high-five. "Good job. I'm proud of you, sis. I can't wait to officially meet him."

I grin. "Thanks! Oh, and Owen said he thinks that the company fixing our water leak can get insulation soon, so I'll probably have a real wall again before long."

"Are you sad about that?" Emerson asks, genuinely curious.

"A little, actually. Because it might mean the end of waking up to sticky notes from him. The one I got this morning said, *Something about today feels like the calm before the…awesome. Or maybe it's the calm before more construction. Jury's out.* And in parentheses, the note said *(I can't wait for the wedding.)* Isn't he just the sweetest?"

"Like a big, fluffy cinnamon roll," Emerson says.

I give him a sisterly smack on the arm, then thank him again for all of his research before heading out to finish preparing for the missions we'll be running early next week. Of course, to do that, I'll have to get my mind off both Owen and how I'm going to dig deeper into whatever it is that Giovanni must be hiding.

———

When I get home from work, Reese and Miles are sitting on opposite ends of the couch, turned toward each other, with their legs in the middle. They each hold a bowl of mini marshmallows that they are taking turns trying to toss across the space between them to land in the other person's mouth.

I drop my keys on the table by the door, hang my bag on the hook, kick off my shoes, and say to Miles, "If it weren't for the fact that you worked out of town so much, I'd be annoyed how often you get off work before me."

"You say that like you're not secretly jealous of my deeply impressive work-life balance." He tosses a marshmallow in the air toward me, so I open my mouth, and it lands right in. "Or my ability to always hit my target."

"Whatever, balance boy," Reese says as she tosses a marshmallow into Miles's mouth. "The scoreboard says you're down by two."

My phone starts to ring, so I pull it out. "Huh. It's Emerson." It's only been maybe thirty minutes since I last saw him. I answer and say in my best cheerful customer-service voice, "Charlie's Pizza Palace—where every call gets extra cheese and zero judgment. Can I take your order?"

"I'm guessing you're at home and you're worried that Owen and/or Reese can hear?"

I glance at the thin and mostly see-through wall that separates my place from Owen's. I can see his fuzzy person-shaped blob at his kitchen counter, possibly making himself a sandwich or something. He'll totally be able to hear this conversation, so I'm not just talking in code for Reese's sake. "Both, actually. We're always happy to offer delivery and takeout."

"All right. I found something. Giovanni made a hefty donation to the La Scala Mare in Naples."

"Oh, one of our Italian specials."

"But the weird part? The building's already been restored. It's been open for years. He specifically requested a solo walk-through. No staff. No publicity."

"So… ordering off the menu."

"Three days before he flew to Maryland to tour The Shadowridge."

Huh. "He didn't order any breadsticks or sauce? He just wanted to be seated alone?"

"Exactly. Like he maybe needed to confirm something."

"Some people like to be super particular about their order. Is there an order history?"

"Still looks squeaky clean on the surface."

"Okay, keep the oven hot and let me know when you've got more ingredients."

"You got it. And if anyone asks, this call was about a disappointing pepperoni shortage."

"Obviously. Talk soon."

I end the call, smiling to myself that I've got at least a first clue to go on when it comes to investigating Giovanni, and then I glance at our shared wall.

"Let me guess," Reese says, deadpanning. "That phone call was actually about what movie he wants to go see?"

I turn to my roommate. "Close. Except it was a stage production." I know that Miles is curious about the phone call, too, so I give him a meaningful look when I say "stage production." I know he'll piece it together and know I was talking to Emerson about The Shadowridge.

Reese turns to Miles. "Do you and your siblings play that 'try to respond to their call as if you're a restaurant' game only with Charlie, or do you do it with each other, too?"

Miles gives an amused smile. "If you want to find out, try it next time you call me and see if I play along."

Reese laughs and then launches a marshmallow at him.

I turn back to my paper-thin wall and the man I can slightly see behind it. How can I be crushing on him when I am actively investigating the guy funding his restoration? Especially when I know how much The Shadowridge means to him. If I find anything, Owen is going to feel betrayed by both of us.

CHAPTER 16

THE TO-DO LIST HEARD 'ROUND THE KITCHENS

OWEN

As I get dressed, I think through my to-do list, and for whatever reason, the tune to *She'll Be Comin' Round the Mountain* pops into my head. Weird, since I haven't even thought of that song in years. But, like I do every morning, I respect the "first song that pops into my head" rule and roll with it, singing my to-do list to that tune, making up the words as I go to get myself properly pumped up for the day.

"The whole crew will be there, all rarin' to go. (Hooray!)

"They'll be staplin' insulation like a pro. (Great day!)

"Luis will work on the ceiling,

"Nate will scrape floor glue that's peeling,

"And delivery truck's at ten with trim cargo."

I've got my work pants on, but remember my work shirts are all still in the laundry room. I grab a pair of socks and put one on as I'm doing a hop-shimmy combo across my room and out to the top of the stairs.

"On break, it's dry cleaner to pick up my suit. (Go there!)

"So, as Charlie's wedding date, I can look cute. (With flair!)

"No, I want to look mighty fine,

"When I show up dressed to the nines,

"So her jaw drops and her words go down the chute."

Then, I attempt to put my other sock on as I'm going down the stairs, doing a much more aggressive hop-shimmy combo.

"Then, send investor pics that make him scream. ('A dream!')

"Gotta sign off on the brackets near the beam. (Check, check!)

"But first, I need a clean work shirt,

"'Cuz I am more than eye dessert,

"And leading shirtless feels like a bad drea—"

I freeze, mid-hop, one half-socked foot in the air as I make it almost to the bottom of the stairs. Somehow, I didn't hear that the Demo Daydream guys had arrived and had apparently been let inside from

Charlie's and Reese's townhome. I also hadn't heard the sounds of them taking down the plastic from both sides of the wall frame, removing what little sight and sound barrier had existed between our two places.

Charlie is standing in her kitchen, yogurt topped with granola in one hand, the fingers of her other hand on her lips, trying to hide a smile. Reese is standing next to her, only giving maybe ten percent effort to try to hide her amused smile. Josh is smiling too, but the one with the biggest grin is Leandro.

"Aaay!" he says, hands outstretched. "Two weeks ago, I was here and there was no wall" —he turns to Charlie—"you came down those stairs in nothing but a towel and covered in bubbles." He holds his hand out toward me. "And your construction-clad neighbor saw, and there was blushing.

"Now, you come down the stairs, all shirtless and self-consciously flexing your abs, your smartly-dressed neighbors saw, and there was blushing. So beautifully reciprocal. So synergetic. Such a full-circle moment." He looks back and forth between Charlie and me. "You two are like one. Man, this is my favorite job site!"

"I'm just going to..." I hike my thumb over my shoulder and clear my throat, "Go get that shirt now."

I and whatever dignity I still have head to the laundry room. I plan to stay in there for a minute or two to give my "blush" a chance to go away, but Leandro just keeps talking to us, louder now for my benefit, so I grab the first shirt I see and tug it on, walking back out as I do.

"And, from your singing about the wedding you are attending together," he says, "I'm guessing things between the two of you have progressed since I was last here, huh? See? Good came from taking down this wall! The gods of broken pipes, or fate, or destiny, or whatever shone down on you.

"And I tell you what," he says, pointing between Charlie and Reese and me, "Josh and I are going to make this place *perfect* for you."

I just wish he could make this moment a little less *im*perfect.

I skip breakfast of any kind to distance myself from what's going on in my kitchen and head back upstairs to finish getting ready.

When I leave my house to head to work, I find a pink note stuck to my truck's window.

Hey, my cute (with flair!) neighbor,

We're having a "The Wall is Up!" celebration at our place at 7:00. There will be appetizers of some sort. Come as you are. (Shirt optional.)

Hope you can make it!

Love, your smartly-dressed neighbors.

I smile as I pull off the note and stick it in my work folio so I can re-read it several times today.

CHAPTER 17
A FONDUE FAREWELL TO THE FAKE WALL
CHARLIE

stopped on my way home from work to pick up a box of appetizers that Reese had ordered. She gave me very strict "No peeking!" instructions, which just really makes me want to. And, it makes me wonder a little if I should be worried about this 3-person party she has planned.

She squeals when I get home and hand her the box, then she pushes me toward the stairs with instructions to go change from "stuffy" clothes to "party" clothes.

Okay, first off, the silky pale pink blouse I'm wearing isn't stuffy. And secondly, I don't think I know what "party" clothes means in her mind. She is wearing a plaid shirt tied over a beehive print knit dress and plaid glasses frames (which I didn't even know they made until Reese wore them for the first time), so I go for a fun and flirty casual dress with a strawberry print.

Since we had workers over today, I do a quick sweep upstairs for bugs and a quick check under beds and in closets for sneaky people. I'll have to check for bugs downstairs after Reese goes to bed.

I go back down and take a look at the kitchen, since I was rushed past it so quickly that I didn't even notice before. We have a wall! It's not painted yet. The place smells like Sheetrock mud, so I'm guessing it didn't dry in time to paint. So my cabinets and countertop are still piled on and around my kitchen table, but there's a wall! The one cabinet that stayed—my lone island—is currently holding what I'm sure are the appetizers Reese planned. But it's also covered by a tablecloth, so I can't actually see them.

A knock sounds at my door, and I immediately know it's Owen. But at the same time, it feels weird because he's only knocked on my door once or twice before. It's strange how quickly we got used to the door cut into our wall. Stranger still is how I already miss it.

I open the door, and I'm practically breathless just seeing him standing there, a beautiful smile on his face, holding a plate of brownies. I can barely manage to get out a super breathy, "Hi." I'm smiling and just taking him in, and he's doing the same right back at me. Gosh, I thought about this man a lot today.

Especially after seeing his cute hopping sock-putting-on while singing his to-do list. I've heard his lists several times before, but I've never seen it at the same time. It was so endearing, and I couldn't stop thinking about it.

And I swear it had nothing to do with the fact that he was also shirtless.

Although I did spend time thinking about that, too.

He holds up the brownies a bit. "Luis and his daughter were baking again."

"They look delicious." *Charlie! You can't just leave the man standing there while you soak him in.* "Come in!"

He looks and smells freshly showered, so I know he's been to his townhome to see the wall. "You've got new Sheetrock on your side, too, right?"

We're to my kitchen, and he nods and says, "My side looks almost exactly the same as yours. Minus this" —he gestures at the appetizers counter that's covered with a tablecloth—"strangely shaped ghost here."

"You are in luck," Reese says, "because I'm about to unmask this ghost." She pulls the tablecloth off with a flourish. "For our The Wall is Up party, we've got 'Wall-Worthy Veggie Planks with a spackle dip.' Do you like how all the carrots, cucumbers, and bell peppers are all lined up like the studs in our wall? And these," she says, Vanna White-ing tortilla rollups, "are 'Painter's Tape Pinwheels.'

"Next, we've got Stud Muffins in both mini chocolate chip and banana varieties. You can decide for yourself if it's a callback to the wall studs or Owen's shirtless moment this morning."

I peek over at Owen and see him blush just a bit.

"And these tasty, flaky, powdered sugar-topped things are 'Drywall Dust Pastry Bites.'" She motions to the brownies. "And we'll call these 'Building Material Bricks.'"

"I won't tell Luis that you called his brownies 'bricks.'"

Reese grins. "And then our gathering activity is to fill out a couple of these certificates for our awards ceremony. Be as creative as you'd like."

"'Gathering' activity?" I ask. "We're all here. There are only three of us."

"Humor me."

So we do. As I'm filling one out, I say, "You know, it's nice it's only been three of us affected. In my college dorm, there were six of us. And we were right next to a dorm with six guys. Can you even imagine how much more chaotic that would've been?"

"I'm not sure I would've survived that," Owen says. "Plus, they probably wouldn't have had pinwheels."

As we finish with the certificates, Reese says, "Okay, load yourself up a plate and come over to the couch."

She doesn't have to tell me twice—I am starving. So I load up my plate and head over to our couches. Owen sits down next to me, close enough that our arms are brushing, and it gives me tingling all up my arm and neck.

Reese stands on the other side of the coffee table. "Okay, we are going to play a game called 'The Wall is Up, But the Secrets Are Out: A Fondue-Fueled Q and A.'" She puts her hands on the sides of a fondue pot. "I've got slips of paper in here, each with a question. We'll take turns pulling out a question, and then the person who pulls it out has to answer it. I was going to put the questions in a bowl, but" —she gestures toward the cabinets piled up in our kitchen—"they aren't exactly accessible. This was on top of the fridge, though. Plus, who doesn't want to see one of these at a party?"

"And we *have* to answer the one we pull out?" I ask, a little wary.

"I mean, where's the fun if you don't?"

"Okay, then," I say, "you start."

Reese makes a big show of reaching into the pot and pulling out a paper. "Okay, it says, *What's something your neighbor might've overheard through the 'wall' that you really hope they didn't? Follow-up: confirm whether they did or not.* Did I have to choose this one?" She runs her hands over her face.

"Okay, Owen. One night when Charlie was

working late, I decided to binge-watch the last few episodes of season two of *Buffy the Vampire Slayer*. I'm really hoping you didn't hear me sobbing my way through the final episode of the season."

In much too innocent of a voice, Owen says, "I must've missed that."

Reese sighs in relief as she takes her seat.

Then, in a quiet voice, Owen says, "*Nooo*, wait! He's Angel again! Don't stab him!"

Reese gasps. "You did hear!" She takes a deep breath. "It's fine. You're going next."

Owen leans forward and pulls out a paper. "*What are you going to miss the most?*" He thinks for a small moment, and then says, "I'm going to miss the sticky notes on my wall. Even the one that simply said, *Is this mildew or is the wall sad?* Because honestly, that got me through a weird Tuesday."

I chuckle. I don't even know what I was thinking when I wrote that one. But I'm definitely going to miss the notes, too.

I grab a slip of paper from the fondue pot. "*What was the most underrated perk of having no wall?*" I hardly even have to think to come up with my answer. "The ease of getting Owen's help, like when I couldn't reach the top of the fridge, or when I desperately needed light."

"Or," Reese says, "to have him come, wielding a drill, ready to fend off an intruder."

Owen chuckles, shaking his head. "I am never going to live that one down, am I?"

"Not if I have any say in it." Reese grabs a paper. "*If you could keep one part of the shared-wall era forever, what would it be?* Hands down, it's how easy it was to eavesdrop. Not that I ever did that!" she says with a sly smile. "I'm just saying that I'll miss the opportunity. The power of knowing I could hear embarrassing moments from both of you and stockpile them for future blackmail… Priceless."

I give her a playful shove as Owen leans forward to grab a paper. "*Tell us about a time you heard something you weren't supposed to.*" He thinks for a moment, then chuckles and scratches the back of his neck. "Okay, so one morning, I was getting ready for work, and I heard Charlie through the wall giving herself a pep talk."

I can already feel the heat rising to my face.

"She said, 'Okay, you've got this. You're smart, you're capable, and your eyebrows are doing exactly what you want them to today.' I wasn't supposed to hear it, obviously—but I was inspired. I gave myself the same pep talk the next morning in the mirror. And honestly? My eyebrows looked great that day. And I accomplished a lot."

"In my defense," I say, "my eyebrows were great that day, and I wanted to acknowledge their contribution."

Reese nods. "And we all know that a strong brow game is the gateway to a strong life."

Shaking my head, I say, "And I was this close to keeping up my 'cool, mysterious girl next door' persona. This is exactly why I now whisper all my pep talks directly to my concealer."

"Honestly," Owen says, "you should start recording them and selling them as motivational voice-overs."

I reach forward and grab out a slip of paper. "*Give an acceptance speech for surviving the Great Wall-less Era.* Okay, I've got this." I stand and walk around to the other side of the coffee table, facing my roommate and the guy I'm falling for faster and faster every day. Then I clear my throat.

"I am so thrilled to win this award. For so long, I didn't think I'd ever get here. I'd like to thank my noise-canceling headphones, the resilience of painter's tape, and the miracle of dry shampoo for getting me through this emotionally trying time. I'd also like to thank Owen for not filing a noise complaint when I sang my way through every girl pop anthem in the shower. And finally, to the crew of Demo Daydreams: your chaos is matched only by your charm. Long live actual walls."

"And to the plastic wall," Owen says, "may your retirement be loud and rustly, somewhere far, far away."

"Here, here," Reese says. "And on that note, I think it's time for… the awards ceremony!" Reese takes my spot, and I sit back down next to Owen. "I'm not going to say who wrote each of these—I'll let you figure it out on your own. Drum roll, please."

Owen and I each drum on our thighs.

Reese picks up the first certificate. They're actual certificates with a blank line that we wrote on. "Okay, the 'Best live performance' goes to… The Hop-shimmy Sock Solo: Owen's shirtless performance of his to-do list song!"

Reese and I both cheer, and Owen stands to take a little bow before accepting his certificate. I love that he's a good sport about this, especially because some-day, I hope to get a repeat performance.

"And the 'Most Cheerful Shower Crooner' award goes to… Charlie, for her belting out of the song *Unwritten* right as the water betrayed her."

My head whips to Owen. "You heard me? But I was upstairs!"

"Yes, but to be fair, it was more a product of the volume and because our bathrooms also share a wall than it was a lack of a wall down here. Although not having a wall down here did make it feel more in stereo."

I take a deep breath, stand, bow, and accept my certificate.

Reese holds up the next certificate. "Okay, the

award for 'Best Backup Wall' goes to… Painter's Tape and Thin Plastic! Since they are no longer here to accept their award, we'll ship it to them in this week's garbage bag."

We all cheer. I am grateful for the painters' tape and roll of plastic that the repairmen put up. We had some good times.

"And the 'Best Rocking out to Music' award goes to… Oh! Me, for 'dancing and singing along to *Livin' on a Prayer* while sweeping.'" Her eyes go wide as she turns to Owen. "Nooooo. You did not see that!"

"It was fuzzy through the plastic, but yes."

"You didn't! I checked for your truck—you weren't home!"

"Maybe when you started, but I came home when you already had the music blasting."

Reese takes a slow, deep breath, waving her hand like she's trying to send more oxygen her way. Then says, "It's okay. I'm over it. Besides, I have great dance moves. Okay, final award. This one, 'Most Timely and Much Appreciated Rescue' goes to Owen, for his 'gift of light in the time of great darkness and cookies in the time of great hunger.' *Awww!*"

Owen looks at me with an expression that I like, but I can't quite read, and I somehow feel the intensity of the emotion deep in my core. Then he gets up, takes a bow, and accepts his award.

I'm not sure how to react to that, so I pick up my

plastic cup and say, "I think this deserves a toast." Reese and Owen pick up their cups, too, so I say, "To the wall!" and we all clink cups. Except it's more of a dull ping than a clink.

Then Owen says, "And to eventually getting a kitchen sink again!" And we all clink-ping. I really can't wait for that day. Owen studies his Solo cup. "You know, it feels weird to use these now that they no longer match the quality of our wall."

"And," Reese says, "To being able to use non-disposable dishes again soon!" And we plink cups.

I'm not ready for the evening to end, and I'm glad that Owen and Reese don't seem to be, either. So we draw more slips of paper from the fondue pot—I swear that Reese made like fifty of them—and keep sharing about this crazy experience. The longer we go, the more we laugh until our guts hurt. And I soak in every minute of it. Gosh, I love spending time with this man.

Eventually, though, the night has to end because Reese and I have an early day tomorrow. As I am walking Owen to our door, he says, "Is it weird that I'm going to miss our plastic wall?"

I shake my head and say, "No." Then I pause. "Well, yes, it is weird. But I'm going to miss it, too."

We stop at the door, and Owen looks at me again like he can see right into me. I can't stop looking at him, either, but I don't seem to have his ability to see into a person. There is so much more about him that I want to know.

"Will I see you tomorrow?" He's tilting his head a bit, his voice is low, and his eyes are soft.

I shake my head. "I'm going straight from work to Mackenzie's to help with last-minute wedding prep."

"So I'll see you next at the wedding? I'm guessing you'll need to be there much earlier than you want me there."

I'm nodding, but I can't stop looking from his eyes to his lips. Then it suddenly hits me. "Oh! We should exchange phone numbers! It's weird that we haven't already."

"We've had such easy access through our wall that I guess we haven't needed it."

So, we put our phone numbers into each other's phones. Then, Owen's eyes fall on mine, and he reaches out and gently caresses my cheek with his fingertips as he brushes a lock of hair behind my ear, sending tingling all down my back.

"Then, neighbor, I will see you on Saturday."

He opens my door and leaves, and I'm left standing in my entry, too stunned by that sweet mega-dose of Owen to even move.

CHAPTER 18
AISLE BE THERE
CHARLIE

Mackenzie, Livi, my mom, Mackenzie's mom, and I all head back toward the bride's room after walking laps around where the reception would've been if today wasn't the most perfect weather ever. It was a nice way to start off what is surely going to be several hectic hours. Mackenzie is coming up on her two-thousandth day of walking for at least twenty minutes a day without skipping a single day, no matter what's going on. Apparently, even on her wedding day.

Over the next hour, all of the bridesmaids show up. With both moms, Livi, Mackenzie's three sisters, Zoe, and me, there are nine of us in the bride's room. It's a good thing the room is meant for big wedding parties like this.

I have a unique buzz set for when a text comes in

from Owen, and my ears are already attuned to it. The moment I hear it, I pull out my phone.

Owen: This was my to-do list song for the day. (Sung to the tune of "Twinkle, Twinkle, Little Star. Don't judge—it's what the tune gods wanted.) I've now checked everything off.

Wake happy to see Charlie

Try to make missing her flee

Ignore that her note was cute

Get dressed up in wedding suit

Resist texting all morning

Give up, text 'I failed' warning.

Owen: That was your warning, by the way. Hi! Good afternoon. I hope all is going well.

Charlie: WHEW. I didn't want to have to be the first one to crack today. You liked the "Weddings make me mushy. You make me swoony. Today's going to be a problem" sticky note on your door, huh?

Charlie: P.S. I'm totally picturing you singing that song while hopping and trying to put on a sock.

Owen: I do my best song rhyming while sock hopping.

Why did we wait so long to exchange phone numbers? We could've been texting like this all along! And why did we wait so long to start dating? Today is technically our very first date, yet already, I have been missing him like crazy. Ever since our wall came down, I've seen him daily. But I'm going on a day and a half now without seeing him, and it feels as if it's been ages.

> Owen: Is there anything I should know about your family before showing up?

> Owen: And are all your brothers as intimidating as your brother Miles?

> Charlie: Oh, they most definitely are. And they WILL grill you, so be prepared.

> Owen: Gulp.

> Charlie: As far as the rest of my family, know that my mom, Evelyn, is the most intimidating and gracious person you'll ever meet. But don't worry—her default is gracious. If she ever aims intimidating in your direction, run.

Charlie: Don't try to out-compliment my cousin, Frederick. He once complimented a 3-bean casserole so sincerely that the dish cried.

Charlie: Note that my great aunt Sissy will pat your cheek if she likes you. She has dementia, though, and you look enough like a younger version of her late husband that I can't guarantee which cheek she'll pat.

Charlie: Seek out my uncle, Dale. He's a fellow history buff. Just know that if you do, you're committing to chatting for at least twenty minutes.

Charlie: Someone will likely say at some point, "Do you know what you're getting yourself into?" Your only acceptable response is: "No, but I'm excited to find out."

Owen: If I survive this, do I get a t-shirt that says "I met the Lancasters and lived"?

Owen: Because I'd wear it proudly.

With all of us doing hair and makeup, the place gets noisy quickly. Eventually, we get into our dresses, which are all magenta-colored, of course. Since it is Mackenzie's wedding, it'd be weird if they were any other color.

But we each got to pick our own style for our

dress. Mine is fitted to the waist before it flares and has a sweetheart neckline. Zoe's is one-shouldered, long, and slinky, and has a daring slit. Livi's is about the same length as mine, but it's a flowy wrap dress with a ruffled hem. Maggie's is vintage tea-length with puff sleeves. Her other sisters' dresses are all just as different from each other. I love it because they show off our personalities so much.

Things start to quiet down just a bit as we all finish getting ready and Mackenzie's hair and makeup artists leave. Mackenzie is standing in front of the full-length mirror, looking at her dress. It's a white A-line with a V-neck and a deep V back, and the bodice is lace with beadwork that trails down into the skirt part. There are two thin bands of ribbon accenting the fitted waistline, and the tulle skirt is all fluffy and beautiful and fun. Plus, she has the most incredible strappy beaded shoes I've ever seen. She looks fancy and stunning without being too elegant to really have fun at her wedding celebration.

Which is exactly what they're calling it—a "celebration," not a "reception."

"You look absolutely perfect," I tell Mackenzie, giving her a hug.

"Thanks! I *feel* perfect. Can you believe that I'm about to be married to Jace! How crazy and wonderful is that?"

Zoe is also standing near us, and she keeps looking

around at everyone, seeming hesitant about something. Then, she asks Mackenzie, "How did you know you wanted all of this?"

"Are you asking about the wedding or the marriage?"

"The marriage."

"Well," Mackenzie says, "the fact that both Jace and I can only imagine a future that includes each other was a good clue. For both of us, when we talk about the future and what we want to do together, it excites us more than anything. Wanting to spend the rest of forever with the other person, which we both very much do, is also a good clue."

Zoe nods, looking deep in thought. I know her mom never married, but she only lived with her until she was about five. She spent most of her years growing up in different homes in foster care. I don't know what kinds of relationships any of her foster parents had with each other, but I kind of get the sense that they weren't good. I can see why witnessing Jace and Mackenzie fall in love and get married is intriguing to her. Maybe she hasn't witnessed that up close before.

The wedding planner comes into the room and tells us that we're five minutes from the ceremony. I hear the faint buzz of Owen's text, so I hurry over to my phone one last time.

> Owen: I'm seated for the ceremony. I can't wait to see you. I'll be the shockingly handsome man in a suit with hearts in his eyes.

Great. Now I have to remember how to breathe *and* walk in heels. This man is trying to kill me with charm.

> Charlie: If I don't see you before I'm standing up at the front for the ceremony, wish me luck that my knees don't buckle. I know what you did to me last time I saw you in a suit, and I'm worried. (Seriously, you should come with a warning label.)

True to her word, the wedding planner comes to get us five minutes later. We meet the groomsmen near the doors leading outside, and we all line up to walk down the aisle. Livi and Emerson are just in front of me, and I've got my arm in the crook of my brother Blake's, with everyone else lined up behind us.

The music starts, and at the wedding planner's cue, we slip through the doors and step onto the stone path leading to the aisle. The tall garden walls wrap around everything like they're keeping the outside world at bay, letting this little oasis exist all on its own. Lush greenery climbs everything it can, and flowers in every color spill from planters and trellises, like the whole garden decided to get dressed up for the occasion.

The ceremony is set up in the left third of the space, and all the guests are seated in rows of white chairs flanking a grassy aisle that leads to a flower-draped arch where Jace is already waiting. The other two-thirds of the space has tables with gauzy linens and low, glowing centerpieces, and an open space in the middle just begging for dancing at the celebration. Stone pathways lead to smaller, more secluded gathering areas in the corners. Everything smells faintly like jasmine and excitement.

Just ahead of us, my three-year-old niece, Heidi, and Mackenzie's four-year-old nephew are very enthusiastically tossing flower petals, with Mackenzie's six-year-old nephew following behind as the ring bearer.

As we near the front and we're splitting off, bridesmaids on one side and groomsmen on the other, I grin at Jace. He grins right back. I don't think I've ever seen my brother happier in his life. He looks so handsome, too!

Then they start the music for Mackenzie, and we all turn to watch her walk up the aisle, her dad at her side. He looks like one proud papa, and Mackenzie's smile at Jace makes her look lit up by the sun. I look back at Jace now that he can see his bride. I was wrong before—*this* is the happiest he's ever been.

I find Owen in the crowd. It looks like he's already made friends with my uncle Dale. He smiles at me, and my knees definitely get weak. He's just such an adorable man. An adorable man who looks downright dazzling in a suit. I have to look back at Jace, Mackenzie, and the officiant just to keep the power of Owen from making me pass out. All eyes need to be on the happy couple, not on me collapsing.

I swear, the moment that Jace begins his vows by saying, "Mackenzie," I start to tear up. Even before he's said anything! And then he goes ahead and continues. Luckily, my dress has pockets, and I pull out a tissue. Yes, I came prepared.

"I've spent my whole life keeping things compartmentalized. Then you walked in and broke through every line I'd drawn. You're the first thing that's ever made me want to stop running and stay.

"I promise to be your constant, wherever we are, however messy life gets. I'll protect you from flying golf balls, purse snatchers, rainstorms, rogue footballs, and any other danger that comes at you."

Mackenzie chuckles as she wipes away a tear, and honestly, the rest of us do, too.

"I vow to laugh with you, adventure with you, climb literal and metaphorical mountains with you, and never, *ever* put the toilet paper roll on the wrong way.

"You're my favorite person. My home base. My

heart. And I can't wait to spend forever making you feel as seen, loved, and cherished as you make me feel every single day."

And now Mackenzie has to give her vows, and I vow to myself at that moment to be the one to go first when it's my wedding. I don't want to have to cry through my groom's vows and then have to try to make my voice come out normal. Mackenzie does a much better job of speaking after emotion, though, than I think I ever would.

"Jace. You are the calm in chaos, the logic in my spirals, and the best thing that's ever happened because of a blind date gone wrong."

Jace smiles. I'm so glad I got to be on both comms and cameras for that one.

"I promise to keep things exciting—whether it's spy-movie marathons, Outside the Bubble Club activities, or just spontaneous cart races in the grocery store parking lot. I vow to remind you, daily, that you are not alone in this world—even when you feel the weight of it on your shoulders.

"I promise to trust you, challenge you, support you, and occasionally distract you with some really fabulous shoes."

Jace chuckles.

"You've taught me that safety doesn't always come from predictability—it comes from being with someone who would go to any length to protect you, body and heart. Even if things get tough—no, *especially* when things get tough—I'm all in, forever, Jace."

They exchange rings, and as they are kissing, I look out at the crowd, and my eyes find Owen's. He's giving me that look that makes me feel like he's seeing right into my soul. I'm giving him a look, too, but I'm not even sure what it is. All I know is that no matter how much I've planned not to, I have thoroughly fallen for this man.

CHAPTER 19
TRIAL BY LANCASTER
OWEN

know that not every guy enjoys going to weddings, but I do. I love them. The excitement in the air, a new future being born, the declarations of love, watching two different extended families interact, and how even the most grumpy relatives loosen up. I love the bad dancing. The bold dancing. The "shoulder injury in the making" dancing. I love all the sincere, the cheesy, the heartfelt, the funny, and the unexpected parts.

This wedding? This is a good one. And not just because Charlie was at the front during the ceremony, so I got to see her reactions to watching the first of her brothers get married. Fun music is playing, the weather is great, and it's not quite time for the meal yet, so everyone is in the open space, chatting and sipping on wedding-themed drinks.

This is definitely not a reception where we're going to hear classical music. The ambiance is fun and lively. The bride and groom are beaming as they move between the clumps of people, chatting and welcoming everyone. It's definitely a vibe of celebration.

Charlie has already led me around to introduce me to so many of her relatives. (Her great aunt, Sissy, did in fact pat my cheek. The one on my face. But she did look like she was considering which one for a moment.) And yes, Charlie's mom, Evelyn Lancaster is easily the most gracious person I've ever met, especially for someone with such a commanding presence. If I was told that she was the president of a country, I wouldn't question it.

The only way into this outdoor part of the venue was through the building, and security was there, checking as everyone came in. I nod to one of the three guards I've noticed out here, and say to Charlie, "I was surprised to see all the security. I don't think I ever have at a wedding before."

"Oh, yeah. This venue really likes that. Oh, come here—I want you to meet Abraham!" She pulls me over to a man in his fifties who's standing next to a woman who I find out is Reese's mom. Charlie tells me that Abraham works with her, that he was her dad's best friend before he passed away, and that he's kind of her substitute dad now.

Abraham shakes my hand and says, "So… you're the one who's been putting sticky notes on Charlie's wall. She's kept them, you know. You're either very charming or very doomed."

"Well, I was aiming for charming, but I guess I'll keep my calendar open for my doom, just in case."

Abraham chuckles, and we chat with him for a few moments. Then his face drops into something more serious. "If Rick were still alive, I'd have to arm-wrestle him for the right to give you the protective dad speech. Since he isn't, I'm doing it for both of us. I assume you've been briefed on the consequences if you ever hurt Charlie?"

"Not yet," Charlie answers for me, glancing over her shoulder to where I assume her brothers are. "But I'm sure it's coming."

I put on a brave smile.

"Charlie deserves someone solid." Abraham claps me on the shoulder. "So far, you seem more granite than gravel. Keep it that way."

As we're walking away, I say in a low voice, "Does that mean I passed?"

Charlie grins. "You passed."

With the exception of Jace, all of Charlie's brothers have gravitated back to one another, and before long, we are there, too. Why do I feel like I'm heading into a big game against a team that is much more formidable?

Charlie introduces me to her oldest brother, Emerson, who seems like a thinker. A very smart thinker. I've already forgotten the name of his date because Charlie introduces me to her next brother, Blake, who is a bear of a man, his date, and his three-year-old adopted daughter, Heidi, who was also the flower girl. I already know both Miles and his date, Reese, of course. I've heard the two of them talking through the wall enough to not be surprised that they're here together.

I meet Zoe next, whom I saw the first night our wall was down, even if I didn't meet her. Then Charlie introduces me to Ledger, who is dating Zoe and is apparently Miles's twin. The two of them probably look the least alike of any of the brothers. I thought Miles was intimidating when I thought he was an intruder. But he's nothing compared to both Ledger and Blake. But unlike Blake, Ledger is wearing a smile that looks like it's always there.

"It's good to see you again," Miles says as he shakes my hand.

I nod. "Especially in a well-lit area, since I didn't bring my drill with me."

Miles grins. "I have no doubt you'd find another creative way to protect Charlie if needed."

"So you're the one who mistook Miles's test break-in for a real intruder?" Zoe asks.

"'Mistook' is a strong word," I say. "I prefer 'enthusiastically overreacted.'"

Her brother, Emerson, sounds thoughtful, and I think he might be joking a little when he says, "So, Owen… What's your long-term plan here? Because if it involves hurting my sister, I've already prepared charts and graphs spelling out a detailed emotional takedown strategy."

"Good to know. I was working on a long-term plan involving baked goods and emotional stability, but I have a great respect for graphs and takedown strategies."

Blake uses a gruff voice that kind of scares me, especially because he says, "But seriously, if you hurt her, you'll have more to face than Emerson's charts and graphs. You'll have me."

And, okay, he doesn't just "kind of" scare me. I swallow hard.

"I assume you're aware that we come as a package deal. You don't just get Charlie, you get all of us." But he adds, "Including family text threads and unsolicited advice," and I realize that maybe he's not quite as gruff as he sounds. Or looks. But he's still scary.

I nod. "I've always wanted to be part of a group chat that both terrifies and emotionally supports me."

Then Ledger says, "Okay, serious question: how are you planning to keep up with Charlie? She's basically a sunshine emoji wrapped in an emergency preparedness binder with a black belt in computers."

Charlie gives Ledger a sisterly smack on his arm.

"Well," I say, "So far, I'm going with caffeinating appropriately, never underestimating her, and hoping I can keep earning sticky notes like they're merit badges."

Ledger nods. "Good. Because fair warning: I know hackers. And if you ever make her cry in a way that isn't happy or laughter-related, I'll have them hack your playlist and replace every song with a kazoo version of *My Heart Will Go On*. For eternity."

I make a show of swallowing hard. "Noted."

Wow. Five brothers is a *lot* of brothers. I've never really realized just how many it can feel like. And there are so many to keep track of. The burly one who's a dad. The bookish one. The one who just got married. The one I thought was an intruder. And the big, athletic one.

"Are you guys done?" Charlie asks, hands on her hips. "Do you consider him properly threatened?"

The brothers all look to each other and nod. "I think we've got it taken care of," Miles says.

I try to not let my breath of relief be too obvious.

Zoe, who I'm remembering is Ledger's girlfriend, asks, "What do you do to blow off steam? Go to any bars?" I'm suddenly wondering if she is looking for a buddy to bar hop with or if I'm still being grilled.

"Yeah, actually." I smile mischievously, letting her know that it's not really about the bar. "There's one I found recently in Baltimore. The place was built in eighteen eighty-nine. It used to be a carriage house for a nearby hotel, and they kept a lot of the original details. Exposed brick, hand-forged ironwork, arched timber beams with the original joinery. Even the stable doors are still there—they just refinished them. It's got these leaded-glass windows that throw crazy patterns of light around at night, especially near the back mezzanine. The acoustics are incredible, too." I shrug. "It's a good place to think."

"A good place to think?" Ledger puts an arm around me. "Have you met my brother, Emerson? I think you two would really get along."

We all start chatting, then a photographer comes over and asks if she can get the Lancaster family together. She starts directing the siblings, along with Zoe and Charlie's mom, to either side of the bride and groom. When they're all mostly in their spots, Blake calls out, "Owen. You getting in on this?"

I hesitate. The photographer is getting a family photo, and I'm not in the family yet.

Yet. When did I start thinking like that?

Emerson says, "You're practically in a group chat now. That counts."

They kind of all pull me in right next to Charlie, and she wraps her arm in mine. And now I'm in the family picture with a very formidable family, trying not to feel out of place at all.

But Charlie is holding onto me, which makes everything right.

As the photographer takes Jace and Mackenzie to get the next shots with another group, Ledger watches as Jace walks away.

"I hope Jace won't go off and get boring now."

"That's not going to happen," Charlie says. "Both Jace and Mackenzie are allergic to boring."

Zoe, whose eyes are also on Jace and Mackenzie, says, "Maybe we should do this, too," before her eyes go back to Ledger's.

"What? Not get boring?"

"Well, we're obviously not going to do that."

"Oh! You mean *this*? Like, get married?" The comment has definitely caught the man off guard.

Zoe nods. "Mackenzie said that if two people can only imagine a future with both of them together, then it's a good clue that you want to get married. And we do that."

"We do. But we've never talked about marriage before."

She lifts a shoulder in a shrug. "Maybe we should."

Ledger nods slowly and kind of thoughtfully. "We should."

Charlie gives me a smile that tells me she's both

thrilled and absolutely knew that conversation was coming.

———

I'm glad Charlie's brothers got all their razzing in before dinner—it let the rest of the meal unfold without the tension of waiting for the next round. Once the plates are cleared, the toasts begin. Emerson, the best man, kicks things off. His speech is everything I imagine he is: sincere, articulate, and surprisingly funny. There's an undercurrent of inside jokes woven through it—nothing obvious, just clever turns of phrase that make Jace laugh and shake his head in a way that says Emerson knows exactly how to push his buttons. But in a brotherly, best-man sort of way.

Mackenzie's best friend, Livi, takes the mic next. She has the whole crowd laughing in no time with her stories of Mackenzie's pre-Jace dating history, then dabbing at their eyes by the end with how perfectly she describes Jace and Mackenzie's relationship.

As she's finishing up, I lean over to Charlie and ask if she is giving a toast. Her eyes go wide, and she shakes her head. "And have all eyes on me? Not a chance. We agreed I wouldn't when Mackenzie first asked me to be a co-maid-of-honor." Then she smiles. "But I wrote a toast—Miles is going to read it." As Miles stands and gives Charlie's toast,

Charlie stays seated, blushing furiously as her words make even the most stoic Lancasters get misty-eyed.

Then, Mackenzie's dad gives his speech. He keeps it short and sweet, and makes everyone laugh at his regret that he didn't know having someone else read it was an option. He sounds like such a proud dad, though.

Jace and Mackenzie stand with the microphone. Jace thanks everyone for coming, and then Mackenzie says, "Now, let's dance!"

The first song is a slow one, and Jace leads his bride out into the grassy area bordered by tables, and they begin to dance. About halfway through the song, others start joining them. So I stand, hold out a hand to Charlie, and say in my best growly voice, "Would you like to dance?"

She laughs and takes my hand. "No need to bring out the growly voice to convince me—I've been waiting all day for this."

When we reach an open area, I put my hands on her hips and she puts her arms around my neck, and we sway to the music under the stars. "You look beautiful," I say. "And so happy."

She smiles. "It's a good day." A moment later, she says, "My brothers love you. My mom, too."

"And apparently, your great aunt Sissy."

Charlie laughs softly.

"I think they're pretty great, too. And I think you are incredible."

She looks at me like she's really seeing me. I can't believe I resisted her for so long.

We dance for a long time. Free-styling fast dances in so many genres, as well as group dances, like the *Macarena, Boot Scootin' Boogie,* and even a Conga line. When Whitney Houston's *I Wanna Dance with Somebody* comes on, everyone sings every word right along with it.

And we don't miss dancing to a single slow dance. Every time, I can't get over how amazing it feels to have my arms around Charlie, dancing closely, whispering in each other's ears, moving as one under the stars. The night is beginning to take on that dreamlike quality where everything feels not quite real. But I also want it to last forever.

Eventually, we start to tire, and Charlie asks, "Do you want to wander a bit on the paths?" So, hand-in-hand, we do, checking out all the fun little spaces spread throughout the venue, all lit by strings of lights above or pathway lights at our feet.

We come upon an alcove hidden away by shrubs, greenery, one canopy-like tree, and vines that grow up and across an archway, and we sit on a bench nestled away inside. I put my arm around Charlie, and she leans her head against my shoulder.

"Thank you for coming with me," Charlie says,

turning her head to look at me. "I know that, for a first date, meeting all the family, extended family included, is… a lot."

"I thought it was exactly the right amount." And I'm really not lying. I had been trying—and not succeeding very well—to distance myself from Charlie. To convince myself that I shouldn't want her or that dating her would be a bad idea. Now that I finally, thanks in large part to my grandma, decided that maybe it wasn't such a bad idea after all, I felt like I had already missed out on so much. So, tonight's mega-dose of Charlie is a gift.

She smiles. "Come on. *Exactly the right amount?*" The light is low in this alcove, but it's enough to see the contour of her cheek, the line of her jaw, the silhouette of her neck as it curves into her shoulder.

"It sounds like you're saying that maybe our second date should be the opposite of this."

"What do you have in mind?"

"Hmm. So we're looking for something more intimate, low-pressure, and the opposite of a full-family, fancy wedding. We could… make dinner together in one of our kitchens, once we get our kitchens fully put back together, of course, or we could set up a movie night in the grassy area behind our townhomes, or we could have a picnic in one of the balconies of the theater in the evening when no one is there."

Charlie raises an eyebrow. "Ooh. I'm intrigued by this picnic idea."

I don't want to wait until next weekend to go on another date with Charlie. I quickly think through what is on the schedule for this coming week—I don't want to take her there right after we made a lot of dust. "Are you free on Wednesday?"

"Yes." She pauses a moment before adding, "Wednesday is a long time away."

"And now we have a wall separating us." I'm glad I'm not the only one feeling it.

"We'll just have to find more creative ways to see each other before then."

I smile. That, I can do.

Charlie reaches a hand up to rest on my chest, and even though we've been dancing together for hours, I swear the touch makes fireworks erupt inside me. She looks so deeply into my eyes, and since I'm doing the same, I catch the moment her gaze flicks from my eyes to my lips. It's only for a second, but now all I can think about are her lips.

I reach up and skim my fingertips along the side of her neck and out to her shoulder.

Charlie bites her lip for a second, and then she leans forward and presses her lips to mine.

I respond by cupping her face in my hands, holding it gently as our lips move together.

She slides her hands around to my back, holding

me close, like she doesn't want to let me go. I sink into it, soaking in the sensation of being so close to Charlie, feeling her pour as much longing into our kiss as I am.

It was sixteen years ago when my grandpa first brought me to The Shadowridge, and I knew I wanted to one day restore it. It was well over a year ago when my career was at a place where I could, and I came back to look at the building again. That very day, I started working through the very long process of making that a reality. I was just so drawn to the building, the town, the possibilities.

I had no idea then that when I would move here to work on it, I'd be even more drawn to the woman who lived in the townhome I'd be sharing a wall with. I think back to who I was on that day—to the *me* who didn't even know that Charlotte Lancaster existed. I wonder how blown away that previous me would be if I'd had any idea what lay in store for me. Or that I would ever experience a night like this with a woman like Charlie.

Or that I would so totally and completely fall for her.

CHAPTER 20
SMOKE SIGNALS
CHARLIE

've led Jace through plenty of missions that required me to come into work before sunrise. Sometimes, even in the middle of the night. I've never come in this early when it wasn't for a mission. But as busy as work has been, this is the only time I have to deal with my sense of uneasiness that only digging through digital paper trails can soothe.

When the elevator dings and the doors slide open, I'm met with the kind of eerie silence that makes it feel as if I've walked into a post-apocalyptic workplace. Normally, the bullpen is buzzing with analysts, operatives, and officers. But right now, it's just me. And I am so ready to get to work.

I turn on my computer and monitor, slip off my shoes, pull my yogurt and granola from my bag, and sink into my chair like I'm settling in for a long flight, but with far more clandestine research and legroom. "Alright, Giovanni. Let's see what kind of secrets you're hiding."

For the past several days, a semi-reasonable voice keeps popping in my head asking me what in the world I am thinking. Why investigate Giovanni when everything about him initially looks clean? Can't I just accept that at face value? Then Owen could continue on with his restoration, and everything would be great.

But then a much louder, more responsible voice (probably the ghost of every intelligence instructor I've ever had) kicks in and says that sketchiness always escalates. Sketchy people don't just sit quietly being sketchy—they build on it until someone gets hurt. And if I don't catch Giovanni's smoke trail now, Owen might be standing in the middle of a burning dream later.

So. Gloves off. Time to dig.

Emerson already did the basics—surface scans, legit databases, eyebrow raises. I'm going deeper. I start with Giovanni's wife, since the whole "here's a random photo of my spouse, don't ask follow-up questions" vibe was the first thing that pinged my internal alarm system.

I don't have the photo he showed me, but Emerson found her Instagram, and since she appears to love posting as much as Mackenzie does, I find that same theater picture. I run a reverse image search and—bingo—it shows up in a promotional graphic for a performance of *The Seagull* in Florence from six years ago. I find the playbill from it, and her name's on it. So that checks out.

Still, something's weird. Despite being married, Giovanni doesn't show up in any of her photos. Not even in the background. Not even in the "My love took me out tonight, look at this blurry plate of pasta" kind of way. Maybe the marriage isn't real, or maybe that's just the way they roll.

Things might be off there, but my gut tells me that I'm not pulling on the right thread. So I move on to Giovanni's luxury import/export business in Alexandria, Virginia. Which, honestly, sounds like a front even before I open the file.

I start combing through shipment logs, customs forms, and tax filings, and bingo again—a shipment from Romania listed as ceramic goods, a 19th-century replica. It arrived just days before Giovanni showed up to ogle The Shadowridge in person. Suspicious? Yes. Illegal? Not on its own. But in spy work, 'suspicious' is the first domino in the tipping line.

I get excited for a second when a travel record pings a low-tier watch list, only to find out it belongs to a different Giovanni Vitale. Probably a charming old guy who just really likes discounted airfare and chain restaurants. Not our guy. But that's okay—I'm not going to get discouraged over chasing leads that turn out to be red herrings.

Next, I turn to the money behind the restoration. The company that's sending funds for the restoration of The Shadowridge is a shell corporation. So I go spelunking. It takes digging upon digging upon digging some more, but eventually, it leads to hits on multiple international properties, including a warehouse outside Marrakesh and a dockyard in Naples. And now I'm *definitely* seeing smoke.

And then it happens—the moment all the digital sleuthing pays off. I find aliases. Several. All linked to Giovanni. The kind of stuff that doesn't show up on a casual background check, but it sets off every internal klaxon I've got.

Hours must have passed because people are filtering in for the work day to start. My yogurt still sits on my desk, untouched, and now warm. I lean back in my chair, rubbing my face. This might not be a smoking gun, exactly, but it's smoke. A lot of smoke. And Giovanni is standing in the middle of it with a flamethrower, whistling like he's innocent.

You may be clean on paper, but I see you, Mr. Vitale. And I'm not going to stop trying to find what you're hiding. Not when Owen—and his dreams, and that vintage marquee he's been talking about—are on the line.

CHAPTER 21
NEVER MINE TO CARRY
CHARLIE

I was prepping for a mission at work today, and every aspect of it was getting thwarted by random things. My ways around it got thwarted. The ways around those took fifty steps… and then got thwarted. I attacked the problems all day long. I had come to work early and even stayed much longer than I had planned. Yet, now that I'm leaving, I feel like I didn't actually get a single thing done.

I don't know how today fits into my whole "I'm on fire at work" metaphor. All I'm picturing from my day is a giant boulder. But I'm not the boulder—I'm just left with a headache from ramming into it repeatedly. I never get headaches.

When I get home, Miles's car is parked out front. I know he has "best friend" status with Reese, but whenever he's not away on missions, I swear he spends more time with her than I do as her actual roommate. When I walk inside, he's standing near the kitchen, towel in hand, as he catches a bowl that had arced through the air to him. "Hi, sis," he says as he dries it.

Reese races out to the hallway from where she was in the kitchen to see me. Then, with two wet, soap-bubble-covered hands, she motions toward the kitchen. "Tada!"

My eyes go wide, and I run to my kitchen. The walls are painted, my cabinets are back where they belong, and the countertop is back in place, which means… "We have a sink!" I run to it, put my hands on the sides of where Reese has obviously been doing dishes, and lay my cheek on it like I'm giving our sink the world's most awkward hug. "I've missed you," I tell it.

My "island" counter is no longer an island—it's the bottom part of my L-shaped kitchen.

"Oh! And we have a table again!" I go over and hug it, too.

"And chairs," Miles says.

Nineteen days. We've gone nineteen days without. I can't believe how good it feels to have a kitchen again.

"Leandro and Josh got here as I was leaving this morning and were finishing up when I got home from work. I decided to celebrate by making chicken stir-fry. Miles and I already ate, but there's a ton left—it's staying warm for you in the oven."

I hug Reese for longer than I normally would, and say, "Thank you times a thousand."

When I finally let go, I give my brother a long hug and say, "And thank you for helping."

He murmurs in my ear, "Unrelated, but wanted to let you know I already swept for bugs and checked for intruders so you wouldn't have to."

"Thank you for that, too," I say, and then finally let go of him.

Reese laughs and says, "Wow, I did not think we would get this much gratitude for feeding you."

"After everything went wrong today, having a restored kitchen and a roommate and a brother who made me food and has it waiting, still warm, especially when I am this hungry, is downright heavenly. You're both angels."

"I don't think you've called me that before," Miles says, "but I'll take it."

Reese nods. "Me, too. Because we are. Okay, we're off to take care of my bees." She glances at the oven and then at the wall that's now an actual wall. "There's enough for two if you'd like to invite a certain someone to come and eat with you."

Yes, I spent the morning investigating the sole donor for Owen's restoration project. Yes, that makes me feel like I should pull back from Owen out of fear that getting any closer to him will make things even worse. I shouldn't be allowed to make decisions when I'm tired and hungry, though, because I have my phone out and texting Owen before Reese and Miles even make it to the front door.

Charlie: Have you eaten? Because Reese and Miles made a chicken stir fry that smells delicious, and before they left, they said there's enough for two warming in the oven. Want to come and join me?

I'm still looking at my phone, waiting for a response from Owen, when I hear a knock at the door. I keep my phone unlocked, looking down at it, as I walk to the door. I pull it open, and Owen is standing there, a box from my favorite bakery in one hand, and says, "I'd love to."

I laugh and pull him inside.

"How was your day?" he asks as we head toward the kitchen.

"Headache inducing. Yours?"

"Good. You've got a headache? Where?"

We stop just in front of the oven, and I pick up an oven mitt. "My temples, mostly."

Owen gently cradles my head in his hands and then places a long, soft kiss on one temple and then repeats it on my other temple. I close my eyes and sink into the sweet touch, like I'm letting it enter right into me. And I swear my headache is gone.

My eyes go wide. "How did you do that? How did you make it go away?"

A smile slowly spreads across his face. "You know, I thought our kisses were magical. I'm pretty sure this is confirmation."

I grin at him, and then pull dinner from the oven as Owen gets dishes—actual, non-disposable dishes—from my cupboard, and then we dish up and go to the table—an actual table—to eat. Now that I'm seeing the food, I'm even more ravenous than I was. My stomach is growling, and the food is tasty, but I force myself to eat at a normal human pace as we talk about our days. With me being vague, of course, and telling about it as if mine were all related to computer network issues I was trying to fix, instead of telling the truth. That the issues I was running into were all related to predictive risk modeling of future high-risk antiquities targets.

After we finish eating, Owen takes our dishes to the sink to start washing them. How sweet is that? I grab a towel and dry as he finishes washing and rinsing each one.

He glances over at me. "Can I ask you something personal?"

"Sure."

"At the wedding, when you were introducing me to Abraham, you mentioned your dad's passing. I didn't know that he'd died. Is that something you don't want to talk about?"

"Although it is hard, I don't mind talking about him at all. He was a great guy and a wonderful dad. It's just something that's awkward to bring up if it doesn't come up naturally in a conversation."

"Oh, I understand, especially since I just brought it up in a way that wasn't natural to the conversation."

I chuckle. "So you understand." I take a breath. "He passed away almost five years ago. I had just turned twenty."

"What happened?"

The truth is, he died during a mission that he wasn't supposed to be on. He'd been trying to recover a drive from a rogue agent that contained information on operatives and assets that would threaten them and their families. When I was a kid, I got fairly used to telling the cover story about it. I'm a little rusty now.

"My dad worked with a lot of our clients who needed computer security consulting, including clients overseas. While he was on site out of the country, there was an incident with a couple of warring crime families that spilled over to where he was working. He was trying to protect someone else and was caught in the crossfire."

Owen gasps. "That's awful."

I nod. "It really was."

As he's letting the water out of the sink and I'm putting away the last dish, he asks,

"What was he like?"

"Super brave. Loyal. Deeply protective of us and his team. He was someone who couldn't walk away from danger if it left others at risk." I smile. "And he was really good at flag football, cooking pancakes shaped like our initials, making up the best bedtime stories, acting like my pet goldfish had a personality, and convincing us that folding laundry was a competition we all wanted to win."

"He sounds like a great dad."

"He really was."

Owen wraps his arms around me, kisses my head, and says, "I'm really sorry you lost him." I let him hold me for a long moment.

Then I take his hand and pull him over to my couch. He sits, and I sit turned sideways with one leg bent on the couch so I can look at him. "Okay, now your turn."

"What do you want to know?"

"You seem like a really happy guy."

He nods. "I am."

"But there's also something behind your smile. Something you try to hide from the world. If you're willing to talk about it, I'd love to hear."

Owen just looks at me for a long moment. "You noticed that?"

I nod.

"You go right to the heavy-hitting topics, don't you?"

"In my defense," I say, holding up my hands, "you started it by asking about my dad."

Owen gives me an amused smile, and then he nods. "Fair enough." He pauses a bit first, absently reaching a hand forward to rub his left knee.

"I told you I played football in high school."

"Quarterback, right?"

"Yep. And I was pretty good at it, too. It got me a scholarship that would cover tuition, my dorm, and even a meal plan. I'd be able to focus all my time and energy on college and football. Everything seemed perfect.

"I had a great final season my senior year. Our team even made it to the state finals. I was on cloud nine throughout our entire end-of-season banquet. They gave out awards as we were finishing our meal, then moved on to the speeches, and then showed our highlight reel.

"I found out later that a few of the guys had snuck out right after the presentation of awards because one of them brought alcohol. They drank all through the speeches and came back just in time for the video. One of them was my running back, Cordell.

"I stayed late to help clean up, and Cordell left to drive some of the guys home. By the time I left,

Cordell had dropped everyone off and was driving back to his house, and I was headed to mine. I had a green light and was going through an intersection when he came from my left, running a red light, and he T-boned me."

I gasp. "Were you okay?"

He shakes his head. "Cordell's truck crashed into my driver's door, pinning my left leg and arm. He had the bigger vehicle, and the impact was mostly on his passenger side, so he only had a few bumps and bruises. They had to cut my car apart to get me out. I was in the hospital for a while. Plus, I had several surgeries, physical therapy for a year, and I missed most of the last half of my senior year as I was recovering. And I lost my scholarship and my spot on the team."

"Oh, Owen. I am so sorry." I know my words aren't enough for something so awful, but I don't know what else to say.

"I did get to go to my senior prom, though! With a knee brace." He chuckles. "I tell you, if you ever need an accessory to go with formalwear, that's one that will get you all the care and attention."

That easy smile of his is back. "And there were a lot of great things that happened because of it. You know, sometimes life doesn't go like you had planned. It takes you down a path that you never saw coming and ends up being pretty amazing.

"For example, I'm left-handed, but because of surgeries, my left arm was out of commission for quite a while. So I had to get good at using my right hand. And for a guy working in construction, I can tell you that it sure comes in *handy* now. See what I did there?"

I chuckle.

"Since I couldn't be on the football team in college, I spent more mental energy on school. And since I no longer had a scholarship, I had to work my way through college, which I did by working part-time for a construction company. Most architectural restoration specialists research, assess, evaluate, plan, and oversee. Which are all parts that I love. But I also love getting in there and doing the hands-on construction work, too. Having that extra experience is a big part of what allowed me to do both.

"It also made me a hard worker. More focused. And it opened a lot more opportunities to me. Sometimes you don't get what you want, but you get what you need, you know?"

I nod and study him for a long moment. Then I say, "It sounds like there were a lot of things that really worked to your benefit in the end."

"Yeah."

"So why is there still a sadness behind your smile?"

He rubs his forehead with his fingertips and then

shakes his head, chuckling. "I should've guessed you would figure out that wasn't all there was to it."

He is silent for a long moment, and I can see him working through things. Finally, he says, "It took so many months of pain and so much effort to get past those injuries. There may have been plenty of good things that came from it, but Cordell's poor choice cost me so much. My knee still gives me pain almost daily. Especially during some tasks or when the weather is bad. It even stops me from doing some things.

"I'd heard that Cordell had driven drunk before, but he'd never been caught. So for our crash, he was considered a first-time offender. He was a good running back—he had a scholarship, too. Since he did, he had such a bright future ahead of him, and no one seemed to want to destroy that future. So the court let him off easy.

"It felt like they were saying that it was okay to ruin my future, but not his. My coach didn't feel the same way, so Cordell was kicked off the team, but at that point, it didn't matter. The season was over, and it was his senior year."

"Do you know what happened to him after that?"

He shakes his head. "I'd like to say that things went poorly enough for him that it seemed like he got what he deserved, but from what I know, everything is going well for the guy. I heard he turned his life around. Maybe he did, or maybe it's all smoke and mirrors—I don't know. I just know that it never seemed like he got any kind of punishment.

"And I know I'm supposed to forgive him. Everyone says that forgiving someone else helps you more than it helps them, but I just don't really know how. I've spent plenty of time putting myself into Cordell's shoes, trying to understand the reasons behind his drinking and what made him think that driving was okay. But no matter what I do, I can't just dismiss what he did or think that it's okay. I can't seem to forgive or forget."

I'm silent for a moment. Then I tell him, "I don't think you're supposed to forget when someone harms you. Because then how would anyone keep from putting themselves into the same situation again if they did?"

"Good point."

"My family went through some hard times when I was little," I tell him. "And then some really hard times when my dad died, especially because it was at the hands of another person." It takes a moment to figure out how to say what I'm trying to say. "When I was little, my brothers and I sometimes did mean things to each other. You know, kid stuff, like taking another's toy, hitting, pulling hair, calling names.

"For a while, when I was probably four, we had a nanny who would always make the person who was mean apologize to the sibling, which was great, but then the sibling who was mean had to ask, 'Do you forgive me?' The one who was the victim was supposed to say, 'I forgive you,' no matter how mad we still were, as if it was part of the process of apologizing. I hated it. I felt like they were supposed to be magic words that would make everything better, except it never really did.

"I think that messed up the way I thought about it for so long. After my dad was killed, I was so sad and angry. I spent a lot of time thinking about what it meant to forgive and why people always said that forgiving was for you and not the other person.

"I don't think it's at all about getting to a point where you feel that what the other person did was okay. I don't necessarily think you need to understand why they did it, either, although it can help. And if you had a relationship with the person who hurt you, I don't think that repairing the relationship—or not— has anything to do with it, either. I don't think the person who caused the harm even needs to know if you've forgiven them."

Owen is looking at me earnestly, like he really wants to hear what I say, so I continue. "Every time I hurt inside because my dad was taken away from us, I wanted the people responsible for it to hurt every bit as much as I did. I wanted them to know how much pain they caused us over such a long period of time. I wanted them to truly understand the full cost of their actions and to feel absolutely horrible that they did it. I wanted them to have to pay as high a price for it as we were."

"That's understandable."

"One day, I realized how much time I kept spending thinking about them and about what I wanted them to feel. At the same time, I was thinking about how much that was doing harm to me. It was making me relive it and feel that pain more deeply. It wasn't making *them* feel any worse—it was only making *me* feel worse.

"I was carrying the responsibility of them feeling bad. Like if I got past it or didn't think about it, then they weren't going to have any consequences. It was such a heavy load.

"That's when it finally clicked for me, and I realized that forgiveness wasn't something that I granted to the other person. It was about me letting go of carrying the mental burden of *their* consequences on *my* shoulders. It was about turning the responsibility for what was going to happen to them that would make things right or balance things out over to God, the universe, the law, karma, a higher power—whatever you believe in—to take care of it.

"It's not *your* responsibility. It was already theirs and had been all along. So, if you hold onto that responsibility, too, then it only harms you. It does nothing to the person who caused the harm. If you turn it over, then you're released from carrying that burden. That's why forgiveness helps the forgiver."

Owen looks at me for a long time, like he's taking me in. But also like he's thinking through everything, so I stay quiet and let him.

Eventually, he says, "I really needed to hear that. Thank you."

I smile. I like it when I can be helpful.

He gets a sly smile on his face and says, "Do you want me to thank you with kisses or with what I brought in that box over there?"

I glance over my shoulder at the pastry box on the table. I've tried pretty much everything that Muffin to See Here makes, and I love it all. But I also really love Owen's kisses. So I turn back to him and say, "Yes." He laughs and stands to go get the box, but I grab his hand and pull him back down to the couch. "Kisses first."

"That, I can do," he says. Then he presses his lips against mine and pulls me in close. I wrap my arms around his neck and hold him just as close as we both sink into the kiss, whatever might be in that pastry box completely forgotten.

CHAPTER 22
NOTHING SAYS ROMANCE
LIKE A FAST ESCAPE
OWEN

It's Tuesday evening, and I am in the middle of looking up some local and federal preservation codes related to my next project. Because my current project always keeps me busy during normal working hours, all the prep work for the next project has to happen at home in the evening or on the weekends.

Normally, I'm in deep focus when doing stuff like this. But I keep thinking about last night at Charlie's place. I just can't get over how good it feels to have someone care about what's below my surface. To really care about the real me, not just about my cheerful front. I'm so impressed that she even noticed. Or could tell. With the exception of my family, who were at my side as I was going through it all, I've never had someone see beyond the smile before.

It has made me realize that because of past relationships and other losses, I had kind of stopped believing in love. Charlie has made me believe again.

Her views on forgiveness were so different from mine. Last night, when I got home, I spent a good amount of time picturing myself physically handing over the responsibility for Cordell's consequences. I'm not all the way to where I want to be yet, but I haven't felt this light in years.

I'm staring at the information on my screen, not really seeing anything, when my phone lights up. It's a text from Charlie.

> Charlie: Miles is heading out of town tomorrow, so he's soaking up time with Reese. They roped me into playing Back Pictionary, which is played in pairs, so clearly, we need a fourth victim. Are you busy? Or are you free to come lose with me?

I have no idea what Back Pictionary is, and honestly, I don't care. I text her back.

> Owen: I've spent the past hour trying to focus on federal code, but turns out all roads lead back to you. I'm in. For the game, the chaos, and whatever version of losing you have planned.

Charlie greets me at the door with a kiss.

"Mmm," I say. "My night has already improved by a thousand percent."

She grins and leads me to their living room. Miles is sitting on a side chair, Reese is on the couch, and in front of the couch sits a pad of big art paper on an easel that Reese borrowed from her work, based on the "Property of Cipher Springs Middle School Library" sticker on its side.

"Great! We've got our fourth!" Miles says as he stands, and Charlie and I take a seat on the couch. "Okay, here's how this works. Reese and I are on one team, and Charlie and Owen are on the other. When it's your team's turn, the person guessing will come up to the easel."

Wait. The person guessing?

"The person drawing will pull a card from the box and show the other team. Then they'll tape a piece of paper to the back of the guesser's shirt, and they'll draw that object on the guesser's back. The guesser has to draw whatever they think was just drawn on their back on the big paper. So they are trying to figure out what the card said based on their own drawing. Oh, and you've got two minutes to guess right."

Oh, okay. Now I get why it's called Back Pictionary.

"Remember to keep your drawing simple," Reese

says. "Or don't. Actually, you two can go full-on Picasso. Miles and I are here to win."

"We're also here to not lose our dignity," Miles says, already peeling himself out of his hoodie like a man preparing for battle. "But mostly to win."

"We'll go first." Reese grabs a marker and a sheet of paper and then turns to Miles. "Guess or draw?"

"I'll guess."

She tapes the paper to his back with enthusiasm. Then she draws a card, flashes it to Charlie and me— Roller Coaster—and starts the timer.

Reese begins drawing what could generously be described as a roller coaster track. There's a steep incline, a sudden drop, and then an unhinged curve that looks more like an EKG reading.

Miles mirrors the chaos on the easel. "Snake?" he guesses.

Reese ignores him and adds four rectangles at the top of the track, connected like a train.

Miles squints at his paper and draws boxes. "Centipede?"

Charlie and I exchange a look. I raise an eyebrow. She bites her lip, trying not to laugh.

Reese draws a stick figure with its arms in the air in the front box. Miles draws something similar, but he didn't guess correctly on where to put it, so his little guy ends up floating in front of the roller coaster like he's leading a conga line.

"Caterpillar?"

I guess it kind of looks like it might be feelers on a bug. Or a nose and whiskers on a cat.

"Nope," Reese says, now rapidly sketching three more people in the remaining boxes.

Miles hesitates. "Parade?"

Reese lets out an exaggerated sigh and begins furiously retracing the roller coaster track over and over again as the timer counts down, the marker squeaking in protest.

Miles watches, squints, tilts his head… then suddenly straightens. "Oh! Roller coaster!"

Reese throws her arms in the air like she just rode one. "Thank you. I was one step away from adding vomit for accuracy." They give each other high-fives.

Charlie gives a tiny golf clap. I lean over and whisper, "Fingers crossed we get a category with fewer individual parts."

We decide I'll guess first, which feels like a mistake the second Charlie tapes the paper to my back with a grin that says she's either about to crush this or completely ruin my confidence in my object recognition skills.

I grab a marker and face the easel, taking a deep breath to prepare myself.

She draws a card, flashes it to Miles and Reese, and starts the timer. Then she begins drawing. Her line starts low, curves outward, then circles around and curves inward close to where it started. I'm pretty sure she drew a line that connected the two bottom lines, so I do the same. Then she draws two lines coming down from the sides, and a box under that.

"Oh! A light bulb!"

"Nope."

No? Really? But this looks exactly like a light bulb. If this were a multiple-choice test, I'd fill in *B: Light bulb* with total confidence.

Now it feels like she's drawing mostly vertical but somewhat curved lines in the middle of the light-bulb-shaped object.

"A multi-colored light bulb?" I guess. Really, I've got nothing else.

"Nope."

I just stare at it, wondering what else it could possibly be. Charlie draws something to the side of the object that I'm thinking might be a flower, or maybe cotton candy, and I draw it, too, the best I can, based just on feeling it. Now that I can see it, I realize it's a cloud.

"A hot air balloon!"

"Yes!" Charlie shouts, and when I turn around, she's grinning, and I give her a hug, spinning her in a circle before I can think twice about it, and she laughs against my shoulder.

Reese guesses next, and first thinks that the oval with two lines leading back to a propeller that Miles drew on her back is a sideways balloon instead of the body of a helicopter. When he adds the landing gear, she asks why it has whiskers. When he finally draws two blades on top, she guesses it correctly.

When Charlie is at the pad, ready to guess, the card I draw is Wedding Cake. I draw it with three architecturally sound tiers, each one sitting atop the one below it. Charlie guesses it's a filing cabinet. I add a cute little couple standing on top, holding hands, and Charlie guesses the Leaning Tower of Pisa. It isn't until I add something that can maybe be considered frosting flowers along the base that she guesses correctly.

We play a couple more chaotic rounds before Reese leans back and says, "Do you know what we should've gotten for tonight? Ice cream."

"Mmm, ice cream," Charlie says.

Miles looks at Reese. "Should we go get some?"

"Right now?"

"Sure. We can just take a halftime intermission on the game." He motions at us. "I bet Charlie and Owen can think of something to do while we're gone."

Charlie raises an eyebrow at me, and I raise one back.

When Reese and Miles leave, I turn to Charlie. "Was today at work any better than yesterday?"

"So much better." She grins. "And, I've been headache-free ever since you kissed it away. How was yours?"

"The frustration that found you yesterday found me today. But Tuesdays are always that way. I'm thinking of officially naming it 'Issue Tuesday.'"

"What happened?"

"We discovered a rare historical element on a wall in the upper floor that leads to the balcony boxes. It was a hand-painted mural that was hidden behind a wooden facade. Which sounds cool, but it was found when a subcontractor—who wasn't supposed to even be in that area yet—accidentally damaged it. So now, the preservation board wants a full report before any work upstairs can be done."

"I am so sorry." I can tell that Charlie feels bad, and her mind is churning, like she's calculating something. Then she says, sounding defeated, "I don't even know how to help with that."

"You don't have to help," I say. "Just listening is enough." She gets an expression on her face, though, that I can't quite interpret, but it doesn't seem good. I want to distract her. I'm sure that when Miles and Reese left, they both assumed that Charlie and I would spend the time kissing. And there's a big part of me that wants to do just that.

But I also want to do something else. I say, "I know you're passionate about safety. The intruder drill you ran with Miles the other day—do you like doing that kind of thing?"

"I used to get my family to do all kinds of drills when I was a kid. Reese, though?" She chuckles. "Yeah, that's not really her thing. She's more of a 'go with the flow, figure it out when we get there' kind of girl."

"I'll do one with you."

She sits up straighter. "Are you serious? You don't have to."

"Of course, I will. Do you want to do it now?"

"Yes!" She lights up more than I would expect a person to light up when hearing that we are going to run a drill of some sort. "How about a fire drill?"

"Lead the way, Chief Safety Officer."

She takes us to the kitchen area, and I stand in front of the stove, pretending to cook something.

"Okay," Charlie says, holding an actual stopwatch, the likes of which I haven't seen since high school, and pointing like a very friendly drill sergeant. "This one starts in the kitchen. Let's say there's a grease fire on the stove and smoke is pouring up from it. What do you do first?"

"Panic," I say solemnly.

She cracks a smile. "After that."

"If it's a small fire, I grab the baking soda and pour it on the fire."

"Very good! And if it's a big fire? Already licking the walls?"

"Exit the building, along with everyone else.

Calmly. Without rescuing the flaming quesadilla that betrayed me."

"Correct. Bonus points for not grabbing flammable food. When do you call nine-one-one for help?"

"When I'm safe outside."

She smiles. "And…" she says, holding up the stop-watch, "big fire starts now. Let's go!" We run out of the townhome, down the stairs, and to the tree in the front yard. Charlie presses the stop button. "That was good. Want to run the drill from upstairs?"

"I can't think of anything else I'd rather do right now."

So we do. She has me start in the upstairs bath-room, and we both test our doorknobs for heat before opening them, then we crawl under an imaginary cloud of smoke on our way to the stairs. She was extra impressed that I handed her an imaginary damp cloth to hold over her nose and mouth to keep her from inhaling too much smoke.

"You know," I say, mid-crawl, "this is exactly how I imagined our evening going."

Charlie laughs. "I knew you were the type to dream of tactical drills."

"I like a girl who keeps me on my toes. And keeps me from catching on fire."

After the third drill, we head back into Charlie's place, both winded but grinning, especially since Charlie announced that we got the fastest time ever. I wrap my arms around her and say, "I'll always do everything I can to keep you safe."

She tilts her head to look at me, and gives me a very sincere, "Thank you. For running the drills. And especially for not making fun of my fears. For just reassuring me."

I smile, kiss her forehead, then whisper, "Always."

CHAPTER 23
CANDLELIGHT AND SHADOWS
CHARLIE

've been dreaming about my picnic date with Owen all day. Okay, maybe not *all* day. I did run support on a mission to scan a briefcase during a staged elevator malfunction in Hong Kong that Miles and Kella did together. But whenever I wasn't decoding the elevator's operating system, which—fun fact—was entirely in Cantonese and had a font I'm convinced was Comic Sans, or perfectly timing a power surge in the hotel to stall the elevator right when Miles sneezed so he could get a scan of the brief-case, I was thinking about seeing Owen.

Owen said he just barely got home from work in time to take a quick shower before our date, and I just got home in time to change into jeans and a sweater, so that worked out perfectly. I mean, as perfectly as "very nearly late" can be.

But we are both ready to just leave everything behind and enjoy tonight. Owen says he already has everything we need waiting at the theater except the food, which he already ordered from Board & Butter, a new restaurant only a block away from the theater. He parks his truck near the restaurant, and after we pick up the bag of food, we walk to a coffee shop closer to the theater to get Italian sodas.

It always amazes me that, in a public place, other people can just be in their own world instead of scanning the faces of everyone they're passing by. Or memorizing who is in the general vicinity, so if that same person shows up somewhere else, they'll know to be cautious. Looking for any suspicious actions. Keeping an eye out for any danger.

It's not just Owen who can walk down the street without a care. I've noticed it with friends, too. They all can just walk, blissfully assuming that nothing will happen.

I know it's a spy thing because everyone else in my family keeps a constant eye out for danger, too. And I'm sure that being on comms and video with Jace while he's on a mission makes me constantly keep an eye out even more, since he's quite often around danger. It means it's extra important for me to also watch for possible issues.

All of Owen's crew has gone home for the day, and the place is locked up, so Owen opens the front doors with his keys and locks them behind him, then leads us up the curving staircase. There are only a couple of lights on here and there that I'm guessing stay on during the night to deter thieves, and there's also enough light filtering through high windows to see just fine.

It's all I can do to keep from asking Owen to take a quick lap through the building with me just to check for danger first. I tell that part of my brain that it can chill out already, because Owen does that before he leaves each day. Besides, I'm with Owen. The guy who would wake from a deep sleep to protect me from an intruder, wielding nothing more than a powerless drill. I am safe with him.

It's only been a week and a half since I last saw this place, but so much has been done since then. No part is completed, yet—everything is still in some state of unfinished construction. It's comforting. It means it's going to be a while before Owen moves on to the next project.

The upstairs is open to the theater, with the exception of the walls and doors for the four balcony boxes. We go into one of them, and Owen closes the door behind us. He's got a picnic blanket spread on the floor, with candles in the middle.

"Owen, this is perfect!"

"Yeah?" he asks as he sets the bag of food on the blanket.

"It's very much the opposite of our wedding date, and I love it." I walk over to the edge of the balcony box where the wall is only maybe two-and-a-half feet tall, and I look out over the open theater. Owen steps up next to me, wrapping an arm around my waist, and I snuggle into him as he tells all about the area where the seats will be below, about the stage, about all the ornamentation throughout. The way he talks about it makes it feel almost magical.

"You really do love this place, don't you?"

"I really do. I think a lot about the people who built it, especially the guy who was in my position originally. I imagine him having a grand vision of what he wanted this place to be and having to figure out how to create exactly what he pictured. And about what he wanted people to feel and experience as they walked inside.

"I've read everything on the original designer-slash-project manager that I could find. And I came across pictures of the crew, too—they had all stopped working to gather for the cameraman, tools still in hand. I looked closely at the faces of each of them and wondered what they might be like and what brought them to this project. Was it simply work that was available in their area? Did they seek it out? What were their lives like?"

Owen shakes his head. "I'm standing on the shoulders of giants as I rebuild this. I have the benefit of largely knowing what the building is supposed to look like when it's restored. Those guys were building from the ground up. None of it had been created. They just went off this one man's vision."

I smile at Owen, soaking in the passion he has for this place.

"And they didn't even have all the tools at their disposal that we have now. They did everything the hard way, and I have so much respect for those guys. I hope that when I'm finished, this place will be something they'd be proud of."

I give him a kiss. "I know they will be. Your grandpa, too."

He smiles, then motions out to the auditorium area. "He was sitting somewhere right down there when he first met my grandma. If it weren't for this place, me, my sister, my dad—none of us would be here."

"Well, I hope the original builders know they accidentally created the cutest love story sequel." When Owen laughs, I add, "And if the building starts randomly playing love songs through the speakers, I'm blaming your grandpa's ghost."

We sit on the blanket, and he starts pulling food items from the bag. "This," he says as he takes the lid off a covered container, "is their Charcuterie-for-Two box."

It has meats, cheeses, olives, crackers, fancy pickles, and nuts, all arranged adorably. Then he pulls out a mini freshly-baked baguette, a little container of some kind of fancy butter, one of fig jam, and two jars with dessert—a chocolate mousse and a crème brûlée.

We are sitting on a blanket in a balcony meant to watch a musical or an opera in a theater we have all to ourselves, with this cute and fun meal. And we are totally cute and fun as we eat it, too. Feeding each other, laughing, making interesting combinations to test out, all of it. (Some combinations are so tasty. Others… let's just say that although elements of bleu cheese, green olive, sweet pickled onion, and fig jam might sound like they could pair well, put them all together on a cracker, and it's pure palate chaos. Zero out of ten, do not recommend.)

And we chat about everything under the sun as we eat. Or, I guess under the candlelight. It's starting to get fairly dark outside, and since we're down on the floor in this balcony box, the candles are providing most of the light. It's so amazing being in our own world inside this little bubble. It's like no worries exist here.

Well, okay, there are worries. For one, it's getting dark, and this is a fairly big place with lots of rooms, and it's not entirely familiar to me, especially in the dark. But I'm with Owen, so it's okay.

And there's another familiar fear that arises, and without even meaning to, I've voiced it. "You keep doing so many things for me, and I haven't been doing anything for you." Why is he even going to want to keep this relationship going if I don't offer enough?

He gets a really concerned look on his face and sets down the jar he just put the lid on. "Charlie, do you think that you have to do things for me in order for me to like you?" He cups my face with his hands, his eyes focused on mine in that way that makes it feel like he's seeing right into me, and says, "I love spending time with you. You're not a Swiss Army knife, Charlie. You're not a tool that I like having near because it's helpful. You don't have to do anything for me in order for me to like you. I like you simply because you're you."

He looks so sincere that it chokes me up a bit. I don't have time to respond, though, because a movement catches our eyes, and we turn to look out over the top of the balcony box wall to the theater below, and we see a man in dark clothes who is moving stealthily. I immediately freeze, but I'm quickly pulled out of it because Owen's first reaction is to move to get up. I pull him down, shake my head, put a finger up to my lips, and then I blow out the candles.

In a quiet but intense voice, Owen says, "We're supposed to be safe in here, and that guy broke in! I need to go do something. I have to confront him."

"No, just stay here." I can tell that adrenaline is

coursing through Owen, and he's feeling a strong need to act, but I desperately need him by me. Safe.

"What if he comes up here? I'm supposed to protect you and this place."

"He's not going to come up here. *Please.*" My own heart is beating so fast, and I can't stop thinking about that time when I was three in the park and a man just picked me up and carried me away. And the time when things looked like they were going to get intense with the man at the café when I was eleven, and my mom told the people in line to protect me.

My breathing is coming fast, and I can't seem to slow it down. Owen must be able to tell a bit about what's going on in my mind and body right now, because the intense expression on his face softens right along with his compulsion to get up and go after the guy. He scoots closer to me and wraps his arms around me, pulling me in tight against his chest.

Both my breathing and my heart rate slow, and the feeling of safety returns. Still, I can't help but keep looking over the top of the wall at the man in the shadows. He came from a side door near the stage that leads to a hallway and the offices. We both watch in silence as he moves along the wall nearest the stage, all the way back to the wall. He silently takes the stairs to the stage and then disappears backstage. He's only gone for maybe ten seconds before he reemerges and takes the same path back out of the theater.

Although it's fairly dark now, Owen showed me where the cameras were the last time I was here, so I know that the man expertly avoided them all, which means he knows where they are. This isn't just a random or ordinary criminal.

Neither of us says anything for a full two minutes. We just hold our breaths, listening for any sound. Once I am sure the guy is gone, I turn to meet Owen's eyes and say in a quiet but urgent voice, "Don't ever go after a bad guy. Staying hidden is staying safe. I learned that from a young age." I wasn't hidden at that park when I was three. I was very easily seen and very much not safe.

Owen cocks his head. "I feel like you know this from more than just hide-and-seek and that experience from your essay."

Yep. From both my lived experiences and loads and loads of training from the CSA. Neither of which I want us to talk about. Owen waits, though, giving me the opportunity. When it's obvious I'm not going to say anything about it, he seems to let his nerves take full rein again, and he looks out across the empty auditorium.

Then he pulls out his phone. "I should probably let Giovanni know about this."

"No!" I say, much too panicked. I quickly calm my voice before I speak again, because I can't tell Owen the truth, which is that my gut is telling me that

Giovanni probably has something to do with this. Or maybe he doesn't have anything to do with it, and everything I've found and seen is just a coincidence. But I can't really deny my spy-dey senses.

So, instead, I tell Owen what seems logical. "Don't bother him with this—Giovanni is a busy man, and he has plenty on his plate already. This will just make him worry while he's on another continent and can't even do anything about it. He has faith in you to take care of things here. Let him. Besides, it didn't look like the guy took anything. He wasn't even here long enough to look around."

He did leave something, though. That much, I'm sure of. I'm also sure that Owen didn't see the hint of a package the guy held.

Owen nods. "You're right. I should go and check the cameras and see if there's anything that the police might be able to go on."

I sigh. "He knew where the cameras were and avoided them."

Owen looks shocked. "Are you sure?"

"I'm sure."

Owen is so wide-eyed and nervous. I don't blame him. "I need to put up some more cameras to cover those areas where that guy just went."

"That's a really good idea. Who knows where the cameras are currently? Your crew? Subcontractors?" I don't ask about Giovanni because I don't want to freak

Owen out, and because I already know the answer to that one—he knows exactly where they are.

"I installed them up high so they aren't easily accessible, but they're not exactly hidden. Anyone who's been in here would know where they are if they were looking for them."

"Maybe the guy just snuck in out of curiosity," I say in an attempt to calm Owen's fears. We don't know anything yet, so no sense in getting him needlessly worried. This place is his baby. And not just because it's a beautiful building that he's already poured so much of his heart into, but also because this place was important to his beloved grandpa. Someone he idolized. I get the sense that he would do anything to honor the man.

We pack up the rest of our dinner remains, and then I ask, "Is there a restroom here, by chance?"

Owen smiles. "The one by the offices is one of the first things we got working."

We head downstairs, and he leads me to the restroom. As soon as I'm inside, I pull out my phone. Jace is still on his honeymoon. Miles just left for a mission. So I text my two remaining brothers at the CSA—Ledger and Emerson—and quickly type what happened, where the man went, and suggest that it might have been a smuggling-related dead drop, based on the man's behavior. Ledger responds first, says he's in Cipher Springs, that he'll retrieve what the man just left, and for me to keep Owen distracted.

When I exit the restroom, Owen is coming back from the front of the theater. "I just checked all of the doors, and everything is locked up, just as it was. I can't see how he got in. Most of the windows are too high. I checked the lower ones in the offices, and they're still locked."

"Who has keys?" I ask.

He pulls his from his pocket. "Only me."

"Maybe he picked a lock."

"They're supposed to be anti-theft. And why did he break in if he didn't do anything?"

He heads back into the auditorium, so I do, too, and we both go up the same steps the man did. When we get backstage, Owen heads left. When he gave me a tour of this place, he mentioned that he showed Giovanni a hidden alcove behind the set storage area, so I go there, and I immediately find the package. It's not too big—about the size of a standard envelope and about an inch-and-a-half thick.

I glance to make sure that Owen is still on the other side of the stage, where he can't see me. Then, I pull out my phone, take a picture of where it is, and quickly text it to Ledger so he won't have to search the whole theater.

Once we've checked everything and don't find a single thing out of place, we grab the bag with our picnic items, head out the front doors, and Owen locks up behind us. As we are walking back up the street to Owen's truck, in an effort to distract him from worrying, at least for now, I look up at the cloudless sky and say, "Isn't tonight beautiful?"

When Owen looks up, I spot Ledger in the shadows. I know he can see me, too, and knows he's clear to go in and retrieve the package.

"It's almost my birthday," I say, so he doesn't focus too much on what just happened. And also because I've been meaning to bring it up all night.

Owen stops walking and turns to me. "It is?"

I nod. "Each person in my family gets to pick some kind of competitive activity for everyone to do when it's their birthday. Well, we actually chose a long time ago, and then they all just kind of became traditions. My brothers all picked some kind of sport with a twist. I chose a talent show. So, every year, my brothers and parents—well, just my mom now—do some kind of performance.

"They don't even have to be real talents. In fact, it's better if they aren't. Anything goes. Like, one year, Jace did a dramatic dialogue of a disgruntled superhero stuck in traffic, and Blake performed a slow, overly emotional ballad about socks. Once, Emerson presented a slide deck roast of all of our worst fashion phases. And they can do it in pairs or alone. One year,

Miles and Ledger performed a synchronized interpretive dance.

"If the weather is good, we do it in my mom's backyard. After everyone performs, I choose a winner, and the winner gets to go home with the trophy and display it with pride until my next birthday. Do you maybe want to join me for it on Saturday?" I'm quick to add, "You don't have to do a talent or anything. You can help me judge."

"I absolutely want to join you."

I grin. Although I am a bit nervous about having him come to see my family in their more natural, less best-behavior-because-it's-a-wedding state. I love my family and don't want their uninhibited, larger-than-life, boisterous natures to ever change. I just hope we don't scare Owen away like we did with pretty much every other guy I ever brought home.

"Speaking of hanging out with families… Do you want to join me when I go to visit mine on Sunday? My sister will be in town for fall break."

"Of course," I say. And I smile the rest of the way back to his truck. I'm going to see where Owen came from.

CHAPTER 24
I'M JUST VISITING
OWEN

Blake hadn't been joking—I did get added to the Lancaster family group text. At least the one that Emerson set up to discuss Charlie's birthday. I have no idea how he got my phone number, since it doesn't sound like Charlie even knows about this particular group text. We mostly discussed what "talent" each brother was planning, along with any pairing up for performances.

Which was how I managed to get paired up in two separate performances. One with Miles, which makes sense, since we bonded over the whole intruder thing. And one with Blake, who still kind of scares me.

I know Charlie said I didn't have to, that I could just help her judge, but I want to. I'm grateful I'll be teaming up with a couple of her brothers because I really didn't want to perform solo in a family tradition

I know so little about. And I love that we've somehow managed to keep my participation in it a secret from Charlie.

On Saturday evening, Charlie's brothers carry an oversized reading chair out to a grassy area in the backyard that faces a wooden platform just below a big tree. They call it the Queen's Throne, and it's where Charlie will sit as she judges the competition. Then, her brothers, her mom, Zoe, Blake's daughter, Heidi, and I all sit on camp chairs surrounding the platform that we'll be using as a stage.

Once we are all seated and Charlie is ready to start judging, her brainy brother, Emerson, and her suave brother, Miles, take the stage and put on a wildly committed sock puppet story, complete with kitchen utensils as props and dramatic background music. The hero sock battles the villain sock with a spatula-saber, and nearly meets his end in the "washing machine of doom," which is played by a salad spinner.

He is rescued at the last minute in a surprise cameo by Charlie's mom, Evelyn, who swoops in from offstage with a leopard-print sock puppet in sunglasses. Declaring she "came back for one last cycle," her puppet saves the day with a spoon chop to the villain. The three of them bow as we all cheer.

Then, Blake and his three-year-old daughter, Heidi, take the stage, and Blake announces that Heidi is a world-famous namer of paintings. He shows a handful of well-known ones, and Heidi names them on the spot. She's hilarious for such a little kid.

I especially love it when Blake shows *The Scream* by Edvard Munch. Heidi takes one look at the swirling sky and haunted, panicked face and declares that it's named, "He's Got a Spider Under His Bed." I also love that when she sees the *Mona Lisa*, she calls it "She Sneaked Some Cookies." I think that will forever remain its name in my head.

Ledger and Zoe take the stage next. As Ledger lies flat on his back, I wonder if the two of them have talked any more about getting engaged since the wedding, and how it went if they did. Zoe announces that she'll be demonstrating "a test of balance, focus, and fragile carbs."

Then she proceeds to see how many Ritz crackers she can stack on Ledger's face while we all count out loud, with very enthusiastic voices, as she places each one. Using multiple piles on his forehead and cheeks, she made a fairly architecturally sound creation as Ledger just lies there, radiating a kind of chaotic confidence.

Eventually, the stacks on his cheeks start to lean inward enough that they rest against his nose, and he sneezes, collapsing the entire structure but producing a lot of hooting and cheering from us.

Then it's my turn. I lean over and give Charlie a kiss on the temple, then stand. She looks at me, confused but intrigued. I don't say a word—I just go to the bag I had Miles stash with the rest of the props and hand him a tape measure and a hammer while I take the level. Then we walk onto the stage with slow, exaggerated purpose, and the crowd immediately hoots. Charlie claps a hand over her grinning mouth, like she's bracing for impact.

Miles pulls the tape measure out several feet and then drapes it across his chest like a royal sash. I hold the level upright in front of me like a broadsword forged by the gods of Home Depot.

Miles bows to the audience and announces in a regal tone, "We welcome thee… to Build-a-Bard."

Then, the two of us improvise a scene in faux-Elizabethan English, very loosely quoting Shakespeare, as we discuss the errors Miles made in building the frame of a wall and how it isn't going to pass inspection.

We end with Miles gasping and looking scandalized before dropping to one knee. "Forgive me, for 'twas the fault of thine cursed manual—written without language, in only hexed diagrams."

"Dost thou mean… the Swedish scrolls?"

"Aye," Miles says. "IKEA hath claimed many brave men before it claimeth me."

We both bow deeply. When we do, Miles accidentally whacks his knee with the hammer, yelps, and mutters, "Ow. The inspection hath failed."

Everyone cheers and applauds. Charlie's laugh carries above everything else, which is really the only stamp of approval I was hoping for. I'm smiling as I take the seat next to her again. Especially because she smiles at me like she thinks I'm even better than her dreams, which I'll take any day of the week.

Charlie's mom, Evelyn, and Ledger's girlfriend, Zoe, carry a card table to the stage. On it is an oddly-shaped box, a roll of wrapping paper, scissors, some ribbon, and a tape dispenser. They make a show of blindfolding Zoe, and then Zoe puts on some work gloves—the type we use at my site.

In a calm, deadly serious voice, Evelyn narrates what Zoe's doing as she attempts to gift-wrap the box, but she tells it like Zoe is trying to dismantle a bomb. She says things like "She's going for the tape… no, she's stuck to the tape, and the timer is relentlessly ticking down." And, "If she can't secure the ribbon perimeter in the next ten seconds, the entire package will detonate into 'slightly crumpled but lovingly attempted' territory."

We're all laughing at the seriousness of Evelyn's voice juxtaposed with the comedic struggles Zoe is having with the gift. Then, as Zoe finishes and holds up the package triumphantly, sporting pieces of mangled tape stuck in random places and a lopsided bow, Evelyn says, "She's done it. The payload is secure. Ribbon integrity: questionable. Corners: classified. Tape application: eh… We'll call it 'legally inadvisable.' But the operation is a success."

When Zoe pulls off her blindfold, Evelyn says with pride, "I trained her myself."

What really gets everyone laughing until they can't breathe, though, is when athletic Ledger and brainy Emerson take the stage, each holding a microphone connected to a karaoke speaker that, by its kiddie look, was purchased when they were much younger.

Ledger starts beatboxing with an impressive level of commitment, while Emerson raps about statistical modeling, of all things. I'm pretty sure that none of us, other than Emerson, even understands much of what he's rapping, but it makes it all the funnier.

While Ledger is holding the mic close, making "Puh-tss-kah, puh-tss-kah—cha-cha-cha- tss—YUH!" sounds, Emerson is saying things like, "I'm talkin' linear regression, straight line obsession. Minimizing errors like it's therapy session. Got a bell curve tighter than Miles's tux, My R-squared's clean—don't need no luck."

It goes on for several verses before they both finish with a spin, hold their mics out straight, and then simultaneously drop them. Emerson, as if he didn't just barely stun us all, calmly fixes the shirt collar of his polo, gives a slight nod, then walks off the stage without any of the swagger he was just showing.

Charlie is wiping tears from her eyes from laughing so much.

I surprise Charlie, once again, when I stand and take the stage so that Blake and I can perform "A Duet in Three Cavities." It's a mock dramatic reading where we combine Blake's profession of dentistry with mine of building renovation in the most ridiculous way possible.

We have a big tooth we've made out of the bottom two-thirds of a gallon milk jug turned upside down, with craft stick scaffolding around it. We hadn't thought ahead about what to set it on beforehand to be the right height, so we grabbed a couple of empty Amazon boxes at the last minute and stood them on top of each other to make a small table barely wide enough for the tooth and scaffolding.

I'm holding a blueprint like I'm reading a newspaper, and Blake has a dental chart. We use a paintbrush instead of a toothbrush and a measuring tape as dental floss. We're both wearing safety goggles from our own places of work as we talk about a cavity in a tooth like it's a crack in an old building.

We get to a part where I say, "A tiny fissure, barely visible. But oh, how it spread," and I step forward to gesture with my arm to show how it spread. But my knee accidentally hits the bottom box and sends both boxes, the "tooth," and the scaffolding crashing to the stage.

"And so," Blake improvises without missing a beat, "the root canal of betrayal began."

I'm laughing inside, but I manage to keep a serious face as I pull my blueprints over the dead tooth to cover it, and say in a mournful voice, "It never had a fighting chance." I guess this skit didn't, either.

Blake crouches down beside the tooth, too, as if he's paying his respects, and says, "Floss in peace."

Everyone cheers, and I chuckle all the way back to my seat. Charlie gives me a smile that is so wide and beautiful that I just want to kiss it.

Ledger carries the card table to the stage, and Evelyn places a laptop on it. "Jace and Mackenzie were sad they couldn't be here with you to celebrate, Charlie. But they didn't want to miss out on your birthday, so they sent in their entry." She presses play on a video.

It starts out with both of them, on a beach, saying, "Jace and Mackenzie present, *How to Stay Undercover While on a Honeymoon!*" Dramatic music plays during clips of things they've filmed while on their honeymoon in the most amazing setting I've ever seen. Charlie told me that Mackenzie was a huge fan of spy movies, and I love that they used that theme in their video.

There are parts of their mini movie where they are very unsubtly sneaking places, trying on ridiculous costumes to avoid being noticed, attempting to blend into lounge chairs, and generally being comedically bad spies. Mackenzie says things like, "Day four. Location: undisclosed. Temperature: offensively perfect. Mission: remain covert… and hydrated."

And Jace says things like, "Most agents rely on earpieces. Amateurs. We use… the coconut comms system," and "Suspect acquired. Repeat: subject is pacing. Wings flared. Possibly hostile."

The best part is that they're filming everything with other vacationers and locals in the background, very much noticing them, with expressions ranging from curious to amused to downright confused. It doesn't seem to faze Jace or Mackenzie.

At the end of the video, Jace says, "In conclusion: stay alert."

"Stay unpredictable," Mackenzie adds.

"And never underestimate a seagull with a vendetta."

Then, together, they both say, "And happy birthday, Charlie!"

Mackenzie adds, "Remember: trust no one… unless they bring snacks."

Everyone cheers just as raucously as we did for the other entries, even though Jace and Mackenzie aren't even present to hear it.

The funny thing is that several of the performances tonight have had a sort of superhero vibe to them. Really inept ones, for sure. But still, if someone were to tell me that this family was secretly superheroes who were actually good at it, I would buy it.

"Are you ready to choose the winner?" Evelyn asks as Miles, who was apparently the one to win the trophy last year, brings it forward and presents it to Charlie.

"I am." She stands and takes the stage, facing us. "We had some truly memorable performances tonight—by which I mean I've seen things I'll never be able to unsee, and I wouldn't trade a single one of them. Thank you all for putting your whole hearts"—she motions at Ledger, "and in some cases, your whole faces—into making my birthday so hilarious and unforgettable. This was the kind of night that makes turning a year older totally worth it."

She holds up the trophy, which is a bobble-head doll that looks an awful lot like her and is mounted on a trophy base. "And the trophy goes to… Emerson for that rap! I did not know you had it in you, but I will forever respect the way you rhymed 'variance' with 'arrogance' and made it work."

We all give the biggest cheer of the night as Emerson comes to the stage and accepts the trophy, "Thank you," he says, as our applause dies down. "I dedicate this win to my calculator and to Ledger, who provided both percussive support and emotional instability in equal measure."

"You're welcome for the chaos!" Ledger calls out.

Then there's cake, and candle-blowing, and an avalanche of birthday wishes. Honestly, I don't think I've ever laughed so much in one night.

But the best part—the part I know I'll remember—is watching Charlie. The way she lights up with every joke, every ridiculous skit, and every off-key birthday song. She's radiant. She's home. And I want that kind of joy for her every single day. I've had fun too—more than fun, honestly. Being here with her family feels surprisingly… right. And I don't want it to be a one-time thing. I want more nights like this.

As things start to wind down for the evening, a weight settles in my chest. I can't stop thinking about Charlie and her family. She is deeply rooted here—this town, this family, this life. And I'm not. My work pulls me from place to place. And before I know it, I'll be in Philadelphia.

Suddenly, the night feels a little too good, a little too borrowed. What have I been thinking, letting myself believe this is something I could keep?

When it's just the two of us out on the deck of her mom's house, taking in the warm night air and the stars, I say, "Thank you for asking me to join you. I can honestly say I've never experienced anything quite like this."

She smiles. "I'm glad you came. And I'm so impressed that you performed. Twice! That was so sweet. And so unexpected."

"I was going for 'Never let them guess your next move.'"

"Well played," she says, and scoots in closer to me, wrapping her arms around my neck. I put my arms around her waist and hold her close, then whisper, "Happy birthday, Charlie," before I kiss her. Everything about tonight has been the kind of thing that dreams are made of, and so is this. Kissing Charlie always feels so perfect, so right. Especially when she plays with the hair at the base of my neck with her fingertips.

After a long moment, I say, "As much as I'd like to stand here and kiss you all night, I've got a present for you."

"A present?"

I nod and let go of her long enough to go to the picnic table and grab the gift bag I had set there earlier. Charlie takes a seat on one of the deck chairs with the bag in her lap, and I sit on the one next to her as she removes the tissue paper and then pulls out the memory box I made for her.

Her eyes fly to mine, wonder all over her face. "Did you make this?"

I nod. "All of the wood is reclaimed from different places in The Shadowridge."

It's all sanded smooth, but it still bears a lot of the character of its past—faint traces of old nail holes, a soft knot in the corner, a subtle curve in one of the planks that makes it look like it's always been smiling. It's roughly the dimensions of a paperback book, but it's nearly three inches deep.

She lifts the lid, which opens silently. I'm proud of that. She sees the sticky note I've left inside that reads, *Happy birthday to the only person I'd do three fire drills and a Back Pictionary rematch with.* Since Abraham told me that Charlie has kept all of my sticky notes, I'm hoping that the sticky note in this will make her think to keep the rest of them in this box, too.

"It's meant to hold memories. Keepsakes. I hope it'll hold a few more of mine." I clear my throat. "I chose this piece of wood for the inside because see how the grain curves upward like it has a sense of motion? I felt like it shows it's carrying your history forward."

Charlie's eyes meet mine, and I see that they are watery. She licks her lips and swallows, like she's trying to hold back emotions. Then, with a voice that comes out a little unsteady, she says, "Thank you. This is the sweetest gift I've ever gotten." She holds it tightly to her, like she wants to hold onto it forever.

And every part of me wants her to do the same with me.

CHAPTER 25
QUIET YARDS, LOUD THOUGHTS
CHARLIE

t takes about an hour to drive west from Cipher Springs to Bridleford, where Owen grew up. I've never been to his town before. It has homes with well-cared-for yards, lots of pedestrians, and fun buildings that look like they've been around for generations.

Owen slows his truck as we turn onto a quiet street lined with tall trees. His family's home sits near the end of the street, with ivy that climbs halfway up the stone chimney. A deep porch stretches across the front of the house and around one side, and has a set of Adirondack chairs on it, facing the hills. There are flowers along the walk and in the window boxes, and the whole place feels like warmth and a deep, relaxing breath.

The yard is pretty big, too, and I can see the woodworking shop where his dad works peeking from the backyard. As we park, get out of the truck, and start walking up to the door, I picture Owen playing in this yard as a kid and try to imagine what he was like growing up. When we get to the wraparound porch, I see a swing gently moving in the breeze that some shrubs had hidden from my view initially, and I wonder how much he sat on that swing.

We go inside, past an outdated but cozy living room, to the kitchen, where Owen's face immediately softens upon seeing his mom, and he hugs her. It's so cute. His dad comes in from the backyard just then, and although he seems like a stoic man, there's a quiet pride in his eyes that's unmistakable when he looks at Owen.

Owen introduces me to his parents, Jeannie and Dean, and they welcome me to their home and say they're glad I came. Jeannie has a bob of brown hair and expressive eyes. She's petite and is wearing a bright blue cardigan, jeans, and comfortable-looking flats. Owen's dad has his same jaw and hair, but his is turning silver, especially at the temples. It's a little tousled, like he was thinking through a problem right before we came. He's wearing jeans, boots, and a flannel shirt. They both have kind faces. Like they fit this place.

Then his sister, Tessa, bounds down the stairs, which is louder with every other step because of the boot she's wearing on her injured side, and gives Owen an enthusiastic hug. She's got the same dark brown hair as Owen's, but hers is long and in soft curls. She's adorable and looks like she's fun.

"Charlie, this is Tessa. Tessa, I'd like to introduce you to Charlie."

Owen looks thrilled to be introducing us, but Tessa is looking less thrilled to meet me. Her eyes quickly take me in—not in an obvious way. More in an "I'm trying to form an opinion of you, but the jury is still out on whether I like you yet" way.

We all stand around, chatting, until Owen's mom hands us all bowls of side dishes to take to the table outside. Owen's dad puts the burgers from the grill onto a plate and brings them to the table, too. They all seem nice and welcoming (well, maybe not so much Tessa for the "welcoming" part), so I'm not quite sure why, but I feel out of place here.

Once we all start eating, Jeannie turns to me right as I take a big bite of a burger. "So, Owen tells us that you work with computers."

I try to chew quickly and not do something like choke as I'm swallowing, just because all eyes are on me. Okay, why did I have to go and think about choking when I'm already not loving all the attention focused on me?

I swallow—without choking—and clear my throat. "Yep. I'm an IT systems coordinator." Both of his parents look at me like they don't know what I'm talking about, so I add, "I basically make sure all the tech at my work talks to each other the right way and stays safe from hackers. If anything goes wrong, I'm the one who figures out how to fix it."

Jeannie's face lights up. "Oh! I get what you do. See, I'm the lead secretary at the elementary school here in town. I was in the middle of juggling three parents in the office, a first grader with a nosebleed, and a kindergartener sobbing because he swallowed a penny. Of course, that's when the computers decided to go on the fritz mid-attendance. You are like the person I called to get it fixed, so that everything wouldn't implode. Because that's what happens when the system is down. I had no idea what the guy on the phone was telling me to do, but it fixed the system!"

"Exactly!" I say. Well, not exactly at all, but close enough.

"Do you enjoy being a miracle worker? Because that's what I called the guy who walked me through fixing the problem."

I smile and blush a bit, and cross my fingers that the spotlight can now get taken off me.

Especially because even though they're being so nice, I just can't shake the feeling that I'm just visiting a world I don't fully belong to. Maybe because in my family, there is always so much going on that every-one's attention isn't on one person so much. At least, not unless they're looking for it, which is often the case with several of my brothers. Here, all the attention is on me.

Which is probably why the conversation isn't flowing as easily as I'm sure it would be if I wasn't here. To help with that and to get the focus off me, I say to Dean, "Owen tells me you have created some incredible things from wood. What's your favorite thing you've ever made?"

He doesn't have to think long before saying, "I did all the carpentry work in the historic courthouse that was restored down on Main Street."

Owen turns to me. "That's the one that made me want to be an architectural restoration specialist."

"After we finished the restoration," his dad continues, "I made a to-scale replica of it, dollhouse-sized, and gave it to Tessa for her birthday when she turned four."

"I loved that thing so much!" Tessa says. "I still have it. I made all the furniture that's inside it. Which you could pretty much tell just by looking at it, because I was probably eight when I made all the pieces."

"He spent weeks building it," Jeannie says. "It was museum-worthy."

Dean really seems to have come alive as we all talk about it, even though he is still using fewer words than most.

It hits me how calm and quiet everything is. I'm not at all worried about a football being tossed over my head at any moment. The conversation has even changed to talking about a bird feeder and what kinds of birds they've seen.

This family is so different from mine. They are all lovely. And so is this life they've built. Is this the kind of life that Owen wants? Because I think it might just take someone calmer and steadier than me. Someone who doesn't live the less predictable life of an intelligence officer at a secret government agency.

As we are all finishing up the meal, the conversation turns to Tessa, and Jeannie says, "We're so proud of our Tessa! She's working toward her Bachelor's in Environmental Design with a focus on Architecture. It's similar to what Owen does, except he works on the building itself, and her field is more of the interior angle. Oh, lands! You should hear when the three of them get talking shop!"

I glance at Tessa, but try to not keep looking at her, because she seems very uncomfortable. Maybe she doesn't like all the attention on her, either. But I aced both Covert Behavioral Intelligence and Applied Psychological Observation, and my gut is telling me that it's because she doesn't like the subject being on her schooling.

"How is school going?" Owen asks her.

Tessa gives a nervous, halting laugh. "Well, let's

just say that my *Building Systems and Codes* class is trying to kill me. Even in my sleep."

Owen chuckles, but his is more genuine. "I took a class like that for my degree, too. I remember feeling the same way. It's a lot."

"Right?" Tessa says, seeming glad to have someone in her corner. "In my head, I've renamed the class to *Managing Legal Risk in Neutral Tones*."

Owen nods. "That fits. And hey, if you ever want help with it, I'm here for you."

"Thanks!" she says, grinning. Then she tosses Owen a look that clearly says, *Change the subject.*

My gut was right.

He clears his throat and says, "After we get cleaned up here, I want to go show Charlie around town. Tessa, do you want to join us?"

She stands and grabs a bowl of macaroni salad to take back inside. "I'd love to."

———

In Owen's tour of his hometown, he takes me to their high school, the adjacent football field where he spent so much time as a teen, and the elementary school both Owen and Tessa went to, which is where their mom works. They also take me to the courthouse that was restored and turned into a reception hall when Owen was ten. It's closed today, but it's gorgeous. I can see why it inspired him.

Since the courthouse is on Main Street, we take a stroll down the cutest section of downtown. This place has adorable shops, and it even has baskets of little purple flowers hanging from every lamppost at the edge of the sidewalk.

Tessa is very, *very* slowly warming up to me. And by "warm," I mean maybe room temperature instead of an outside-in-the-dead-of-winter temperature. She's mostly been standing on the opposite side of Owen and directing what she says to him.

But after stopping to look in some shop windows, Tessa and I end up walking side by side, so I try to connect with her. I don't actually know enough about her to talk to her about more than school, her child-hood dollhouse, or the injury that has her foot in a boot. I decide to stick with school.

"So… are you hating all the classes related to your major, or just your *Building Systems and Codes* one?"

She looks over at me, alarmed. "I never said I hated it."

Okay, so that failed. I stay quiet.

After a moment, she says in a quieter voice, "But you're right. I do."

I look over at her, hoping she'll continue.

She does. "It's just that instead of letting you dream or imagine, it's constantly telling you what you can't do. I don't feel creative in the class at all. I feel like a box-checker." She pauses a moment, then asks, "How did you know I hated it?"

"I read people well." Which is true. I did even before the CSA trained me. "Plus, while we were eating, you had your phone on the table, and a grading notification came up for that class. You turned your phone over. Which is natural—I know I never wanted to think of school when I wasn't there. But I saw the expression on your face, and it was more than that. I could tell the class causes you a lot of stress. Does it make you worry you're in the wrong major?"

Tessa gives a little nervous laugh and glances at me from the corner of her eye as we walk. "You got all that from me turning my phone over? That's... freakish."

"Hey," Owen says. "Watch it."

"I'm just saying, do you ever wonder if your girl-friend has mind-reading superpowers?"

Owen chuckles. "I have, actually. But I've always been amazed and impressed by it."

Tessa looks at me. "Also, that's kind of a leap to go from not wanting to think about my class to being in the wrong major."

I grimace. Inwardly and outwardly. "I'm sorry."

"Don't be. Because you are right." Tessa swallows and glances past me to Owen. "I really *want* to want my major. But I keep questioning whether I'm cut out for it. Even though I'm passionate about design. But I don't know. I want the freedom to create atmospheres and moods—not just spaces that meet code."

Owen says, "You've never liked being boxed in, not even when you were a toddler. So, I can see how you'd feel that way. Is there a different major you've been considering?"

Tessa lights up when she says, "Design, Technology & Management. They have a concentration in Theater Design & Technology that sounds so cool! I'd still be using spatial creativity, but for story-telling and visual impact. They've got classes on things like stage layout, theming, and even art direction." Then her face falls, and she says, "But I don't know."

She stays quiet for long enough that I know she's not going to offer more on her own, so I give her a nudge. "You're unsure because you don't want to disappoint your dad? And Owen?"

"Again, freakish." She looks at me for a long time before she says, "Exactly."

"I've got five older brothers. Four went into fields related to business solutions. But not my brother, Blake—he's a dentist. Do you want to know what has made me super proud of each of them? When they've found the career that most perfectly suits them. The one that really allows them to shine."

Tessa stops walking and turns to Owen. "What do you think?"

"I want to see you shine in a career that perfectly suits you. I'm betting Mom and Dad do, too."

"Really?"

Owen nods.

"You wouldn't be disappointed?"

"Nope. I'd be proud of you for figuring out what you most wanted."

I smile at Owen, and he gives me a little smile back.

Tessa looks forward again, smiling like a woman whose whole world just opened up to her. She links her arm in mine, and we start walking again. Then she says to me, "You're really easy to talk to, you know?"

"Freakishly easy?" I ask. I do feel like I kind of need to walk on eggshells around this girl, but the humor just slips out. I glance at Tessa and only see a smile. Success! I look over at Owen and grin. He reaches out and holds my hand. Okay, I am feeling a lot better about things here now.

I get in about five steps of actually feeling good when I step in someone's discarded gum right as Tessa shouts, "Audrey!" And then she unhooks her arm from mine and runs forward awkwardly with her one foot in a walking boot toward a woman who's standing on the street, looking surprised to see her.

I don't have anything resembling a napkin to use

to get the gum off my shoe, and I don't just want to scrape it on the sidewalk for someone else to step in. I don't have a lot of choices here, so I decide to scrape it off on the asphalt of the road. Not a great option, either, but it's the lesser of two evils.

As I veer right to the road, walking awkwardly to keep my shoe from putting the gum right back onto the sidewalk, I nod to the woman with Tessa and ask Owen, "Who's that?"

Owen sighs. "That's my ex, Audrey."

"Oh." As I'm stepping off the sidewalk and trying to take in Owen's ex, I bonk my head on the underside of one of the hanging flower baskets. "Ow," I say, mid-step, followed closely by a much more enthusiastic "Ow!" because not only did I bonk my head, but my hair got caught in the basket and really got yanked. And now I'm tethered by the hair to a hanging basket.

Owen rushes over to help. Since I can't look up without it pulling on my hair too much, while he's working on untangling this mess I got myself into, I check out the woman who, thankfully, has all of her focus on Tessa.

She is beautiful. Her chestnut hair is pulled back into an elegant low bun, and she's dressed in dark wash jeans, heels, and a flowy blouse that make her look like she belongs on a magazine cover. She also has a look about her that says she never forgets to register her car or comes down the stairs sporting only a towel and a head full of shampoo, not knowing her new neighbor can see her. I bet she's never even burned cookies.

"Okay, I think I got it," Owen says.

I slowly and gingerly step away from the basket, the few remaining strands pulling their way free. Until the last couple get stuck and are yanked from my scalp. I rub my head as I look back up at the hanging basket, feeling betrayed by it. Then, I start scraping my shoe on the asphalt, trying to get all the stickiness off so I won't leave a trail behind me.

Then I take the most fortifying breath I can, muster what dignity I have left, put my hand in Owen's, and head toward Tessa and Audrey. As we get closer, I start hearing part of their conversation. Tessa is saying, "My flight's not until tomorrow morning. You should come over! There's tons of food leftover from lunch. Besides, how long has it been since you've seen my parents?"

"They had me over just a couple of weeks ago. But I'd love to come and see you before you head back!" Then she sees that we've caught up to them, and she says, "Hello, Owen. It's great to see you."

I glance at Tessa to see that she's looking at my hair with her brow furrowed. My hands fly to the top of my head, and I feel the tangled mess that is supporting the part that I'm sure is practically sticking straight up. The movement catches Owen's attention, and he tries to help, which doesn't make things any less embarrassing.

By way of explanation, I motion back to the betraying basket. "The hanging flowers decided to attack. Hi, I'm Charlie. It's nice to meet you."

Cool. Very cool. Nothing like minor public humiliation to reinforce that I'm the quirky chaos goblin and Audrey is grace in heels. Plus, Tessa loves her. Owen's parents love her enough to have her over when neither of their kids is in town, so she obviously fits in with his family well. She seems perfect for Owen, and right now, I feel anything but.

It's fine. I'll just walk directly into the nearest pothole and let the shame swallow me whole.

CHAPTER 26
SMILE AND SECURE THE EXIT

OWEN

'm sitting on a padded folding chair in my makeshift office in one of the balcony boxes, my laptop sitting on a card table, as I scour the video feed from over the weekend. I have the new cameras installed, which means more cameras to check. As I scrub through them, I don't see anything out of place, which gives me such relief. Weirdly enough, I'm getting in even more of a funk as I sit here than I've been the rest of the day, which is saying something.

The weekend was great, though, and the hour-long drive to my parents was totally worth it. Charlie was amazing with Tessa. She isn't the easiest person to connect with, yet Charlie did, *and* she helped her in a way I couldn't have, since I hadn't even sensed there was a problem. I swear, Charlie is just magic when it comes to seeing into a person's heart.

My parents love Charlie, too. My mom has texted me a good five times since we left their house yesterday to tell me so. Charlie seems to be pulling back, though. I felt it to some degree almost the whole time we were in Bridleford.

And for some reason, it feels like The Shadowridge is pulling back, too. I worry that someone is going to break in again, even though I've taken ample precautions. I love this place and don't want to lose it. I just need it long enough to get it fully restored and looking the way my grandpa hoped it would look again someday, back when he first showed it to me more than fifteen years ago.

I keep thinking that maybe if I hold onto it tightly enough, including obsessively checking the security camera footage, it'll know how much I care, and I'll get to keep it. I know that doesn't make rational sense, but it's what I've got. Even though I know that life is under no obligation to be fair.

My crew is all leaving for the day, so I'm surprised when I hear a knock on my doorframe and turn around to see Luis.

"Hey, boss. Can I come in?"

"Of course." I motion to the extra folding chair, and he takes a seat.

"I just wanted to check in and see how you're doing. You've seemed off today."

Normally, in a situation like this, I would paste on

a smile and say that I'm doing great. But for whatever reason, I say what I'm thinking. "I don't know. I just feel like everything is on the verge of falling apart."

"With Charlie?" he asks, concern in his voice.

I know there was some awkwardness when we ran into Audrey, just like there is any time anyone runs into an ex. I don't know how much that is playing into Charlie pulling back. I'd like to think it isn't at all—I mean, there's a reason Audrey and I broke up. When I brought it up on the drive back to Cipher Springs, Charlie said everything was good. And really, there is nothing concrete with any of my worries. It's just a feeling.

I answer Luis by saying, "With everything. No one is going to stick around when things get tough."

"And you anticipate things getting tough?"

"Seems to be the way things go."

There haven't been any signs—at least not signs that Luis would've seen—about things not going well for The Shadowridge. Really, there's nothing concrete with that, either. Not besides a single super-quick break-in where nothing was stolen and nothing was damaged. They're just hunches. But that leaves Luis to assume that I must be talking only about Charlie, because he leans back in his chair and asks, "Have you ever dated someone while on a job?"

I shake my head. "Charlie's the first in a while. I'm kind of breaking my own rule."

"That because of all the moving around?"

"Yeah. New place, new project, new start. Feels easier to keep it simple."

He nods like he gets it. "So…what happened with the last ones? Before Charlie."

I raise an eyebrow. "What is this, therapy hour?"

He shrugs. "Hey, you're the one who said you feel like everything's about to fall apart. I'm just trying to figure out what 'everything' means."

Fair. I blow out a breath. "Okay, well. With Audrey—who Charlie and I ran into yesterday—things were always kind of surface-level. Never got deep. Celeste… I think she mostly liked that I could fix things. It was less love, more free handyman."

Luis snorts. "Oof."

"Right? Then Lily. I was swamped with work and school, and started pulling back without meaning to. I figured she'd fight for us or at least ask what was going on. She didn't. We just… faded out.

"And then there was Alina. We liked the same stuff, but we were heading in different directions, and neither of us wanted to course correct."

Luis is quiet for a beat, then says, "So basically… either they weren't really in it long-term, or you weren't, which reinforced your belief that no one sticks around."

I blink. "Wow. Thanks, Dr. Phil."

He holds up a hand. "I'm just saying, now you're

with someone who might actually stay, and your brain's already halfway packed for the breakup."

That hits a little too close to home. "You think I'm pushing Charlie away?" Am I? Is that why she's pulling away? Or maybe she's in the same place and I'm the one pulling away?

Luis shrugs. "I don't know. But you should probably ask yourself that before she starts believing it too."

I nod because I should. But not right here, and not right now. Whining to a friend about my fears is not the way I operate. I channel my normal self and paste on a smile. Not only does it generally keep me from conversations like this, but it usually makes me feel better, too.

I shut my laptop and stand. "Do you know what? Everything is going to be fine." I clap Luis on the shoulder as he stands. "Everything works out in the end, so if it hasn't worked out yet, it isn't the end, right?"

Luis is looking at me like he doesn't really trust that I am fine, but I keep my smile in place. "Come on. Let's go home. You've got a great wife and daughter waiting for you." Then we both head down the stairs, and I make sure the building is locked up tightly before I leave.

CHAPTER 27

PROCRASTINATION: IT'S NOT JUST FOR FRIDGE LEFTOVERS

CHARLIE

I t's Roommate Night, so as soon as Reese and I get home from work, we change. Me, into knit shorts and a t-shirt, and Reese into yoga pants and an oversized short-sleeved sweatshirt with the neckband cut out. Her pants are plum color and her sweatshirt is a lavender, yellow, and cyan plaid, which looks cute together, but they totally clash with the leopard-print glasses frames she's still wearing.

And no, Roommate Night doesn't mean watching romcoms while eating grocery store sushi and cookie dough by the spoonful. It means cleaning out the fridge that we ignored when we didn't have a kitchen sink, and then going grocery shopping for food that is less... fuzzy. Reese takes the lid off something that's been marinating in our fridge, and then shows it to me. "Any idea what this was?"

"I'm pretty sure it used to be some kind of vegetable. Now it's a threat."

Reese dumps it into the garbage we've got right between us. "This is what happens when we pretend leftovers are 'future meals' instead of fridge clutter with commitment issues."

I pull out a box of takeout leftovers that I know are weeks old and toss them into the garbage without even looking at them. Then I grab a container of something, pop the lid just enough to release a horrendous smell, then immediately close it again before even seeing what it used to be. "What do you think? Should I just throw the whole container away?"

"It's the only merciful option."

As Reese is checking the expiration date on a bottle of ranch dressing, I ask, "Have you ever been dating a guy, then met his ex-girlfriend—who seems absolutely perfect for him—and it makes you feel so much less sure that you are?"

She tosses the bottle. "Nope."

"No? Really?"

"Yep, because the key word in your sentence was 'seems.' She *seems* absolutely perfect for him. But a) first impressions can be wrong, b) some people are very good at presenting themselves in a way that isn't true to who they really are, and c) you can't get the full story by just briefly meeting someone. I always tell myself that they broke up, right? That means that no matter how perfect they *seemed* to be for each other, they weren't. Simple as that."

"True," I say as I pull out a Ziploc bag containing half a red onion that looks like it was put in a food dehydrator. "But there were probably areas where the ex was really strong, and he loved those parts. And maybe those parts are where you're weak."

Reese tosses a jar of vinaigrette. "Well, yeah, there will always be that. I just tell myself that the best parts of me will so blindingly outshine those that he won't even care."

"I wish I had your built-in self-assurance."

"Yeah, it's helpful. Except when I'm very vocally confident about something… and then find out I am wrong." Reese shrugs. "It's less helpful then." She pulls out a plastic container, pops the lid, and sucks in a quick breath. "I think it just hissed at me." She takes the lid off completely and then holds it out for me to see. "What do you think this was?"

It doesn't even look like it was ever food. "I'm going with a science experiment that failed and then mutated."

Reese dumps out the contents. I'm looking for the expiration date on a tub of sour cream, but I'm not making any headway. Probably because my mind is on other things. "I haven't told Owen that I was kidnapped as a kid."

"Girl," Reese says as she pulls out a bag of decomposing broccoli, "you and I have been friends for what? A year and a half? And you didn't tell me for most of that."

"Yeah, I'm sorry. It just happened so long ago! I was three, so it's been twenty-two years. And, I mean, it's not like I told you about the time when I was six, fell off my bike, and broke my arm."

Reese gives me a look. "That's not the same thing, and you know it."

I sigh. "Yeah. And I feel really bad that I haven't told him. I know I should. He's opened up to me so much, and I'm not reciprocating. But it's also hard because the kidnapping shouldn't still affect me. I've lived—" I quickly do the math—"eighty-eight percent of my life after it happened. But I'm starting to realize that maybe it does affect me more than I've been willing to admit."

I give up on finding the date, pop the lid, and give it a sniff. It's probably still good, so I put it back into the fridge. "Plus, I don't want to just dump my problems on him, you know?"

"I don't think he'd see it as dumping your problems. He seems like the kind of guy who'd love to know so he can support you."

I nod.

She pulls out a jar of salsa, tips it back and forth, and then tosses it into the garbage. "I get it, though.

You know how I had Hodgkin lymphoma when I was fifteen?"

"Yeah."

"The part I haven't told you is that during treatment, I had to have high-dose chemo and pelvic radiation. It saved my life, but it cost me my fertility."

"Oh, Reese," I say, my stomach just dropping for her. "I am so sorry."

She brushes away my comment with her hand. "That's not what this conversation is about. The point is that I get why it's hard for you to tell him. I don't like to talk about my past trauma, either, and I am pretty much never the one to bring it up. I like to just go on with life, acting as if it didn't happen, until I come upon a situation where I can't, then I act like it doesn't really affect me.

"But I know it did—*does*—affect me. And I understand that ignoring that fact doesn't make it stop affecting me. But sometimes it's just easier to pretend it never happened, you know? It makes it less heavy."

I nod. I really do know. "I think I've been pretending it never happened for too long."

"So, you're going to tell him?"

I nod as I dump out a container of mystery stew. "Yep. I'm going to do it."

"Good timing," Reese says as she stands. "Because I think we're done here."

"I'm not going to go tell him right now!"

"I'll take this bag of stinky, gross food remains out to the dumpster if you do."

"No. I'm not going to go knock on his door and when he answers, say, 'Oh, hi, Owen. I just wanted to pop by and tell you about that time when I was three and got kidnapped.'

"Plus, we already agreed that tonight, I was going to clean out the fridge and go grocery shopping with you, and he was going to go through some structural assessments. I don't know exactly what those are, but they sound like they take focus, so I'm not going to interrupt. Besides, I'll see him tomorrow."

"Swear to me that you'll tell him then. No backing out."

I take a deep breath. "Okay, I swear I will if you still take out the garbage."

CHAPTER 28
SPY MOM, FAUX DAD, REAL CRISIS
CHARLIE

As I'm walking from my car in the underground parking garage to the elevator, I see that the Clandestine Service Agency's director (a.k.a. my mom) is already there, standing at the retinal scanner before she breathes into the DNA scanner. The light turns green, the doors open, and she steps in and holds them for me as I jog the last bit and get in, too. As the doors are closing, I say, "Oh, monkey bolts! I also forgot my water bottle!"

My mom's finger hovers over the button to take us up. "In your car?"

I sigh. "No. At home. We can go up."

As the elevator is taking us to the main floor, my mom looks over at me. "You seem a little distressed this morning. Is everything okay?"

I rub my fingers over my forehead. It's barely eight a.m., and already my day is bad. "Yeah."

"Is it work or home stuff?"

"Home."

"Do you need me to be your mom for a minute?"

I look over at the polished director. She's wearing a navy pantsuit with a white shirt, looking as professional as can be. "Yeah," I say. "I really don't want to share this with my boss."

Her demeanor softens as the elevator comes to a stop. "Let's grab a conference room."

When we step into the room, she takes off her lanyard—a sure sign that she's switched from director mode to mom mode, and then she darkens the floor-to-ceiling glass so that no one from the floor can see inside. We both take a seat.

"I got a ticket on the way to work."

My mom cocks her head. "You don't speed."

"It was for having an expired car registration. And I left my water bottle at home. And I'm not even wearing clean underwear because we were doing other things last night, and I forgot to do laundry. We won't even mention how I didn't have enough time to make my lunch, or that I put my phone in the fridge and a yogurt in my purse. Oh, and I stabbed myself in the eye with my mascara wand.

"Sometimes I feel like I can mostly stay on top of things, but that's when there's not much going on. The rest of the time, I feel like I'm...chaotic. I'm on fire at work, but I'm flooding at home." I meet her eyes. "Other people don't let basic things fall through the cracks. Why can I not get my life together?"

I can't help but think about Owen's ex and wonder if that's the kind of person he really needs in his life. Someone who is more polished and doesn't mess up this much. Part of me loves feeling like Owen sees the real me that I don't let others see often. The part of me that hates being in the spotlight, though, is terrified that if he sees enough, he'll discover how much I'm lacking.

"Sweetheart, everyone has things fall through the cracks sometimes. I do, too. I was supposed to renew my driver's license by my last birthday, but somehow it never made it on my radar. And I even have an assistant to help keep me on top of things! Do you want to know how I found out that it had expired?"

"You got pulled over?"

"No. That would've been preferable, actually. I found out because I had to go to a meeting with the Director of National Intelligence, along with the directors of a lot of other agencies. CIA, NSA, FBI, DIA, NGA—basically the whole alphabet soup of intelligence agency directors. As Director of the CSA, my badge got me past the gate. It was at check-in inside the ODNI lobby that I found out it had expired.

"And let's just say that the security officer I'd

handed it to wasn't discreet about it, either. Pierce, the CIA's director, had checked in right before me and was on his way to the elevators. The director of the National Geospatial-Intelligence Agency was right behind me. A few junior staffers were also in the mix. And the security officer said that I couldn't proceed until they got the 'situation' resolved, and that he'd have to call over a supervisor."

My face is burning just imagining being in that scenario, with all eyes on me.

"Needless to say, I got to the meeting late, and everyone who hadn't already known exactly why found out when Pierce updated the whole group. So, don't beat yourself up over letting something fall through the cracks. We all do at times."

I am blown away that my mom forgot something like that. I thought she always had everything together. Oddly, it does make me feel better to know that even she can mess up.

"And I need to apologize to you," she says.

"You do?"

She nods. "I probably should have a long time ago. After your kidnapping, your dad and I made sure we all got therapy. We knew it was a big thing to process and that it could have some real lasting effects. We even took you all to a therapist who specialized in trauma in young children."

I nod. I was only three, but I still remember quite a few things about going.

"We both figured that all of you very possibly would have fears of it happening again, that you weren't safe, or even fears of parks or open grassy areas, like the one where you were grabbed. What I hadn't anticipated—and really, hadn't even recognized for years—was how much we had all shifted into "protect Charlie" mode.

"And not only were we all focused on protecting you from danger, but I think all of us tried to protect you from everything." She shakes her head. "That was such a disservice to you. It sent the message that we didn't think you could handle things on your own, which was very much not the case. It also kept you from experiencing and learning to do things that you had a right to learn and do. And for that, I'm truly sorry."

Our chairs are facing each other, but she scoots even closer, and she holds both of my hands, like she really wants me to take in her next words. "You need to know, Charlie, how much faith I have in you. I know what you're capable of because I see you in action every day. You are not just 'fire' at work and 'flood' everywhere else." She chuckles softly. "Although you are definitely 'fire' at work. And you are definitely 'fire' in the way you look out for others, no matter where you are.

"The thing is, you're the same Charlie at work as everywhere else. You are just muting the fire version of yourself outside of work because that's what we inadvertently taught you to do. But make no mistake, Charlotte Florence Lancaster, you have it in you to be fire everywhere."

A scared, little, tentative bud of hope builds up inside me. "You really think so?"

"Without a doubt."

I stand, and my mom does, too, and I wrap my arms around her in a tight hug, and she hugs me right back for a good long minute.

―――――

After many meetings and hours spent researching and finding answers to things I didn't really want the answers to, it's finally lunchtime. And since it's a Tuesday, it comes with the added bonus of eating with Abraham.

I take the elevator down to Sub-level One and head over to his workspace. The corners of his eyes crinkle into a familiar smile the moment he sees me that is equal parts mischief and dad-energy. He pushes aside a disguise-in-progress—false teeth, tinted glasses, and something rubbery that I'm guessing is a nose or fore-head appliance—to make room for our lunch.

I flop down in the chair across from him.

"Exhausting day?"

I nod. "It even started out that way. But, I have a working kitchen sink, and my water didn't shut off mid-shower, so at least I've got that."

A lot of times, Abraham and I each bring our own lunches. Since Reese and I went grocery shopping last night, I had planned to make a veggie wrap this morning. But with how my morning went, I ended up grabbing a protein bar and an apple instead. So I was thrilled when Abraham messaged earlier and said he made dinner last night, that there were plenty of leftovers, and he brought enough for both of us.

"Maybe this will help give you some energy back," he says as he pushes a container across the table to me and pulls the other in front of him. "Warmed them up moments ago." I take off the lid and breathe in the creamy mushroomy sauce as Abraham says, "It's chicken marsala with garlic herb orzo and roasted broccolini."

"Did you always know how to cook like this, or did this skill magically appear once you started cooking for Annette?" I stab a piece of chicken and a mushroom and take a bite.

Abraham laughs. "It's one of my many skills—just one that I've kept more covert. Are you exhausted because you ran a mission today?"

I shake my head, and after I swallow, I say, "Ooh,

wow, that is good. And no, I'm exhausted because I had a meeting with Emerson just before this."

"He brought out the spreadsheets, didn't he?"

I laugh. "No. He basically confirmed that I can trust my gut. Which is good. But it's also so bad."

"Oh. This is about The Shadowridge's investor you told me about last week, isn't it?"

I nod.

"I stopped by The Shadowridge a couple of days ago and Owen gave me the tour."

"You did?"

"What kind of a substitute dad would I be if I didn't more thoroughly check out the guy you're dating? He's a good one. And he's doing a mighty fine job on that restoration."

I nod. "He really is." Then I blow out a deep breath. "Upstairs, we've all been working hard at finding out who the man is behind the thefts of a bunch of ancient artifacts that are being sold on the black market.

"This morning, I took a bunch of pieces of the puzzle that I've been finding about Giovanni—the investor—and realized they're connected to the puzzle we've all been working on. He's the guy. The one we've been searching for. He's been right here, under our noses, this entire time. Well, mostly in Italy, actually. The man funding Owen's entire project is running an international smuggling ring and is using The Shadowridge as a drop point."

Abraham's eyes go wide. "Well, that is rather unfortunate, isn't it?"

"I'm sure you saw, as you were touring the place, just how passionate Owen is about it. It's where his grandpa and grandma met. And he told his grandpa before he died that he would one day restore the place. Abraham, how in the world do I tell him that his investor is going to be arrested soon and that the building he loves so much could get seized in the process?"

"Oof. That's a tough one. Are you going to let him know who you really work for so he knows how you got that information?"

"Probably not. I submitted the forms to read him in and he was vetted last week, but it doesn't really feel fair of me to say, 'Oh, hey, I've been lying to you about what I do and where I work' at the same time that I drop the bomb about his baby, throwing its future into the unknown."

"Yeah, that's a lot. Have you thought about just not telling him about his investor? I mean, he'll find out on his own eventually."

"I really like Owen. And by that, I mean that I love him, even though I haven't told him yet. I think he's the one. How can I know about this humongous thing that will personally affect him so much, and not tell him simply because it'd be hard? What kind of a relationship does that set us up for?"

"Okay, admittedly, not a great one."

Abraham takes a bite of his chicken marsala as he ponders. He always thinks before answering big questions, and I'm grateful for that. I take a bite, too, but I can't focus on the food—only on Abraham's face and what he's thinking, and how I am supposed to tell the man I love that his dream is in big trouble.

Eventually, Abraham takes a deep breath and says, "He's going to want to know how you have this information, since it isn't knowledge just anyone can get. If you don't think now is the right time to tell him about the CSA and your job—and I think that's a good choice on your part—then I suggest keeping things about your source vague but honest. Avoiding direct lies will keep your integrity intact, and it'll let you say later, 'There's more I didn't tell you, and here's why.' Then, when you do tell him about the CSA, hopefully everything will click into place instead of feeling like a shock."

I nod. "That's good. I can do that."

"As far as what to tell him about Giovanni and The Shadowridge? I'd keep that honest, too. Give him details, because if you don't, he'll assume the information must be wrong. But don't give him too many details, or you'll overwhelm him and he'll shut down. It's tricky to get the balance right."

"Yeah, that does sound tricky."

"You'll get it, though."

"Do you think?"

"During our lunch two weeks ago, you told me you thought something was up with the investor. Last week, you told me that Emerson's initial search showed he was clean, but you started investigating him on your own anyway. Those instincts of yours knew something was wrong even when all signs pointed to him being fine, right? Those same instincts will help you figure out how to tell Owen."

I sure hope that's the case! Because the words I choose when telling Owen could mean the difference between crushing his hopes and dreams—his whole world—and… Okay, it's going to crush his hopes, dreams, and world either way. But maybe one way will help him to mentally prepare. Maybe even have a little hope. And the other will just leave him crushed.

We chat more as we eat, with Abraham telling me stories about when he was a field operative and had to give people information they didn't want to hear, and gave it in a way that made it easier to digest. I try to take it all in. Hopefully, it'll help me break the news to Owen.

After we finish eating and clean up lunch,

Abraham says, "Well, I'm not going to tell you, 'Good luck, have fun, and don't die,' because that just feels inappropriate for this situation. So instead, I'll just say, good luck, speak gently, and try not to obliterate the man's soul."

CHAPTER 29
HALFWAY BUILT, HALFWAY BROKEN
OWEN

f it were morning and I was singing my to-do list right now, it'd be singing to the tune of *I'm Walking on Sunshine*, because that's what's been running through my head since this afternoon. In the auditorium part of the theater, the electrical, insulation, and new Sheetrock have all been installed, so we got to work on putting up new trim today. It's one of those steps where the potential of the space starts becoming clear to everyone. All my guys were walking on sunshine today, too.

And not only that, but after I take a quick shower, I get to see Charlie. She's working a bit late, so she'll be meeting me at Keyhaven Park on her way home, where we're going to walk along the nature trail before heading to her favorite ice cream shop.

When I arrive at the park, the sun is getting lower

in the sky, but I'm still walking on sunshine. Well, more like floating on sunshine once she pulls into the lot and smiles at me. I go over to her car, and when she gets out, she drapes her arms over my shoulders and gives me a kiss as I put my hands on her waist, holding her close.

She pulls back enough to meet my eyes and says, "You are looking mighty happy today."

I give her one more quick peck before I switch to holding her hand and starting to walk in the direction of the trail. "How could I not be? The auditorium part of The Shadowridge is past the parts where demolition makes it look worse, and is to the point where it's looking more incredible every day. And I get to spend the evening walking hand-in-hand with you."

Charlie smiles at me, but there's concern showing just under the surface. Whatever kept her late at work must still be weighing on her. I ask, "How was your day?" to see if she wants to talk about it.

"It was…hard."

I pause my walking right as we get to the trail. "Should we not do this tonight?"

"No, no. We should."

The trail starts out in the park, but it winds around into beautiful wooded areas where it feels like the rest of the world ceases to exist. For a good distance, the trail runs between old train rails, with crushed stone forming the path. It's just the two of us, the wind through the trees, and the first of the crickets that are starting to chirp. Even with the breeze, the weather is nice—it's not even bordering on too cold.

We cross over a long wooden bridge-like area where the wooded hills on both sides rise, the wooden path barely fitting between them. We aren't too far past it when we come to a bench, and Charlie pulls me toward it. Once we both sit, she turns to me and takes my hands in hers, which is sweet. I'd be loving this moment if it weren't for the ultra-serious expression on her face combined with the stress-filled vibes I've been getting from her. Now I'm just nervous.

She looks at me like she's trying to figure out how to start. Which, honestly, is giving me heart palpitations. She shifts on the bench, and then she says in a soft voice, "I didn't want to keep anything from you, but I had to wait until I had facts. And now I do. I also can't tell you everything about how I know this—not yet. But I promise the information I'm about to tell you is legitimate."

So this talk isn't about our relationship. That's comforting. My stomach still tightens, though, because this sounds serious. For a moment, I worry that it's about Tessa. Then, suddenly, I know. "This is about The Shadowridge, isn't it?" She nods, and I have an immediate pang in my gut. I don't know what has been making me feel like it was pulling away, but I knew it was.

"I looked into Giovanni because something just didn't feel right," she says. "What I found was pretty serious, and I think you should know."

I swallow hard and brace myself.

"But this is privileged information. So you'll have to use a lot of discretion so you won't tip him off."

"Okay," I say, my voice coming out wary.

"The man we saw break in that night of our picnic? He had a small package with him when he went back-stage, and when he came out, he didn't have it with him anymore. When we went to check everything out, I remembered you said you showed Giovanni a hidden alcove behind the set storage area. I looked there, and I found the package."

"You did?" My mind scrambles to remember that night exactly. Had I seen the man holding a package?

"Yes. I got in touch with a contact at a government agency, and they retrieved the package. I didn't bring it up because I hoped it was nothing, and I didn't want you to have to stress even more about the break-in if it was. But the package contained ancient coins from a known cache that went missing. They were confirmed as illegally trafficked antiquities."

Now my mind is whirling, trying to process this information. "So the package was…What? Some kind of black market thing?"

"Yes," she says, then takes a breath. "But it's even more than that. Giovanni has been running an illicit artifact smuggling operation internationally, and he's using the theater as a dead drop location."

I lean back hard against the back of the bench, feeling like I was just punched in the gut.

"He targets historical buildings," she continues, her voice gentle but steady. "That's why he chooses them as restoration projects. It could be because he genuinely appreciates their beauty—he did seem to truly love The Shadowridge. Or maybe because they're full of forgotten spaces and clever hidey holes. Either way, he disguises what he's doing behind philanthropic restoration funding."

My throat feels dry as pieces click into place. "Those questions you asked Giovanni when you first met him. You already sensed something was off and were trying to get information out of him?"

Her eyes don't leave mine. "Yes."

I close my eyes for a moment, as if the enormity of this situation wouldn't enter if I did, before I have too many questions to try to block it. "When you asked if he flew in just to see The Shadowridge, he mentioned that he had other business in the area to attend to. Was that related?"

Charlie nods. "He's got a luxury import/export business in Alexandria. That's how he connects with international buyers, moves things overseas, and keeps everything looking legit on the books. He's good at it, too. It kept his less-than-legal activities hidden for a long time."

I stare out at the trees that rise up just on the other side of the path, my thoughts tangling.

"So The Shadowridge… It's not just a passion project to him. It's a front." Saying the words out loud makes it feel even more real. Even more devastating.

"I'm so sorry, Owen." Her voice cracks just a little. "I know how much restoring it means to you."

I nod, but the motion feels brittle. I turn to her. "How do you possibly know all this?

"It's… complicated," she says, carefully. "I can't go into details yet. Not because I don't want to. But the short answer is, at my work, we investigate people like Giovanni.

"Officers and agents have had eyes on The Shadowridge since that man snuck in that night we were there. They arrested the person who showed up to retrieve the package he left. So far, they haven't seen anyone else come to drop an artifact or to pick one up. But they might be lying low because I'm sure they know that the location's been compromised."

I'm gripping the edge of the bench and trying my best to stay calm. "So what happens now?"

"It's hard to say. Giovanni might get arrested right away. Or they might hold off for a bit so they can gather more evidence or find couriers in the chain. But if Giovanni's people have gotten spooked, it might be a while before anything else happens. Or, it's possible things could happen quickly."

Silence hangs between us for a long moment.

Then Charlie really looks at me, and her voice drops a little. "I didn't want to tell you this. I was really hoping all my fears were unfounded and that the answer I'd get today would be that my gut was wrong and I just shouldn't trust it. But now that I know, I had to tell you so you won't be caught off guard. I don't want you blindsided if things do start to move fast."

I search her face. She's clearly not saying everything, but I know that what she has told me is the truth. And somehow, I trust her more for not pretending this is simple.

I ask the question that I'm afraid to ask, yet at the same time, I can't not ask it. "What does all of this mean for The Shadowridge?"

Charlie studies me. "There are several factors. How much of it do you want? I don't want to overload you."

"I think it's safe to say I'm already overloaded. But give me all you've got. I need to know what I'm facing."

"I totally understand that. There's a lot that I don't know, but I can give you my best guess. I think the biggest thing The Shadowridge has going for it is that the building is owned by a historical trust—Giovanni was just funding the restoration. If he owned the building, it'd likely be seized, and that would put things in limbo for years.

"Since he doesn't, odds are better that you'll be able to continue, possibly in a limited capacity, depending on funding. You'll for sure have to find new donors. I don't know how long what Giovanni's already paid will last, but he'll likely not be able to send more."

He didn't pay a lump sum up front—in the contract we signed, it was scheduled to come in a series of five payments, and we've only hit the benchmarks for the first two. "It's not enough to finish." I feel like I've got a brick in my stomach.

"I know you said that finding donors is the hardest part, and that it takes a while. I'm so sorry, Owen."

I sit there for a moment, staring at the pathway like it might offer some answers.

Giovanni is a smuggler. He was using The Shadowridge. He was using me.

My stomach turns. I feel stupid for not seeing it and for placing so much trust in him. And I'm angry. At Giovanni, at myself, maybe even at the world, for letting something this good get tainted.

I look over at Charlie as she sits right beside me. Her shoulders are tense, but her eyes are steady. She didn't have to tell me any of this. She could've let it unfold on its own, and I would've just found out when everything exploded. But she didn't. She came to me with the truth. That matters more than everything else crashing down.

Yet, I still can't help but think of all those things that are crashing down. I shake my head. "Nothing is ever guaranteed, is it?"

"It isn't." I'm looking down, but she gently puts her hands on my cheeks and turns my face to meet her eyes. "So, that means that a bad outcome—or the outcome you're fearing the most—isn't guaranteed, either."

Giovanni's assets will probably be seized and his accounts frozen. The likelihood of my being able to finish the restoration of this building I love and honor my grandpa's memory by doing it is slim. Especially because a partially finished project is always more difficult to secure funding for, because then there's a stigma attached to it. New investors almost always assume that a project is doomed if a previous investor pulled out.

The implications of it all start to hit me. How quickly the funds we've already received from Giovanni will run out. That all my crew will be out of a job. That I won't have a reason to stay in Cipher Springs and will need to move on to the next job. That it might greatly affect my relationship with Charlie.

And if I do somehow miraculously find a way to secure new funding, there will still be a loss of momentum on the project. And the all the uncertainty will likely cause so much stress every step of the way.

I'm trying not to show how much I am freaking out. But it is so hard to hold in. My chest just feels so tight, and although I'm breathing fast, I'm not getting any air. I'm so dizzy. How did it get so hot? Suddenly, I'm standing, and I say, "I need to think. I'm sorry. I have to go."

And then I head back along the pathway, speed-walking, leaving Charlie behind.

CHAPTER 30
ALL SYSTEMS OVERLOADED
OWEN

When I get to my truck, I start driving with no plan as to where I'm going. I find myself on a road out of town that's narrow, with no shoulder, where most of the time, I have green fields spread out on one side and lots of trees on the other. Only an occasional home. I've never been on this road before, and I don't care where it's taking me.

I only make it about fifteen minutes out of town before the road has a shoulder again, and I pull off to the side. The moment I do, I get out my phone and open the app that shows the cameras in The Shadowridge. Not that I'm expecting to see Giovanni, some courier dropping off a package, or even a hint out a window of whatever officer or agent is watching the building. I do it because I need confirmation that this place I love is okay. Fifteen minutes. That's as long as I made it.

I keep switching between each of the cameras, looking for nothing, yet not being able to bring myself to stop. I can't believe I never clued in on Giovanni's plans to use The Shadowridge as a front. When I look for investors, I usually find them through networking in my field, researching philanthropists who may be interested in projects like mine, or talking to past donors of similar projects.

I found Giovanni through a mix of those. Initially, through research, then through someone I didn't know well, but whom I'd seen at several networking events. He made the introduction, and Giovanni seemed interested, so we talked and I pitched the project to him. I look back at that initial phone call through the lens of the information I learned tonight, searching my mind for any clues. I don't remember anything that seemed off.

Over the next several weeks, I met with him via video call often, showing him the space, my proposal, discussing the scope, history, impact, timeline, funding needs, all of it. Every step of the way, he seemed as excited by the project as I was. Was he excited because of its potential as a drop location for his illicit business, and I just interpreted it as excitement for the restoration itself? Had I just been projecting?

He'd sent out a team to look at the site, and I didn't notice that anything was off. We worked through a draft of the funding agreement with lawyers together, negotiating the timeline and restoration conditions for nearly two months.

From that first phone call up until now, I've given him updates at least weekly. How could I have been so blind to such a big issue? I must not have checked everything as well as I thought I had. And now everything is about to collapse.

I know that everything can change in a single night. It did when my grandpa died. And it did the night of the football banquet when I was injured in that accident. I was blindsided by both of those events, too, just like tonight. Why does badness come after me? I rub my knee that is suddenly hurting. Maybe I haven't come as far as I thought I had in forgiving Cordell because right now, I'm mad at him again. It just feels like there's no justice.

I cycle through all the cameras again. My heart is already aching for the loss of it that's on the horizon. As much as I love this building, I love Charlie even more. When I decide that I'm all in on something—which is what I've done with both The Shadowridge and with Charlie—then I'm all in. What if I lose her right along with the building?

It's possible the building won't be lost. I know there's a glimmer of hope. But I also know it won't be easy, even if it does end up being possible. What if new funding takes a long time to secure? What if I have to go through the approval process and get all new permits? What if the timing doesn't work out with the Baltimore train station restoration? Will it take so much time that I won't see Charlie even if she does stick around?

My crew needs work. They didn't like being off for two days when I couldn't get the insulation. They won't be able to just wait around for me during whatever delay is caused after Giovanni is arrested, before I can even start looking for new funding, and then during the months it'll take to finalize it. And that's if I can even find funding. It won't be like finding it the first time around.

My regular crew has already melded. It always takes a bit, but now they're working so well together. I'll likely not be able to get them all back—if I can get any of them back. They'll have to move on to other jobs.

And what will Charlie do when I'm working further away? When there's so much more than a single wall separating us? Will she move on, too? Probably. I think back to what Luis said about me choosing people who reinforced my belief that people always leave. But I didn't do that with Charlie. And yet, here we are.

I know I'm spiraling. I can feel it. But I also can't

seem to stop it. There are just so many unknowns. I like being able to wake up in the morning and sing my to-do list because I know what to expect of the day. What will tomorrow bring? Another day where I can go to work and make progress, ignoring The Shadowridge's impending doom? Or will it be the day that things implode? Can I ever tell my crew if I can't tip off Giovanni? Charlie gave me advance warning. Will I not be able to do the same for my crew?

I close out of the camera app and get out of my truck. I lean my back against the bed, close my eyes, and breathe in the night air slowly until my body calms and I can think straight without the spiral.

This whole situation sucks. That's just the way it is. I tell myself that it's okay to grieve this place I love so much. But just like Charlie said, the outcome I fear the most isn't guaranteed. And Luis warned me that my brain was already halfway packed for a breakup with Charlie. I can survive losing The Shadowridge. I can't lose Charlie. I have got to find a way past this, or I think I'll be guaranteeing that's exactly what will happen.

CHAPTER 31
OPERATION: FIND MY FAVORITE HUMAN
CHARLIE

I managed to get off work early, which is good, because I can't stop worrying about Owen. When I told him about Giovanni and The Shadowridge, he left. I could tell he needed some time to process, and following after him wasn't going to give him that. When I finally heard his truck pull into the driveway last night, I was already in bed, but I hadn't even begun to calm my mind enough to fall asleep. Knowing he made it home safely helped.

Which was good, because I had to go into work so much earlier than normal today to help with the search for Giovanni. The package going missing that the courier had left that night in The Shadowridge—the one that Ledger snuck in to take after I found it—must've really spooked him because he's gone underground.

I've been tracking his credit cards, wire transfers on any of his accounts, watching for hotel stays or purchases that match his or any of his aliases' spending patterns, and tracking his phones and tablets. It was all going well until suddenly, there was nothing. No hints of him anywhere.

He has to still be in Italy, though, because I've also been using real-time facial recognition software to scan airport terminals, major metro stations, train stations, toll booth cameras, gas stations, bus station CCTV, customs lines, and I've been monitoring coastal surveillance systems, and he hasn't appeared on any. Which makes it so much more difficult to arrest him.

When I leave work and make it back to my place, Owen's truck isn't in the driveway, which isn't strange for this time of day. He probably won't be home for another hour. But I still don't let my phone out of sight as I head upstairs to change out of my pink work dress and black cardigan and into jeans and a dark gray tee. I've been texting him all day, but haven't heard a single thing from him. I'm really getting worried. I dumped a lot on him last night, and I need to know if he's okay.

I'm hurrying down the stairs so I can head to his work when Reese gets home. She's hanging her school lanyard and keys on the hook as I round the corner, and she looks at me, anticipation all over her face. "I never saw you last night, and I've been dying for an update! So, did you tell him?"

It takes me a moment of just staring at Reese, wondering how she knew I was going to tell Owen about Giovanni and wondering why she's acting excited about it, before I realize she's asking if I told Owen about my kidnapping.

"Oh! No, I didn't."

She puts her hands on her hips. "Charlie, you swore. *And* I took out the nasty garbage."

"I know. And I will do some other nasty chore to make it up to you. But he got some devastating news, so I couldn't."

Her expression immediately changes into one of concern. "Is everything okay?"

I shake my head and say, "I don't know. I need to go find him."

———

Owen's truck isn't at The Shadowridge, but I still park and head inside. I find Grady working to prep a long wall for painting, and I ask if he knows where Owen is.

"Not a clue," Grady says. "He was here until this afternoon, but he hasn't been himself all day."

Trent came over when he saw me and adds, "Yeah,

normally the guy has a smile twenty-four, seven. I don't think he smiled once today."

Then Grady tells me, "He said he got some bad news and needed to blow off steam right before he left, but he didn't say anything about where."

I thank them and head back to my car, worrying about Owen even more than I had before going inside. Where would he go if he were upset? Obviously not to me or one of the guys he works with. Home to Bridleford? That hour-long drive might've been what he needed.

That doesn't feel right, though. To a park? To visit a friend at one of his previous site locations? His sister is back at college in Boulder, so visiting her wouldn't be easy. Hopefully, he didn't just hop on a plane without telling anyone. Maybe he went for a run? Nothing feels right, and I'm racking my brain trying to figure out where he could be.

Then it hits me. At Jace and Mackenzie's wedding, Zoe had asked if he ever went to bars to blow off steam. He'd mentioned one in Baltimore. Not by name, but said he liked it because of the architecture and because it was a good place to think. What had he said about it? Oh! That it was a carriage house for a nearby hotel, built in…1880-something? I pull out my phone and start Googling.

Apparently, there aren't too many carriage-houses-turned-bars built in the late 1800s in Baltimore, so I find it pretty quickly. It's called Loose Reins, and my phone says it'll take forty-two minutes to drive there.

When I pull up to the building, it's easy to see why Owen said he loves this place. It has the same character and attention to detail as the courthouse in his hometown and feels drenched in history. I head inside, where there's exposed brick on the walls and on the front of the bar, timber beams, and a lot of ironwork. It has a partial wall dividing it from the other half of the space. A few people sit at tables on this side, but not Owen, and what little sound I'm hearing is coming from the other side. I head back there.

Everyone starts cheering just as I round the wall. There are quite a few more people here—probably twenty-five or thirty. I spot Owen sitting alone toward the front of the space, and I finally exhale in relief at seeing he's okay. Well, okay, but not great. His back is to me, but his face is turned just enough for me to see that he's wearing an intense expression of focus.

I'm just about to wind my way through the tables and chairs to go to him when a man steps up to a microphone on a stage that's maybe a foot higher than the floor. "Now," he says, "let's give it up for our next performer, Owen Hollis!"

Owen stands, and I feel so clueless about what is going on right now. As he walks to the stage, I take a seat at an empty table toward the back. There's a chair on the stage, and Owen sits on it, pulls the microphone from the stand, and looking down at a spot on the floor that's maybe ten feet in front of him, instead of looking at the crowd, he starts to talk.

"The One with Arched Beams and Terrible Timing." He clears his throat and then says, "You were built in nineteen thirteen. Back when wood spoke in curves. When ironwork still wore the blacksmith's breath. When blueprints whispered like love letters to possibility."

I gasp quietly. Is this a spoken word poetry night? I look around at the people sitting at tables. All eyes are on Owen.

I think back to when the power had gone out and Owen and I were chatting in my dark living area. I had asked him to name something that made him smile. He'd said something along the lines of using his vast knowledge of random historical facts, and one of the only ways it was useful was in writing epic poetry. Why had I not asked more about that when he'd said it? I hadn't even pictured something like this. Maybe I could've talked him into doing it more.

I know his subject matter is The Shadowridge. He speaks with the careful timing of someone sculpting words, and he tells about how they don't make entrances or lay bricks like hers anymore. Like permanence was a promise. Then he says, "And I care. I care too much. Which is the problem.

"See, they told me not to fall for you. Not in so

many words. But in red tape and grant applications. And that one guy from zoning who thinks joy is a code violation."

I chuckle, right along with most of the others watching. I know that Owen is hurting. I also know that he prefers to have a smile on his face, even when things are hard. It's comforting to know that even when everything must feel like it's crashing down around him, he can still find the humor. He's still my Owen.

He continues. "They said, 'Don't get attached. It's just a job.' But they didn't see you in the morning light. When the dust catches the sun through leaded glass. And your floorboards creak like an old soul stretching its limbs.

"They didn't run their fingers along your balustrades. And feel the past rise up under their touch. You've got stories in your moldings and a heartbeat in your beams. (And possibly mice in the balcony, but we don't talk about that.)"

Gosh, I love this man. This is so beautiful and is absolutely breaking my heart. Even more than the words he's saying or the cadence he's using, it's his earnestness and the way it feels like he's baring things deep in his soul. He's pouring so much feeling into every line.

"And maybe I got in too deep. Maybe I should've just done the job. Hammer, level, plaster, paycheck.

But I kept seeing more. More than just what you were. More than what you could be. I saw *you*. Becoming fully alive again.

"And maybe that's what hurts the most. Because still… I might lose you."

I dab a knuckle under my eye. He's going to make me cry.

"I might have to walk away and never touch that stage again. Never fix the last cracked tile. Never leave my own mark on your long line of caretakers. But even if I do…

"You'll still be the one. The one who taught me that love is sometimes made of sawdust and scaffolding. But also the one where I learned that love doesn't have to be planned to be right. That love comes in sticky notes, and patio talks, and concern through a taped-closed door."

He was talking about me! I hold in a sob so I won't miss anything.

"The one who proved I could dream in brick and light and shadow. The one with arched beams and terrible timing.

"I don't know what happens next. But I know this. Some things—even me—are worth fixing. Even when the world says they're already lost."

Owen bows his head and places the microphone in his lap. Everyone in the place starts cheering, and I stand and cheer, too. Owen stands, puts the mic back, and dips his head in a bow. Then he looks out at the audience, and our eyes meet. Surprise and disbelief cross his face, followed quickly by happiness. Whew! I was kind of worried that he didn't want me here.

He hurries off the low stage and winds his way between the tables of people toward me. When he reaches me, he's searching my face. "You came. How are you even here?"

"I was worried about you."

He hugs me tight for a long moment, and I squeeze him right back, not releasing until he does. Then he pulls back enough to really look at me and asks, "How did you find me?"

"Well, let's see. A hint from your crew, remembering you talked about an old carriage house at the wedding, some Googling, and a bit of driving. I can't say I was expecting it all to lead me to spoken word poetry."

"Well, we all grieve in different ways."

We both walk around the partial wall to the other side of the bar and slide into one of the few booths. "I can't believe you found me with that little to go on."

If he only had any idea how little I need. Or how experienced I am in finding people who don't want to be found. "Well, we all worry in different ways."

He chuckles, and I ask him how he's doing.

"I'm working on getting to acceptance. But I've mostly been stuck on a merry-go-round of the other stages." He pauses a moment, then says, "I want to go to The Shadowridge tonight. I know that at some unknown point, things could move quickly, but since I don't know when it will suddenly be my last day inside the building for a while, or possibly ever, I want to make sure I get a chance to give a proper goodbye. Do you want to go with me?"

I nod. "I would be honored to."

CHAPTER 32
WELL, THAT ESCALATED QUIETLY
OWEN

'm glad that Charlie is here with me. And I'm glad that she thwarted my plan to wallow alone at open mic night. I had also planned to be alone when I gave my goodbye to The Shadowridge, but I'm so glad she's here with me, too. Without even saying I needed it, she has offered the kind of security and emotional steadiness I've been craving in a partner my whole life.

We go through the front doors, and I lock them behind us. I had planned to walk through the place, taking in every inch of its beauty in its unfinished state. To fully feel the longing I have for it, even though it isn't gone yet. And to apologize to my grandpa for not being able to finish it like I had promised.

But now that we're here, that's not exactly what I

want to do. Charlie and I walk hand-in-hand into the auditorium, right through the middle that I hope will one day be filled with refurbished seating, and we go up the stairs and onto the stage. Then we sit on the edge of it, our feet dangling, looking out at the space for several long minutes.

Right now, everything is mostly shades of Sheetrock dust and primer white. I can picture exactly what it'll look like once everything is fully restored and in full color, though. And as we sit, I realize I came here for two purposes tonight. I thought it was just to say goodbye, but that's not what's grabbing me the most. I turn to Charlie. "Do you want to be a spy?"

She looks at me in shock.

"Well, more of a detective, I guess. I rewatched the video footage of the night we saw that guy sneak in. Several times, actually. And it's been niggling at me ever since."

"Yeah?"

"He came through that door," I say, pointing off to our right. "Sure, he avoided the cameras as he moved through the area, but there were also cameras on all the doors into this place. Yet no matter how many times I watch the footage, even if I go clear back until the moment when we left the building for the day, I didn't see him come through any of the doors."

Charlie cocks her head. "Do you think he was

already inside? Or do you think he found another way in?"

I shrug. "He could've come in earlier in the day. I could watch the footage from each of the cameras from the moment I opened the doors for my crew that morning. But I don't think he was. I check everywhere before I leave each day."

Charlie sits up taller, and I can see a bit of excitement on her face. "Do you want to check the place out for other ways he might've come in?"

I love that she wants to. I smile and nod.

We start in one of the offices that we've been using as a makeshift supply room and grab a couple of flashlights. We search that room, then the other three office rooms. We look at the windows, of course, but I'd also checked those the night of the break-in, and I hadn't seen any signs of entry.

So, we also open every closet and cupboard, looking for… I don't even know. Secret entrances, I guess. Most don't even make logical sense that they could contain a hidden way in. We'd probably be more successful searching the outside of the building for anomalies.

But it's kind of fun sleuthing around The Shadowridge with Charlie, so we search every nook and cranny. When we finish the offices and hallway, we head through the side door that leads backstage and begin searching there. We sneak up to closed doors to closets or storage spaces and pull them open quickly, like we're about to catch someone, and honestly, it's the lightest I've felt since Charlie dropped the Giovanni bomb on me yesterday.

We yank open the door to a maintenance closet near the dressing rooms and shine our flashlights around the space that's only a few feet wide but probably twice that deep. Nothing. But as we turn to leave, I accidentally smack my elbow into the door frame and drop my flashlight. When it hits the floor, it makes a hollow clunk.

Our eyes immediately fly to each other's. I pick up my flashlight and drop it just outside the closet, and it makes a very different sound.

"Do you think there's something below it?" Charlie asks.

"It's concrete," I say, confused. But we both shine our flashlights all around the space inside the closet, anyway. Then we spot a recess in the concrete that is just big enough for a handhold. I put my fingers in it and lift. It takes a bit of shifting to figure out which way to pull and where to stand, but I'm able to raise up one side. We both gasp when we see it's just a thin layer of concrete over a trap door. I open it all the way and shine my light inside.

It's musty-smelling. And there's a short vertical drop leading to a set of steep, uneven brick ledges that work as stairs. It's deep enough for a person to stand fully, and it might be the opening to a tunnel.

I look at Charlie. "Maybe this leads to another location, and they got inside the building through here! That'd explain why I never saw them coming through the doors."

"And it's probably why the officers never saw anyone else when they were watching the building." Charlie immediately pulls out her phone. We both shine our flashlights down into the tunnel as she takes a picture, then she backs up to take a picture of the maintenance closet that was hiding it.

"Should we go down there and see where it leads?"

Charlie's attention flies from her phone to me, and she hisses, "No! Remember what I told you? We don't go after bad guys. Hiding is best." She takes my arm and pulls me further from the closet, as if I'm going to sneak down when she's not looking or something.

Then she starts muttering about who to text—Jace won't be back from his honeymoon for another two days. Ledger and Miles are both out of town. Her mom is at a meeting in Virginia or something. She murmurs, "I'll text Emerson and Blake."

I'm standing next to her, looking down at her phone as she attaches the two pictures to a text. She has typed in the words, *We are at,* when we hear a menacing voice behind us say, "Put the phone down and turn around slowly."

Charlie slides the phone into her pocket, and as we turn around, I do it in a way to put my body between the man and Charlie. Then I pull back in surprise to see it's Giovanni standing there, a gun in his hand, aimed right at us. There are two other guys with him, too. They're all standing near the tunnel, so either they heard us when we opened the hatch—or saw the light of our flashlights shining down—and came up, or they were already inside The Shadowridge and snuck into the room quietly.

Giovanni shakes his head. "You weren't supposed to find this entrance. I liked you, Owen."

I don't know exactly what he means by using "liked" in the past tense. I'm having trouble focusing on anything with that gun aimed at us. It's the first time in my life I've been face-to-face with one, and honestly, I didn't know it'd make me freeze in terror like this. Especially when it's held by someone that, until very recently, I really respected.

Giovanni says that he can't have us up here, thwarting things, so he takes both of us down into the tunnel with him.

CHAPTER 33
NOT MY FIRST KIDNAPPING
CHARLIE

I am a highly trained technical operations officer in an intelligence agency. I can't believe that when we first saw the opening to the tunnel, I didn't immediately call Emerson and request backup. Nope. Instead, I have us shine our flashlights down it! And then just take pictures to attach to a text!

Okay, granted, we thought that Giovanni was on a different continent. I guess we should've realized that a smuggler as skilled at evading detection as Giovanni is would've figured out how to smuggle himself. And we've seen so little movement with this building that it didn't occur to me that anyone might be around.

But still. Had Jace, or Miles, or Ledger done exactly what I did, I would've given them so much grief for it! And they are highly trained in the field and could hold their own in a situation like this. I am not.

What I am is someone who is currently getting every childhood fear of hers triggered as we walk down a tunnel that has probably been around since Prohibition. (And I'm not just basing that off the number of spider webs in the corners. The floor is packed dirt, and the walls are brick. Not that I'm a brick expert, but they do look like they've been around since at least the 1920s. I bet Owen could probably tell exactly what year they were made. Maybe even *where* they were made. That's probably one of those random historical facts he has memorized.)

As far as tunnels go, they're decently-sized. Nearly three-foot-wide hallways, tall enough that no one has to crouch, not even Giovanni's taller stooge, and there are several spaces that are much wider. They were probably used for alcohol storage. Now, at least one of them is being used as a smuggler's compartment and one as a sort of command center, where a third stooge is standing at a table with some papers and a lamp on it.

So we have enough space, but we're still trapped. This place is nothing like the warehouse where I was kept as a kidnapped preschooler, but I immediately recognize the fear I'm feeling that my family won't know where I am as the same. My hands are clammy, and I am simultaneously uncomfortably hot and freezing cold. I shiver, and Owen puts his arm around me.

It seems that Giovanni and his guys are in the middle of trying to get the items they have down here moved elsewhere, especially because they know they have government agencies watching them, and preferably moved to buyers that they already have lined up. He seems too busy to deal with us yet, and maybe also like he doesn't have the spare brainpower to figure out *what* to do with us. So, they stick us in one of the wider spaces that they haven't filled with something else. A space that is right in their line of sight, so there's no sneaking out.

Owen and I are sitting on the ground, our backs against a brick wall (that I definitely checked for spiders before leaning against). I can't keep my eyes off the gun at Giovanni's waist. The silent threat.

"Are you okay?" Owen asks.

I nod without taking my eyes off the gun.

"Charlie," he says, and waits until I look at him. "We need to get out of here."

I look back at our captors. "We can't. We're trapped." My mind just keeps swirling around that one fact. We're stuck down here. They're watching us. They have a gun. This is the guy that my whole department has been trying to find for weeks. And they have us. I'm supposed to be safe behind a computer! Not in the field. Not captured. Not where no one knows where I am.

The hair is lifting on my arms, my heart is racing,

and I'm struggling to keep the shaking in my hands from being noticeable and my breathing from being too fast. Every part of my body is telling me to hide, yet there is nowhere to hide. There's only out here, in the open, where I can most easily be seen.

"Charlie, look at me." I manage to tear my eyes off the men and look at Owen. He puts his hands on the sides of my face, holding my focus on him. "We're going to be okay."

I nod a bit. I like the words. I don't believe the words. *We're trapped. We're trapped. We're trapped.*

"Breathe with me."

I know I need to listen. I try to focus on the rise and fall of Owen's chest. Feel his hands on the sides of my head, the brick wall at my back, the dirt on the ground, the way his bent leg is pressed up against mine. And I breathe. Slower. Deeper. More sure.

After a few minutes, the swirling fog in my mind begins to subside, and I can think a bit more. When my heart rate feels like it's not racing quite as fast, I glance back at the men. They seem to be focused on their own issues, so Owen drops his hands from cradling my head and straightens his leg as I slowly slide my cell phone from my pocket and unlock the screen. It still has the text open that I was getting ready to send to Emerson and Blake. "No bars," I breathe. There's not even a hint of a bar.

Owen's eyes go wide.

I sneakily type the words *CAPTURED* and *HELP*. I don't even bother to say that we are at The Shadowridge—they're smart enough to figure that one out. Then I tap send, even though I know it won't go through until we are out of this tunnel, which will be kind of pointless then, and slip it back into my pocket.

I can tell that Owen's mind is spinning, so I pull myself together. I am almost never in any actual danger, but I have proximity to danger all the time. I experience it vicariously every time I guide Jace through a mission. Owen doesn't. I need to be calm for him. I know how Jace thinks from watching him in situations similar to this, so I can handle this.

I breathe slowly and deeply still, and I think. Silent but Scary keeps looking at me like he's worried I might bolt, so he needs to keep himself prepared to tackle me at any moment, and it's making that regulated breathing a bit more difficult. *Be strong for Owen.* He just calmed me—returning the favor is the least I can do.

I remember I have something I can tell Owen that will help keep him from being overly focused and stressed about our situation. And Reese will be so proud of me if I do. Besides, what better time to tell the story about when I was so vulnerable and exposed than at a time when I'm feeling most vulnerable and exposed?

Well, probably any other time—during *any* other situation—is a better choice.

I take a deep breath and hold it for a moment, because it came in shaky and I need it to not come out the same, then I exhale. I can do this. Owen and I are sitting so close that our bodies are practically touching from shoulder to ankle, so I can talk softly and he'll still hear. "This is not my first time being kidnapped. Well, technically, we aren't kidnapped; we've been abducted. Or held against our will, I guess."

He looks over at me in shock. "This isn't your first time?"

I shake my head. "I was three years old. I was with my brothers and our nanny at a park. Blake and I were playing in the woodchips in the playground area when a woman with a dog walked by. Blake loved dogs, so he ran after her to see if he could pet it. I like dogs, so I followed, but I got distracted along the way by a caterpillar. The next thing I knew, I was being lifted up by a man who then ran with me across the grass to a van that was waiting. As soon as we got inside, the van took off before he even pulled the door shut."

Owen sucks in a breath, entwines his fingers in mine, and gives my hand a squeeze.

Outside of telling people when it first happened, I don't think I've ever talked about it more than just saying that it happened when someone else brings it up, like Zoe did. Then I shut down all thoughts of it. A part of me wants to do exactly that right now. To hide. I push through it, though.

"I always say I don't really remember it, but there are parts that I do. We were in some kind of open space, probably a warehouse. There were five men and one woman there—none I had seen before. I remember being afraid. I knew there was nothing I could do, and I felt so helpless. Not that you don't feel pretty helpless as a three-year-old at any given time anyway. But I knew that my family wouldn't know how to find me."

"How long was it before they did?"

"Almost twenty-four hours. But I couldn't see the sun where they kept me, so I thought it was much longer. I'd never gone that long without my family before. But I wasn't hurt. I made it back all safe and sound.

"It was hard on everyone in my family. Blake, especially, because he doesn't think it would've happened if he hadn't gone over to pet the dog. It really spooked all of us. It had just been an ordinary day, you know? No one saw it coming. We had all felt pretty helpless."

Owen wraps an arm around me and pulls me tightly to him, and it calms my nerves.

"When I was standing out in that field, squatting to get a good look at that caterpillar, I was in a wide open space. I was so exposed to danger." I glance around and force a chuckle. "Kind of like how I'm feeling right now."

Owen reaches his other arm around to give me a squeeze, and I just soak in the feeling of being safe in his arms for a long moment.

When he drops his arm, I decide I want to continue. For the first time since I was three, I didn't downplay what happened or brush it off. I showed more of myself to Owen than I ever show to anyone. I can let myself be fully seen by him. "I like to believe that getting kidnapped was something that only affected me when I was three. I mean, that was a long time ago! I didn't want to believe that something that happened when I was so little could still affect me as an adult.

"But since we met, I've been starting to realize how many things that I just assumed were part of my personality—like not wanting to be seen—can be traced back to that. I'm sure there are even more parts that I haven't realized yet. And I don't know what to even do with that information." I let out a breath of a chuckle. "I guess it just makes me feel like I'd felt when I was three and captured—helpless. And I really don't like that feeling, so I try to stay away from it."

"You're not helpless," Owen says in a low voice. "There are just parts that you haven't given yourself time to figure out yet. You will, though. I mean, look at you—you've been brave since preschool! And you're one of the smartest and strongest people I know. On top of that, your sunny outlook is so bright that it can turn even the darkest corners into day. It can find every crack that fear tries to hide in. I've got no doubt that you'll figure this out. And I'll be here for you in whatever way you need me."

Instead of sharing with Owen being dangerous, like I've always felt it is, it somehow feels like the safest thing I've ever done. Which is saying something, given the fact that Giovanni, Man Bun Menace, Silent but Deadly, and Shoulders-for-Days are all hurrying around and talking in stressed tones.

"I'm sorry it took me so long to tell you. Especially since you trusted me with your trauma much sooner."

"Hey, someone had to kick off the Sad Backstory Olympics. I took one for the team."

I laugh. Quietly, of course. We've got bad guys in the room, after all. And I'm still me, so I don't want their attention on us.

I'm glad I told Owen. It feels good that he knows. It feels good to no longer carry around the weight of not telling him. And it feels extra good because it has definitely calmed him and taken his focus off the stressful situation, which was kind of the point in the first place. Well, that, and fulfilling my promise to Reese.

I hear Giovanni say a buyer's name, and log it in my head. The whole time we've been down here, I've been keeping an ear out for names that Giovanni or his goons mention, trying to memorize them. I wish I could type them on my phone without being noticed. My brothers are so good at memorizing everything because they have to be. I don't. I always have my computer right there, so I'm not as practiced. And there have definitely been times when I've been focusing on Owen and not paying attention at all.

As long as Giovanni is giving orders to pack up specific artifacts and giving instructions to Silent but Deadly and Shoulders-for-Days on where to take them, there's not much we can do. And if Owen and I stop talking, we're both going to go back to being stressed out and anxious.

Plus, I realize how much I trust Owen. I know he'll be with me through thick and thin.

I look at the four men we share this secret tunnel with. Not only are they at least a dozen feet away, but they're all scrambling to take care of everything quickly. I know they can't hear our quiet talking, so I guess now's as good a time as any. "Since we're on the subject of sharing things we never share, I've got another doozy for you."

CHAPTER 34
THE SECRET LIFE OF CHARLIE LANCASTER
CHARLIE

"Oh, yeah?" Owen shifts the way he's seated just a bit. "Okay, I'm ready for the doozy. Hit me."

"First, I need to swear you to secrecy. This stays between us."

Owen makes a motion of zipping his lips.

"When we were sitting on the stage, you asked if I wanted to be a spy. I've wanted to pretty much my whole life."

"Really?"

"Yep."

"Because you were kidnapped?"

"I'm sure that factored in."

"That's pretty cool. But wow. I was prepared for more of a doozy than that. I guess I should tell you that when I was five, I wanted to be a magician who solved crimes. Basically, if Sherlock Holmes had a top hat and a rabbit."

I chuckle quietly and give him a playful push. "That wasn't the doozy part. Stay in that prepared state, because I'm going to tell you something I haven't told anyone before." I take a breath. "You know how I told you that I work for the family business?"

"Yeah."

"Lancaster Business Solutions isn't actually the family business. That's just our cover."

Owen cocks his head.

"The family business, or at least the business most of my family is in, is the spy business, although we don't actually call it that. I work for a top-secret government intelligence agency."

Owen pauses a moment, then says, "Wait. Are you being serious?"

"One hundred percent. IT Systems Coordinator is my cover job title. I'm actually a Technical Operations Officer. Tech op for short. Or handler, whichever you prefer. Tech op is better, but I prefer handler because I don't know. I guess it makes me feel like I have more control, even though the term is most used for an intelligence operative with their asset. I'm the one who's behind the computer while the intelligence operative is out in the field, doing a mission."

"Oh. So you're the one who hacks into traffic

lights and security systems, and guides the operative in the field through a laser-grid hallway while chewing on gummy bears and being wildly underappreciated."

"And who says things like 'I've got eyes on you' and somehow knows everything even while sitting in a windowless van. Yep! That's me." I give Owen a minute because he looks like he needs it.

Eventually, he says, "So… it's like the CIA."

"Similar. Except the CIA isn't a secret agency. We are."

"Oh, right. So, back when we were lying on the blanket in the grass behind our townhomes, you said you'd been recruited into the family business. So, that means you were recruited into a top-secret government spy—"

"—intelligence."

"—agency right out of college?"

"Yes. It's a lot to take in, I know. Well, I mean," I gesture to our surroundings, "so is being kidnapped."

"Abducted."

"By the guy who was single-handedly funding your dream and secretly bulldozing it at the same time."

"And you work for?"

"The Clandestine Services Agency. Or you can call it the CSA. We do."

"And I can't tell anyone."

"Right. No one. Not even Tessa. Reese doesn't even know what I really do."

"Oh, wow. Okay. And that was how you found out about…" he glances at Giovanni, "our host?"

He's using good instincts to not mention Giovanni by name. People are always attuned to their name. "Yes."

"And is… your work…" He makes a complicated hand motion that I'm guessing is supposed to mean "the ones taking down Giovanni."

I say in a quiet voice, "Several agencies working together, both here and in Italy, in conjunction with local law enforcement." I look around. "I just keep thinking, what would one of my brothers do if he were the one who was captured? Well, one of my field operative brothers, of course, and—"

"Wait. You said it's a *family* business. Your brothers are spies!" he hisses, and then looks over at the men to make sure he wasn't loud enough for them to hear.

"Yes. Jace, Ledger, and Miles are intelligence operatives in the field, and Emerson is an analyst."

Owen leans back against the brick, staring at nothing. Then he says, "That actually makes so much sense."

"Oh, and while you're taking it all in, I should also mention that my mom is the director of the CSA."

Owen puts his hands over his face for a moment before running them up and through his hair. "So, when you said at the wedding that if your mom ever aims 'intimidating' at me, then run, you weren't being overly dramatic. She could probably kill me three different ways using only whatever she had on her person at the wedding."

I look up, counting. "Four different ways. *But she wouldn't.* That's the important part. Oh, and my dad was the director before my mom. That story I told you about him dying on the job? That was true—he just had a different job than what I'd said."

I remember back to yesterday, which feels like it happened days ago, when I was having lunch with Abraham. He told me to give Owen enough information but not too much information, or I'd overwhelm him, and that it was a balancing act getting it just right. He was referring to me telling Owen about Giovanni, not about my secret double life, but the sentiment is the same for everything.

Yeah, I've clearly not scored high points on that balancing act. Owen is overwhelmed. His arm is still around me, but I give his other hand a squeeze and wait patiently, trying not to add to the overwhelm.

Eventually, he shifts the way he's sitting so he's turned a bit more toward me, and he runs his hands through his hair. "Wow. I am in love with a woman who's a spy, in a family of spies. Sorry, *intelligence operatives*. That is wild."

I tilt my head. "You're in love with me?"

"Of course I'm in love with you, Charlie. You're everything."

I smile with my whole face. "Well, I'm in love with you, too."

Owen leans in closer, his mouth just a breath away. "Well, that works out very conveniently for us, doesn't it?"

"I think so," I breathe, moving in even closer.

Owen reaches a hand up to cup the side of my neck, his fingertips in my hair, and he kisses me.

CHAPTER 35
ESCAPE PLAN: TRUST THE GIRL
OWEN

"You know," I say quietly to Charlie, "I wouldn't choose to be captured by a gun-wielding criminal who had made me believe in my dreams and then be held in a dark tunnel with my very near future unknown. But since I have to be, there's no one else I'd rather be here with than you."

Charlie smiles. "What about Chuck Norris? Or Liam Neeson?"

I work to hold back a smile. "Chuck Norris and Liam Neeson probably wouldn't keep me laughing and smiling through the stress. I think I'm still going to have to go with you."

I cannot believe that I've been dating a spy. *Tech op.* Someone who works for a top-secret intelligence agency. Oddly enough, I'm glad she told me down here. It feels somehow appropriate to find out that the normal things you thought about your girlfriend were only part of her cover story—and that her real story is so far outside of what I've known as normal—while in a place and situation that is also so far outside of what I've known as normal.

Had she told me all of that while we were in one of our town homes, walking down the street, or out getting tacos, I would've probably... been just as blown away as down here, actually. Maybe I'm just glad that she told me. As strange and not-typical as it is, I like knowing her non-cover story. Her kidnap experience, too, even if it makes me feel worse that I suggested we go sleuthing, since that's what got us caught and trapped down here, reliving her childhood trauma.

Also, I totally called it that hers was a family of superheroes.

It hits me that sometime in the past couple of days, I've come to the realization that Charlie isn't going to leave when things get tough. I wasn't even conscious of the change as it was happening. But now I know with certainty that she's dedicated to our relationship every bit as much as I am.

Giovanni and his men seem to be picking up their pace as they pack things up and figure out the specifics of their plans. I have to admit that my focus has been almost exclusively on Charlie and not on the specifics of the bad guys. But since she has spy training, I'm hoping she has paid attention more than I have. So I ask quietly, "Do you know what's happening?"

She nods and keeps her eyes on me, so if one of the men glances over, it'll look like we are just chatting instead of talking about them. I do all I can to keep my eyes on her, too, as she talks. "They need to get all this stuff removed from here because they can tell that authorities are closing in. They can't take it all out at once, though, without drawing too much attention in the restaurant, so they'll have to take two trips."

"Restaurant?"

"The other end of this tunnel is heading toward the buildings on the street that runs parallel to this one, behind The Shadowridge. I bet if it weren't for the trees, you'd be able to see the back of Lantern House from the back of The Shadowridge. My guess is that's where they're exiting. And with a restaurant, they'd have deliveries at all times of the day, so they could bring goods in, sneak them down here, and not be too noticed.

"If you think about it, it's the perfect setup for them. The buildings aren't too far apart, but because they're on different streets, people won't tie anything they see happening there to The Shadowridge. We don't even have officers watching that street. It's brilliant, really."

I nod as I watch the men wrap up and box things. Ancient-looking things. "So, where did all this stuff come from?"

"Archaeological finds, museums, things on their way from archaeological sites to museums, stuff like that."

My stomach churns as I watch them roll up stolen history in bubble wrap like it's an eBay shipment. Ancient artifacts—things that belong in public museums, in the hands of people who would honor their stories—are being boxed up to disappear into the vaults of private collectors. My jaw tightens, and anger simmers deep in my chest. These aren't just objects—they are whispers from the past, the kind of treasures that had survived wars, time, and obscurity, and they're being treated like contraband.

"We have to do something," I say. "We can't just sit around while all this stuff gets sent off to wherever it's going and doesn't have a chance. What was that you were saying about what your brothers would do if it were them here?"

"Hang on. He's telling Shoulders-for-Days to deliver a couple of objects to a buyer who will meet him at his business in Alexandria. That's a ninety-minute drive, so we won't be seeing him again tonight."

Shoulders-for-Days? I glance at the men. Ahh. Okay, that one.

"He's sending Silent but Deadly off to meet a different buyer. He might be gone a while, too. Giovanni and Man Bun Menace, though, are each taking some of the items—I think ones that they haven't lined up buyers for yet—to… I'm not sure where. I get the sense that it's nearby, though. Like, not too far out of Cipher Springs. I'm sure they're the ones who will be back for the second load."

"You want all of us to leave?" the man Charlie calls "Man Bun Menace" asks. "And do what with the lovebirds?"

"Do you have more zip ties in there?" Giovanni asks, and the man pulls some out of their packing supplies. "We'll tie them up. Lock the entrance to The Shadowridge from down here, and we'll lock the one in the restaurant from the other side."

I throw Charlie a panicked look. The only thing not making me freak out is the fact that we haven't been bound. But she gives me a look back that says everything will be okay, so I believe her.

There isn't much down here to zip tie us to, so they opt for tying our wrists to the shelving where they have the artifacts, moving the remaining objects further away from where we're bound. The look Charlie had given me had said she was okay with this, but now she's trembling. I try to position my body in a way to feel like I'm giving her a hug, but it's too awkward.

Giovanni tells Man Bun Menace to hold back so he can turn off the lamp, but then Charlie says in a voice that's trembling as much as she is, "Don't turn it off! Please. I'm terrified of the dark."

"She legitimately is," I say, looking at Giovanni and pleading with my eyes.

He pauses for a moment, probably considering the good relationship we've had, and then he gives Man Bun a head motion that tells him to leave it. Then the four men head down the tunnel leading away from The Shadowridge. We see the light from their flashlights for a distance before they climb up through a hatch.

As soon as we hear the hatch close, Charlie switches from fear to urgency. "We need to get out of these zip ties."

"Were you faking being terrified?"

She gives me a head shake that is both a yes and a no, but finishes with a yes that's slightly stronger. "They underestimate you when you're small and afraid. I've seen it over and over." She's turning her hands and wiggling, and manages to pull one hand and then the other free.

"How did you do that?" I ask in wonder. There's no way I can get my hands through.

"When they were putting on my zip tie, I just positioned my hands in a way that would make it feel like they tightened it well, but wouldn't actually be tight. Yours is actually tight, though. Okay, we just need to find something to mess with the little tab in the locking part." She finds a pen on the table and goes to work on mine, and I swear she has them off in five seconds.

"See? This is why I'd choose you over Chuck or Liam."

She grins, pulls her cell phone out and turns on its flashlight, and then we head down the tunnel in the same direction that the men went. The hatch on this side is wooden, and there is a metal ladder installed against the wall leading up. Charlie climbs the ladder and pushes on the hatch, shining her flashlight around the opening, shifting her position to try to see along its edges.

Then she gets a notification on her phone, looks at it, and says, "My text just went through! So there's service here." She immediately makes a phone call and puts it on speaker.

A moment later, a panicked voice answers. "Charlie?"

"Hey, Emerson. Okay, so the good news is, we found out how Giovanni's guys are sneaking into The

Shadowridge. There's a secret tunnel. The bad news is, we're trapped in that tunnel." She looks down at her phone. "Blake got the text, too, and you can probably see that he's also freaking out. Can you loop him in to this call?"

She climbs back down while Emerson gets one of her other brothers on the call and says to me, "Pull out your phone and see how far we can get from this opening before we lose cell phone bars."

I start walking to check it, but don't have to go far. We can't even get three feet from it without losing reception.

Blake joins the call, and Charlie updates them both on our situation and what Giovanni and his men are doing. "So we need someone to come over here now so we can save what is here."

"There's no one to send," Emerson says. "Jace, Ledger, and Miles are all out of the country. I don't even think Mom is back yet. I could come, but I'm still at work, and it would take at least twenty minutes. Everyone else here has already gone home."

"And I might need you there," Charlie says.

"I'm already driving," Blake says, "and I'm fifteen minutes away, tops."

"Do you want me to call local law enforcement or the FBI to get someone there more quickly?" Emerson asks.

That sounds good to me, but Charlie says, "And

have them come in all noisy and flashy, guns blazing? They'd be able to recover the remaining artifacts, but Giovanni will be in the wind."

"True," Emerson says. "Which means it has to be you."

"Me?" Charlie's voice comes out as a squeak. I reach out and give her shoulder a squeeze. "What do I even do? And how can you guide me through this when I can't even step away from the far end of the tunnel?"

"Even if you had reception," Emerson says, "I'm not sure I *could* lead you through it. There's a reason why I'm an analyst and not a tech op—when I need to figure something out, I shut out the world and focus. I usually get time to think. I don't have to give an answer right in the middle of stressful things. I have no idea how you do what you do.

"But Charlie, you *do* know what to do. Right in the heat of things, you know. You just need to trust your instincts. You knew Giovanni was committing crimes before anyone else had the slightest clue. Trust yourself. If Jace was the one down there, and you had him on comms and cameras, what would you tell him to do right now?"

Charlie visibly calms. "I'd tell him to get photographic evidence of everything, making sure to put it all exactly back as it was, then to zip tie himself back up before Giovanni returns. Then I would watch street cameras for Giovanni to come back, and I'd send in the cavalry as soon as he was back in the tunnel." She lets out a long exhale. "I wish I could have you go to my computer and show you how to bring up the cameras on the street in front of the restaurant so you could watch for Giovanni, but it'd take too long."

"I can tell you when he comes," Blake says. "Heidi and I will head to the restaurant, find the hatch, and then keep an eye out for him. When we see him, I'll call you, Emerson, so you'll know to send in the noisy, flashy suits with blazing guns."

"That's perfect!" Charlie says. "Tell them to go into The Shadowridge, too, so he doesn't escape from that direction. Those pictures I texted are of a maintenance closet backstage, near the dressing rooms. It's locked from down here."

"Got it," Emerson says.

"And Charlie, if anything happens to you…" Blake adds.

"I know. You'll have even more bitterness toward the CSA than you do right now. Don't worry. We'll be careful."

Charlie ends the call, and we both run back to the table that Man Bun had been working at. I take a picture of how everything is on the table, and then I start opening folders, and Charlie starts taking pictures as I flip to each page, holding my flashlight on them so she'll get a good image. It looks like these papers show where every piece has gone. Hopefully, it'll mean they can get them all back.

When we finish, we look at the picture on my phone and get the table back the way it was, and then we do the same to the artifacts. We're working so fast our hands are shaking from all the adrenaline. We hear a sound at the far end of the tunnel, so we turn off our phones' flashlights and put them in our pockets. Charlie quickly grabs two zip ties, and we sit at the base of the shelving just like we were.

"Put your hands like this," Charlie says, holding her fists out and pressed together, palms down. So I put my fists like that on the other side of the bar, and she zip ties me. "If they check your bands, turn your hands like that again, and they'll feel tight." Then she puts a zip tie around the same bar, keeping it loose, then slips her hands into it.

We've still got adrenaline coursing through us, so we're breathing heavily, but hopefully Giovanni will just interpret it as fear. "You are amazing," I whisper to Charlie. "You know that, right?"

She gives me a smile that's beautiful in the dim glow of the lamp. She looks like she's pretty proud of herself, and I'm proud of her, too.

We see Giovanni walking in the tunnel back toward us first. It's maybe a minute later before Man Bun joins him. As soon as Giovanni is to us, Charlie says in that same trembling voice that she'd used before, "Thank you for leaving the light on for me."

He just grunts a response, and he and Man Bun start packing up the rest of the artifacts.

Charlie turns her head to me, mouths, *They're going too fast. We need to stall them.*

Now that's something I can do. I have plenty of questions I've been dying to ask Giovanni.

CHAPTER 36
DISTRACT AND CONQUER
CHARLIE

Giovanni had been gone for long enough that I'm sure Blake found his way into the Lantern House restaurant, hopefully found the hatch, saw Giovanni return, and notified Emerson. I'm sure Emerson already had the FBI, or at least local law enforcement, on standby, ready to storm in. But still, it takes a bit to get them from wherever they were to be in place, ready to capture Giovanni and Man Bun Menace when they leave.

Luckily, I am tied up next to a man who knows just how to stall Giovanni.

Owen looks up at Giovanni from where we're sitting on the floor. "Can I ask you a question?"

Giovanni hesitates a moment, his hand stopping halfway toward what I think is a rolled parchment in a fancy case. Then he nods and turns his attention fully to Owen, which tells me that the man must really respect Owen.

"Did you care at all about The Shadowridge, or any of the other restorations you financed? Or did you just choose historical buildings because they made smuggling more convenient?"

"There are a lot of paths I could choose to make smuggling more convenient. I choose to finance restorations because there's something sacred about reviving a place that time tried to forget. These buildings—cathedrals, opera houses, theaters—each one carries the soul of the people who walked their halls a hundred years ago and the bones of craftsmanship that no one bothers with anymore. Each time I walk into a space that was nearly lost to history but is alive again because I made it happen... Well, that's the closest thing I know to immortality."

I'm watching Owen's face as warring emotions cross it. This man obviously feels the same way that Owen does about historical places, yet he's also a criminal mastermind. And the reason why Owen is about to have his dream of restoring The Shadowridge ripped away.

"Why did you choose The Shadowridge?"

I know that the answer Owen is really asking is, why did it have to be the place he loves? Why couldn't he have chosen anywhere else that would allow him to keep his dream? But Giovanni answers the question Owen actually asked.

"That was because of you. And that spark in your eyes when you talked about The Shadowridge. That reverence for the past, the sense that these walls aren't just brick and plaster, but witnesses to history. I thought, finally, someone who understands that breathing life into something ancient is about legacy. I didn't just finance The Shadowridge, Owen. I backed someone who believed, as deeply as I do, that the past deserves a future."

The two men just look at each other for a long moment, a certain respect passing between them. There's more, though, and I can't even begin to guess what all is going through Owen's mind right now.

"It's all going to be ruined, you know. They aren't going to let me finish."

Giovanni gives a heavy sigh. "That's the biggest tragedy in all of this. For what it's worth, I'm sorry you won't be able to." He turns back to his tasks of helping Man Bun Menace pack up the remaining objects.

Owen asks, "Then why smuggle artifacts? Why not something else? *Anything* else."

"Maybe because I like working with people who also appreciate the past. Those are the buyers I want to seek out. The people I want to do business with."

"But how can you have so much appreciation for

the past, yet try to take it away from people?" Owen gestures at all the antiquities the men are packing up. "Everyone should be able to appreciate those."

"Because not everyone does. So, why not give them to people who are willing to pay a lot of money for them?"

"Why smuggle at all?" I ask. "Why not use that brilliant mind of yours for something less illegal?" Like something that doesn't require me to investigate you, leading to your takedown right along with the takedown of my boyfriend's dream.

Giovanni gives me a sly smile. "Now, where's the fun in that?"

Ahh. It's about the challenge for him. Could he not find some other way to be challenged?

"So what's next for you?" Owen asks him.

That's a great question. He and Giovanni seem to have quite a rapport. I'm hoping he'll give Owen a really good answer. Especially since Giovanni sees me as a scared little girl, not the woman who works for an intelligence agency who, when it comes to her work, is on fire. Not the tech op who executes plans like a boss, and is responsible for his current predicament.

"What's next?" Giovanni echoes, almost to himself. "Let's just say that there is always history looking to change hands. And not every exit is an ending."

As Giovanni and Man Bun Menace each finish putting their final bubble-wrapped object into one of two big canvas packs, I ask, "What's next for *us*?" Because, honestly, I'm getting a little scared. I think we've stalled him for long enough, but I don't think the agents are going to come down into the tunnels— they're going to wait for Giovanni to go up. And I don't know what he plans to have happen between now and then.

He looks at me for a moment, then at Owen. "I like you, Owen. If it were anyone else, my answer would be different. Obviously, I can't have you calling for help before I get far enough away to avoid being caught, so I'm going to leave you here. Once I am safely away, I'll have an associate call in an anonymous tip on where to find you." He glances at me. "I'll even leave the light on for your girlfriend."

Man Bun Menace gets his pack on first and heads down the tunnel toward the restaurant, flashlight in hand. Giovanni puts his pack on and then says, "Goodbye, Owen. I wish you the best in your future projects." Then he turns to follow Man Bun.

We watch as Man Bun reaches the ladder at the end, steps up a rung, and opens the hatch above him. He steps up another rung before he sees what is surely a bunch of FBI agents, probably in full tactical gear, surrounding the opening. He gets the bright idea to step back down, but he barely moves before they reach down to pull him up.

Giovanni started running back in our direction the

moment he spotted trouble, and he races straight to the opening leading up to The Shadowridge as agents pour into the tunnel from the restaurant. He quickly unlocks the hatch closer to where we are, only to find that there are just as many agents waiting for him there.

I grin at Owen as we both turn our hands to slip out of the zip ties and stand. Owen wraps his arms around me and turns me in a circle, like he's so happy we found our way out of this that he has to spend the excitement somehow. "Can you believe we did it?"

I slide my arms around his neck and move in close. "Because you, Owen Hollis, have excellent stalling skills."

"And you, Charlotte Lancaster, are way better than Chuck Norris or Liam Neeson." I laugh, and he adds, "You are incredible."

"Would you say I'm on fire?"

"Very much so," he breathes, and then he kisses me as the buzz of agents in black tactical gear swarms around us and at both ends of the tunnel.

I don't want the kiss to end. But eventually, an agent taps me on the shoulder. "I'm guessing the kiss means you're both okay, yes?"

I turn to him, a little sheepish. "Yes. Sorry."

Looking a bit amused, he says, "Do you think we could trouble you to go up for a debrief, then?"

As we head up into The Shadowridge, I realize I

don't feel so "fire at work, flooding at home" anymore. I am only fire. I mean, I'm not exactly field operative material, and I don't ever plan to be. But I do know that my instincts are strong and reliable, and I know I can trust them. Especially because we get out to the auditorium just in time to see Giovanni taken out in handcuffs.

By the time we've finished talking to the agent in charge, Blake is just walking in from the side door, holding my little three-year-old niece's hand, and I can see that Emerson is rushing in from the front doors, looking a bit stressed but very relieved to see us. Blake and Heidi reach us first, so I tell him, "Thank you. We couldn't have done this without you."

"Seriously," Owen says. "Thank you."

Heidi, still holding Blake's hand, starts jumping, posing with each jump, as she says, "We helped catch the bad guys!"

"You sure did," I say, just as Emerson joins us. Then I turn to Blake. "Look at you, doing spy work for the CSA."

He narrows his eyes at me. But what are sisters for, if not to poke the bear every once in a while?

Heidi looks up at Blake. "Daddy, you should let me stay up this late and catch bad guys all the time."

I chuckle at the horrified look on Blake's face and turn to Emerson. "And thank you. Seriously, we couldn't have made it without you both."

"Eh. We barely did anything. This was all the two of you."

Owen turns fully to me. "Do you realize how huge tonight is? The girl who was afraid to read her essay was in the spotlight. Exposed and vulnerable to abductors. Yet she didn't hide."

I smile. "Or pass out."

He nods. "Or pass out."

"Instead, I tackled it like a boss."

He chuckles and wraps his arms around me. "That you did. I'm proud of you."

"I'm proud of myself, too—but I'm just as proud of you. I mean, after everything I dumped on you tonight —my real job, the whole childhood kidnapping thing —you still jumped right in and stalled Giovanni like a pro, with no hesitation. This mission wouldn't have been a success without you."

Owen grins at me. "We are pretty great when we're together, aren't we?"

I grin right back. "Yes, we are."

EPILOGUE ONE
HIGH-VALUE TARGET ACQUIRED

Owen

I made the two and a half hour drive from Philadelphia earlier today, and I've been at The Shadowridge ever since, getting everything ready for opening night. We've got a sold-out crowd, a brand new staff, plenty of new systems, a traveling theater company performing, and we're even doing a ribbon cutting. So plenty of things have kept me busy since I arrived. The Shadowridge is the star tonight, and she's ready to shine.

I glance at my watch. Charlie should be here in about twenty minutes, and my family will not be far behind her, so I'd better hurry and go get ready. Once we got the offices in the side hall restored, I moved my office there to free up the balcony boxes for their restoration. I'm just about ready to move the last of my stuff out, though, so the people running the day-to-day of this theater can use it for other things.

But for right now, it's my changing room. I could've worn my dark suit for opening night—it would've been totally appropriate for it. Instead, I decide to wear the suit that Charlie picked just over a year ago when I had knocked on the wall frame separating our townhomes to get her advice on what I should wear. The vintage-inspired one that reminds me of cedar and old books. The one that made Charlie's words come out a bit choked when she told me the suit said, "You can trust me with your beloved building." It feels even more appropriate for the occasion.

That moment seems like a lifetime ago. So much has happened since then.

I step in front of the full-length mirror and make sure my hair looks good, my tie and vest are straight, and my sports coat is smooth and looking good. I put the index cards containing my speech notes in a pocket, take a deep breath, and leave to go start the evening that I've been dreaming about for ages.

I head out to the front of the building. We've got people directing cars to the parking lots on both sides of the building, and Cipher Springs has closed off the road directly in front of the theater for the ribbon cutting.

As people start to gather in the street for the grand opening and I'm checking on the last few things out here, I turn and see Charlie step around from the side of the building into the light of the lowering sun, and for a second, I forget how to breathe.

Her dress is a deep sage green—just a shade or two lighter than my jacket—but in satin that catches the light like moonlight on water. The soft flutter of her sleeves brushes the tops of her arms, and the fitted waist and subtle vintage stitching make her look like she's stepped out of the same era as *My Fair Lady*, but better.

Her hair is pinned up in soft waves, and she's wearing antique-inspired jewelry. When she smiles at me, the sparkle in her eyes is brighter than everything around her. I thought The Shadowridge would be the shining star of the night. It turns out, it's her.

And she's looking at me like she did that morning when she first saw me in this suit—like maybe I take her breath away, too. There's half a building's space between us, and I cross the distance quickly. I wrap my arms around her waist, and she drapes hers over my shoulders and gifts me with a brilliant smile.

"You're looking mighty spiffy, Mr. Hollis."

I smile back. "And you're looking rather radiant, Ms. Lancaster." I take in all the details of her face. It's only been five days since I last saw her, but it was about five days too long. "You are such a sight for...

well, not exactly sore eyes, since they've been taking in The Shadowridge. But definitely longing eyes."

"Are you all ready?"

I nod. "I've been ready for as long as I can remember."

Charlie's eyes shift to just over my shoulder, then she smiles and makes a movement with her head that tells me to turn around. So I do, and I see my grandma, my mom, dad, and Tessa, all dressed to the nines. We walk over to greet them, and see that my grandma has tears in her eyes that are threatening to spill over.

"Oh, Owen," she says as she looks up at the front of the building, taking in all the brickwork, trim, and the fully restored sign that reads The Shadowridge. "She's even more beautiful than I imagined!"

"Just wait until you see inside."

More and more people are gathering in the street, and it isn't long before the manager of The Shadowridge comes over and tells me that it's time to start. I look at Charlie. "Are you ready?"

"I can't say that I've been ready for as long as I can remember, but I'm ready now."

I told her that she doesn't have to be at my side as I give my speech. That it was totally fine to just stand with my family if she wanted to stay out of the spotlight. But she chose to, and I couldn't be more proud of her.

Margaret, who is President of the Cipher Springs Historical Preservation Society and a woman I've worked with closely through this entire restoration, steps up to the pulpit on the stage they have on the sidewalk in front of the building and introduces me.

Charlie and I step onto the small platform, and I begin my speech. I tell a little bit about The Shadowridge's history and about my grandparents' history with The Shadowridge. Then I thank the historical preservation society and the donors who made it happen.

When Giovanni was first arrested and we lost all funding from him, I went to every contact that I had and tracked down every new contact I could get a lead on. With each of them, I pleaded my case as earnestly as I could, and I tapped into all the skills I possessed to paint a picture for them of what this place had the potential to be.

It took so many long days and sleepless nights, and I don't think I've worked harder in my entire life. But before long, several investors stepped forward and offered to fund part of it. That got us close to the amount we needed, but it wasn't enough. That's when the cities of both Cipher Springs and Cloakwood banded together to raise the rest of the money.

I get choked up in my speech as I thank them. It had been an amazing thing to watch, and I've never felt a sense of community or belonging stronger than I did as everyone came together.

I take Charlie's hand in mine and smile at her. "And I'd like to thank Charlotte Lancaster. She's been at my side through all of the ups and downs, helping to make it all happen, and I know without a doubt that we wouldn't all be here today if it weren't for her."

Charlie smiles back at me, and I'm struck with an intense awe of her. She constantly blows me away, and I know how fortunate I am to have her in my life.

After my speech, we do the ribbon cutting with the comically large scissors. I'm up there with Charlie, the investors, and the historical preservation society board. And joining us are the guys on my crew—Luis, Grady, Trent, and Nate. Because of the gap in time with no funding, I was only able to get Luis and Trent back when we started up again, but all four of them left such a mark on this place.

They all look pretty decent and very different from how I normally see them, all cleaned up, wearing suits, and grinning like they're so proud to have had a hand in restoring this place to such a beautiful state. And they very well should be. Honestly, they all deserve medals of some sort.

We head inside, and Charlie and I walk through the place, hand-in-hand, showing my family every part of it. My grandma takes in the beauty with a sense of nostalgia. My dad looks at everything with an eye for craftsmanship, taking in every detail. When we finish the tour, my dad gives a nod. Like a stamp of approval. Then he says, "Good work, son. Grandpa would be proud of you."

My grandma nods. "He is."

Back when my grandpa came to this theater and first met my grandma, he kept his ticket stub, knowing that it was a night that would forever change the trajectory of his life. My grandma still has it.

And because they saved it, I know exactly what seat he'd been sitting in, and I am able to seat my grandma in the same seat he'd been in when he first saw my grandma on stage in *My Fair Lady*, as we watch the same musical tonight. But this time, his seat is surrounded by all the people in his family who wouldn't be here if it weren't for that night.

———

Later, as Charlie and I are carrying a couple of blankets onto the grassy area behind Charlie's town-home, I'm still feeling the adrenaline from the night coursing through me. Especially because we've been talking about the grand opening nonstop since we left the theater. Nothing beats seeing people enjoy the space that your vision and perseverance helped to restore.

Charlie drops her blanket onto the grass before helping me to spread out the other one. "And did you see your grandma's face when the cast came out and she got to meet the actress who played Eliza Doolittle?"

I nod. "I thought she might cry."

"It meant a lot to her that you were able to get that specific musical there for opening night."

"It meant a lot to me, too."

We lie down on the blanket, and I spread the second blanket over us. We're both wearing pajamas, just like we did back when the wall between our town-homes first came down, right after we'd raced around the grass to help get us past wallowing over mistakes made at work. But unlike that night, this one is a bit chillier.

There are still just as many townhomes on all four sides of us with their back porch lights on, including the townhome I used to live in. The couple who live there now has a barbecue and a couple of chairs on their deck. Since their deck isn't empty, like mine was, it makes it harder to imagine that I still live there. It gives me a sudden and intense longing for the place I lived while falling in love with Charlie.

"Hey," Charlie says. "Eyes over here."

I chuckle and turn to look at her. She's lying on her side, her arm bent at the elbow, her head resting on her hand as she gazes at me with eyes twinkling in the light of the moon. She's right. I have everything I need right here.

"And did you see how I was at your side during your speech, fully spotlight-adjacent?"

I smile, remembering back to that night out here on a blanket when she told me she couldn't be in the spotlight, and I echo her words. "Instead of being in the bathroom, either throwing up or passing out from hyperventilating? I did."

Charlie nods. "Now that's what we call growth."

"Indeed. Although I feel like you've been getting more comfortable being in the spotlight for a while now."

"Oh, I have. It's just sometimes good to acknowledge the awesomeness all over again."

"Kind of like you still acknowledge the awesomeness of having a kitchen sink and a shower that doesn't stop providing water right in the middle of washing your hair?"

"Don't forget a table and chairs. And it's because those things are worth acknowledging the awesomeness of daily."

"And that's just one of the many reasons why I love you."

"I never got a chance to ask you how your drive was."

"It was good. But really long, especially because I was dying to tell you news the whole time."

"News?" Charlie says, sitting up and turning to face me.

I sit up, too, facing her. "Part one: I've been working through the schedule and budget on the train station. I have all the building materials ordered and on site. My guys have been begging for overtime, and now that we have close to final numbers in, I know there's enough in the budget to let them have it."

Charlie perks up. "Oh, yeah? So when do you think you'll finish?"

A smile spreads across my face. "Two weeks."

"For real?"

I nod. The funding for finishing The Shadowridge came in close to the same time I was under contract to start working on the train station in Philadelphia. So, for the past five months, I've been working double duty. I've spent most of my time in Philadelphia because, well, because The Shadowridge has had Luis. He knows just what I want and just how to manage the crew and all the sub-contractors, so I know I can trust him to take care of things while I'm in Philadelphia.

It has meant that I've only gotten about three days every two weeks to work hands-on at The Shadowridge, but it was worth it to get the place to where she is now. And it's amazing that both locations are wrapping up so close to the same time.

"And part two: I got a call this morning that my next project, the Inn in Cloakwood, was greenlit."

Charlie lets out an excited shout that echoes off the buildings surrounding us. "Owen, that is so great!" She wraps her arms around me in a hug and squeezes tightly. After a moment, she pulls back, leaving her hands on my shoulders. "So, are you saying that in two weeks, you'll be able to be back here? We'll no longer have to switch off driving two and a half hours every weekend to see each other?"

My grin is wide. "That's exactly what I'm saying. In two more weeks, we'll be able to see each other daily. Then I can acknowledge the awesomeness of you all over again, in person, every single day." These past five months have been hard, especially since we had been so used to seeing each other all the time. But the five hours spent in the car every other weekend were completely worth it. I would drive ten times that distance if it meant seeing Charlie.

Charlie is just looking at me, grinning as wide as could be, and I question whether I can even make it another two weeks before being back here, seeing her every day.

"So, since we'll be back together again soon, I've got a question for you. And I am one hundred percent prepared to use my growly voice, if that's what it takes."

Charlie cocks her head, trying to figure out what I

might be asking. I put my left hand in the pocket of my pajama pants, my fingers wrapping around the box.

"I may not be trained in espionage, but I know a high-value target when I see one. And Charlotte Lancaster, you are it. You've hacked my heart, infiltrated my life, and somehow made me fall more deeply in love with you than I ever thought possible. There is no one I want to be with in the world more than you. You're my person. You make me feel like I am finally home. I want to go hand-in-hand with you through a life filled with laughter, tech jargon I don't understand, sticky notes, and anything and everything that life throws at us.

I pull out the ring box and open the lid. "Will you marry me, Charlie?"

She gasps when she sees the ring, which I'm pretty sure is a good thing. It's got a pink sapphire instead of a diamond, and a white gold band, which sets it off beautifully. The band has a kind of twisting pattern near the sapphire, with some small white diamonds set into it. It's clean and uncluttered, yet it feels like it was carved by a master craftsman.

Charlie's eyes are wet as she looks at me. "I think this is the most beautiful thing I have ever laid eyes on!"

I let out half a breath of relief that I had chosen

correctly. The other half of my breath is still waiting for her answer.

"Of course, I will marry you, Owen! You are my favorite infiltration ever."

I slip the ring onto her finger, and she admires it for a beat. Then she bursts forward to wrap her arms around my neck with enough enthusiasm that it knocks me onto my back. I chuckle softly for the smallest moment, and then her lips are on mine, we're kissing, my fingers are tangled in her hair, and I am blown away by thoughts of being able to spend forever with this woman.

EPILOGUE TWO
CHARM, DISARM, REPEAT

Miles

I've done some pretty ridiculous things to get inside a restricted area before. I've forged a film crew permit, rerouted a delivery truck to hitch a ride inside, and coordinated a flash mob to use as a distraction. One time, I even faked an engagement to a diplomat's daughter.

But this time, the golden path Jace and I had planned didn't pan out. Neither did our silver nor bronze paths. So now we're left with no time and no props. Just my "player" reputation and Jace's annoyingly smug faith in it.

He nudges me with his elbow as we lean against the railing of a sidewalk café in downtown Lisbon, acting casual. "That woman right there wearing a lanyard—red blazer by the gate."

She's standing just inside the security perimeter of the modern art museum that also happens to house a very not-public underground storage vault that contains a ledger we need to acquire. I nod. "She might be able to get us there. Do you have a plan?"

Jace shrugs, and like it's no big deal, he suggests, "Why don't you go work your charm-and-disarm routine and get her to take you there?"

I grin. "Oh, is that all?" I push myself off the railing, adjust the collar of my button-down, and run my fingers through my hair, smoothing it after being in this breeze. "Any chance you want to offer backup or maybe a distraction?"

"I'm the guy watching the perimeter," Jace says as he pulls out his phone to look at it so it won't appear to onlookers as though he's doing exactly that— watching the perimeter. "You're the guy who makes women forget what job they're doing."

I roll my eyes. "One of these days, that's going to stop working."

"You? Give up the bachelor's life? I have a hard time picturing it, but maybe someday. Today is not that day, though."

I head toward the woman, already putting on the persona. I toss her a smile—just the right mix of charming and sheepish—and strike up a conversation about the art exhibit. Turns out she's passionate about modern art and aesthetics, and I pretend to be interested in a non-existent sculpture exhibit that I tell her is in the museum's off-limits wing.

Within five minutes, she's smiling and touching my arm. By seven minutes in, she's offering to walk me there herself. On our way, she's talking about marble inlay floors, and I'm complimenting her attention to detail. And I do what I always do—lean in just close enough to keep her distracted, say just enough to keep her curious, and steer the conversation exactly where I need it to go.

Does it bother me that everyone sees me as a player? No. It's much better than them seeing the alternative, which is that I'm hopelessly, pathetically in love with my best friend, Reese, and have been for years.

I'm reminded often that the sentiment is completely one-sided, though. It wasn't too long ago when Reese told me that I'd make some girl very happy one day. Like it wasn't even a possibility it might be her.

At least this version of me doesn't come with rejection by the one person I can't seem to stop falling for.

So I flirt. I charm. I disarm. I offer the smile I know will always get people to let their guard down. And I let everyone keep believing what they want to believe.

Because this? This is safer.

Even if it is a complete lie.

Get Miles and Reese's story in *Spies Don't Fall for Their Best Friend*.

ABOUT MEG EASTON

Meg Easton is the *USA Today* bestselling author of
contemporary romances and romantic comedies with
fun, memorable, swoon-worthy characters, and
settings you'll want to pack up and move to. She lives
at the foot of a mountain with her name on it (or at
least one letter of her name) in Utah. She loves
gardening, bike riding, baking, swimming before the
sun rises, and spending time with her husband and
three kids.

She can be found online at www.megeaston.com

Sign up to receive her newsletter and stay up to date with new releases, get exclusive bonus content, and more.

If you liked this book please leave a review. Your review can help other readers find books they might fall in love with.

youtube.com/@megeastonauthor
bookbub.com/authors/meg-easton
instagram.com/megeaston_author
facebook.com/MegEastonBooks
tiktok.com/@megeaston_author

www.ingramcontent.com/pod-product-compliance
Lightning Source LLC
Chambersburg PA
CBHW021228190726
48289CB00005B/1228